TALES

D0000131

Jack London – his real name was ⟨...⟩ ⟨...⟩urful youth on the waterfront of San ⟨...⟩ ⟨...⟩e left school at the age of fourteen and worked in a cannery. By the time he was sixteen he had been both an oyster pirate and a member of the Fish Patrol in San Francisco Bay and he later wrote about his experiences in *The Cruise of the Dazzler* (1902) and *Tales of the Fish Patrol* (1905). In 1893 he joined a sealing cruise which took him as far as Japan. Returning to the United States, he travelled throughout the country. He was determined to become a writer and read voraciously. After a brief period of study at the University of California he joined the gold rush to the Klondike in 1897. He returned to San Francisco the following year and wrote about his experiences. His short stories of the Yukon were published in *Overland Monthly* (1898) and the *Atlantic Monthly* (1899), and in 1900 his first collection, *The Son of the Wolf*, appeared, bringing him national fame. In 1902 he went to London, where he studied the slum conditions of the East End. He wrote about his experiences in *The People of the Abyss* (1903). His life was exciting and eventful. There were sailing voyages to the Caribbean and the South Seas. He reported on the Russo-Japanese War for the Hearst papers and gave lecture tours. A prolific writer, he published an enormous number of stories and novels. Besides several collections of short stories, including *Love of Life* (1907), *Lost Face* (1910), and *On the Makaloa Mat* (1919), he wrote many novels, including *The Call of the Wild* (1903), *The Sea-Wolf* (1904), *The Game* (1905), *White Fang* (1906), *Martin Eden* (1909), *John Barleycorn* (1913) and *Jerry of the Islands* (1917). Jack London died in 1916, at his home in California.

Andrew Sinclair was born in 1935 and educated at Eton and Trinity College, Cambridge, where he wrote his first two novels, *The Breaking of Bumbo* and *My Friend Judas*. His major trilogy of novels is *Gog* (1967), *Magog* (1972) and *King Ludd* (1988). He has also written *Prohibition: the Era of Excess* and *The Better Half: the Emancipation of the American Woman*, which won a Somerset Maugham Award, as well as several biographies, his subjects including Jack London, J. P. Morgan, John Ford, Sam Spiegel and *The Other Victoria*, the Empress of Germany. He has also edited a further collection of stories by Jack London for Penguin Classics, entitled *The Sea-Wolf and Other Stories*. He frequently appears on television and radio as a critic and is a fellow of the Royal Literary Society and of the Society of American Historians.

JACK LONDON

TALES OF THE PACIFIC

INTRODUCTION AND AFTERWORD BY
ANDREW SINCLAIR

PENGUIN BOOKS

PENGUIN BOOKS

Published by the Penguin Group
27 Wrights Lane, London W8 5TZ, England
Viking Penguin Inc., 40 West 23rd Street, New York, New York 10010, USA
Penguin Books Australia Ltd, Ringwood, Victoria, Australia
Penguin Books Canada Ltd, 2801 John Street, Markham, Ontario, Canada L3R 1B4
Penguin Books (NZ) Ltd, 182–190 Wairau Road, Auckland 10, New Zealand

Penguin Books Ltd, Registered Offices: Harmondsworth, Middlesex, England

Published in Penguin Books 1989

Printed and bound in Great Britain by Antony Rowe Ltd.,
Chippenham, Wiltshire
Filmset in 10/12 Linotron Baskerville

CONTENTS

INTRODUCTION

'Fallible and frail, a bit of pulsating, jelly-like life – it is all I am.'
So Jack London characterized himself before sailing across the
Pacific on his new ketch, *The Snark*, after the San Francisco
earthquake of 1906. 'About me are the great natural forces –
colossal menaces, Titans of destruction, unsentimental monsters
that have less concern for me than I have for the grain of sand I
crush under my foot.' Against the elements and dangers of the
great ocean that lay between America and Asia, London saw
himself matched and triumphant. 'It is good to ride the tempest
and feel godlike. I dare to assert that for a finite speck of
pulsating jelly to feel godlike is a far more glorious feeling than
for a god to feel godlike.'[1]

Yet the cruise of *The Snark* was a sad illusion. It was begun to
show off Jack London's physical and mental dominance, but it
ended in his collapse. After reaching Hawaii, the ketch needed
extensive repairs. London and his second wife Charmian saw the
life of the island and visited the leper colony on Molokai. The
ravages of the disease brought out compassion and horror and
fear in the Londons. They took the Pacific Traverse 2,000 miles
down to the Marquesas – no other sailing boat was known to
have made the journey. It took two months of beating in variable
winds and lying in the doldrums and roaring before the trades to
reach the islands where Gauguin had come to find his own
disillusion and death. It was a voyage of vast solitude, for no
other ships were sighted. Jack London was in his element, the
entertainer of his little world as he read aloud Melville, Stevenson
and Conrad in the evenings, the lord of the sea as he pitted his
pride and skill against the sudden squalls.

As usual in his philosophy and in his fiction, he saw the
struggle for existence about the ship, particularly among the
flying fish, which tried to elude the gunys in the air and the

bonitos in the sea, only to leap against the mainsail of *The Snark* and be devoured by its crew. He caught dolphins, too, and, like Lord Byron, he admired their change into all the colours of the rainbow before they died, as mutable and doomed as himself. He found it hard to sleep after catching one, so he wrote to a poet and friend, 'The leaping, blazing beauty of it gets on my brain.'[2]

At Nuku Hiva in the Marquesas, Jack London rented the clubhouse where his boyhood idol Robert Louis Stevenson had lived. He and his party rode out to Melville's paradise of Typee, the valley of Hapaa. Tuberculosis, leprosy and elephantiasis had decimated Melville's perfect warriors and had turned many of the survivors into freaks and monsters. The noble savage described by Rousseau and seen by Melville was now the ignoble sufferer from the white man's plagues. Jack London was almost driven to the conclusion that the white peoples flourished on impurity and corruption, but he discarded the idea. An immunity had been built up through natural selection, and the Polynesians must undergo the same bath of organic poison before they could lay the foundations of a new people.

After sailing on to Papeete in Tahiti, Jack London found a noble white savage, one of the first of the pioneers in organic living, whom he called 'The Nature Man'. This city child from Oregon had been dying of pneumonia, when he cured himself by vegetarianism and by living in the sun and the woods. Hounded out of America by various authorities because of his insanity, he had cleared a plantation in Tahiti and lived like a prophet of the simple life, preaching the cooperative commonwealth and the flesh-free diet. Jack London admired him and rejected his advice. He was too bound to the reward system and raw meat, to his vision of the capitalist society red in tooth and claw before the eventual victory of socialism. In the autobiographical novel he was writing on the voyage, *Martin Eden*, his hero finally committed suicide because of his disgust at fame and success, for there was no reasonable alternative to the relentless pursuit of them.

Sailing on to Tahiti, Jack London discovered financial disaster back on his ranch in California. He had to return there by steamer, sort out his affairs, and go back to Tahiti to resume his voyage on *The Snark*. His temper and body and spirit began to deteriorate. By the time the ketch reached the New Hebrides and the Solomon Islands, where head-hunters still attacked the black-birding schooners trying to kidnap the tribesmen for forced labour on copra plantations, London was sick from many tropical illnesses including yaws and ulcers and a skin disease which seemed to be leprosy caught at Molokai. His elbows became silvery and his hands swelled to the size of boxing-gloves as their skin fell away, layer after layer. The burning sun of the treacherous islands of the Pacific seemed to be destroying him. He appeared to be on board Rimbaud's *Bateau Ivre* on a voyage of delirium and madness and despair. He had to abandon ship and take a steamer to a hospital in Sydney in Australia, where remedies based on arsenic cured his flesh and affected his nerves.

So ended the voyage of *The Snark* in illness and failure. As a young man, Jack London had been on a sealing expedition in the northern Pacific and had sailed off Japan and Korea as a war correspondent; but the effect of his two-year voyage through the southern hemisphere brought darkness to his imagination. The extremes of his experience showed in his first tales about the South Seas. 'The Chinago' demonstrated the injustice and the indifference of the white masters to their workers, while 'Mauki' revealed a pleasure in telling of sadistic brutality and suffering met with total revenge. In its horrific details, London seemed to be working out his own agonies of the flesh in a terrible retribution. There is an understanding of local cultures in 'The House of Mapuhi' and 'The Whale Tooth', but greed for the price of a pearl, a typhoon and the killing of a missionary are devices used to penetrate the thoughts of the islanders. Yet in his initial *South Sea Tales*, London wrote best about the characters whom he understood. In 'The Seed of McCoy', he presented a descendant of the mutineers of *The Bounty* holding together the scared crew of a burning schooner by his seductive and compelling presence, a mysterious emanation of the spirit. In that tale of humble certainty mastering brute terror and adversity, London set down his rare hope for his own future and for those who could still command their fate.

There is a different feeling in London's stories about Hawaii, his island of rest, his serendipity. Although his fear of becoming a leper himself haunted three of the six stories published with *The House of Pride* as a book in 1912, an understandng and love of Hawaii permeated the other tales. 'Good-by, Jack' might not be the best of them, but it was the most revealing. In it, using his own Christian name, London confessed to his fear of isolation for life in the leper colony of Molokai. If he had been sent there, he would have tried to escape, as did 'The Sheriff of Kona'. Or, if he could not escape, he would have aspired to the legendary defiance of 'Koolau the Leper', who would not accept what society and his disease demanded of him. Where London confused himself with his heroes, he wrote his best stories of the individual struggle against the forces of human or natural law.

Before his early death at the age of forty, Jack London spent twelve of the last eighteen months of his life in Hawaii. It was the place where he chose to forget the slow internal disintegration of his body and the horrors of the First World War, which had begun in 1914. The sea and the surf soothed his illnesses, and the easy hospitality appealed to his need for love and approval. The warm island seemed to him to be a true melting-pot of the peoples of the earth, which might contradict his dark Darwinian prophecies of racial struggle and final destruction. He was reading Freud and Jung's *Psychology of the Unconscious*; he was growing into a new understanding of the power of myth and dream in the search for self-awareness.

Most of the Hawaiian stories, published posthumously as a book, *On the Makaloa Mat*, were the reverse images of London's bleak early view of Alaska and the Klondike. No longer did he identify himself with a young Anglo-Saxon hero braving the frozen northland in a struggle for survival against cold, hunger, beasts and lesser breeds. Now he told his stories from the point of view of the Hawaiians, talking of their traditions and myths to sceptical foreigners. Ancient wisdom confounded modern materialism. In 'The Bones of Kahekili', an old Hawaiian islander recounted to a quizzical American rancher the story of the corpse of a chief which would not sink into the womb of the waters. 'When Alice Told Her Soul' demonstrated London's occasional sense of satire as the converted Alice revealed that there was social hypocrisy even in Hawaiian society. And in 'Shin-Bones', a prince of the royal line, educated at Oxford University and a trained critic, talked of diving into the burial lava cave of his ancestors – a psychic return to the womb. From the cave, the prince took away the bones of two of the heroes of his people's sagas. It was not that he believed in the mystery stuff of old times, 'And yet, I saw in that cave things which I dare not name to you . . . This is the twentieth century, and we stink of gasoline.'[3]

So, at the end, London began to reveal the power of his dreams and his unconscious rather than parading his defiance of nature or his bitter realism. When the old fisherman in 'The Water Baby' told him that the local Prometheus named Maui had lifted up the island from the sea by hooking it to heaven and had stopped men from walking on all fours by raising the sky, London (under his Hawaiian name John Lakana) recalled that a volcanic eruption had originally pushed up Hawaii from the Pacific, and that men were once brutes who walked on four feet. He acknowledged the prehistoric and scientific basis of myths, and he was liberated into the conscious description of his own unconscious. He no longer saw himself as a speck of pulsating jelly mastering the ocean, but as a creature returning to his mother the sea to be reborn. In his last tales of the Pacific, London surrendered himself to the ocean that he sought to dominate and to the islanders that he once patronized.

It was a tribute to London's enduring mental fight that he succeeded toward the end of his short life in transferring his analysis of himself and human society from the imperatives of Darwin and Nietzsche and Marx to the self-awareness suggested by Freud and Jung and to a Proustian reaching back to childhood in order to explain the contradictions of his adult personality. Nietzsche had already suggested to London that in dreams, 'the whole thought of earlier humanity . . . manifests its existence within us.' London had used the idea in his extraordinary

neanderthal story of 1906, *Before Adam*, and he was excited to
find this theory of atavistic dreams confirmed by Jung and Freud,
to whom myths corresponded to the distorted residue of the
fantasies of whole nations.

But personally the most significant text in London's later life
was Jung's *Psychology of the Unconscious*. In his marked copy, he
underlined two phrases in the introduction: 'Freud sees a definite
incest wish toward the mother which only lacks the quality of
consciousness,' and, 'the often quite unbearable conflict of his
weakness with his feelings of idealism'.[4] Jack London began to
recognize some of the unadmitted neuroses of his life, his search
for a mother's love in the many women he had called 'Mother-
Girl' or 'Mother-mine', his denial of his physical breakdown in
the myths he wrote about himself as a superhero in search of
human brotherhood. 'Mate Woman', he said to Charmian in the
last months of his life before his death in 1916, 'I tell you I am
standing on the edge of a world so new, so wonderful, that I am
almost afraid to look over into it.'[5]

What the reading of Jung had done was to begin to separate
in his mind the validity of the ancient myths that illuminated the
best of his later work about Hawaii from the racial prejudice that
darkened the worst. One of his last projects was a story of the
discovery of America by the Vikings, no longer motivated by
their blood lust and urge for mastery, but by the myths from
their own unconscious. He had wanted to write a sexual biography of himself, 'delicately realistic, beginning low down and
ending high up'. Yet by early January in 1916, a note on his
night pad read: 'My Biography – The dark Abyss of Sex – rising
to the glory of the Sun God. All darks and deeps and fluxes of
the abysmal, opening itself in God, and basing itself on hell.
Write Jung and Freud, in sex terms of fiction.'[6]

Only the last Hawaiian tales and the final Klondike story,
'Like Argus of the Ancient Times', testify to the deepening self-
awareness of Jack London's last years. His own character became
elusive to him as he began to recognize the terrors and contradic-
tory desires behind his effort to project a consistent image of
power and candour. He reported one recurrent nightmare to

Charmian; it was a confession that he had long wanted to submit his own fierce ego to a darker power or to a mystery beyond his own belief in materialism. He saw in this dream an imperial figure, inexorable as destiny and yet strangely human, descending a cascade of staircases, while he looked up at it and waited to be vanquished. The Nemesis never reached him, but he knew that he must yield to it.[7] He even intended a novel to be called *The Pearl Man* or *The Sun God*, in which a magnificent specimen from the South Seas hated human society like Koolau the Leper and was convinced of the futility of all art and human illusion, holding that there was something bigger behind it all, and that he must strive for it.

In this way, Jack London matched his will to live and his questing mind against the chronic pain of his last years. He felt himself purged through suffering, become a prophet of mankind through his many experiences. He planned a series of bold, truthful essays to expose the self-delusion of modern men. He would make them aware as he had been made aware. He would tell them that, if some women were prostitutes, so were most men. Hypocrisy and secret sinning ruled society. The gods of the Constitution and the flag and the law were tin gods. The struggle between capital and labour was absurd in an economy that was managed inefficiently. Man was both a brute and an angel, who chose to exist in a limited and cowardly way. If he would only live by his finer passions and his rationality, he could master the earth and harness the stars. Otherwise he would skulk in the shadows like the helpless cave man, afraid of the ferocious beasts in the open, terrified of nature's hostility.[8]

It was a bold concept of humanity, as extreme as Jack London's own manias and depressions, his heroic myths of himself and his periodic revulsions from his own kind. The most haunting of his final novellas was 'The Red One'. In it, an explorer is dying slowly in the large hut of an old shaman in cannibal Melanesia. The explorer has passed through all the stages of savagery himself, and he waits for his inevitable death from the shaman's knife as he watches the old witch doctor cure the heads of other white men. Both explorer and shaman have left behind the desires of the body. 'Where was the appetite of yesterday?' Only one mystery remains unsolved, the melodious siren call that has lured the explorer into his particular heart of primitive darkness. The shaman tells him that the bewitching note comes from the Red One, which is also the God-Voiced, the Sun-Singer and the Star-Born.

Before he dies, the explorer reaches the source of the mystery. His final discovery is not that of Conrad's Kurtz in the Congo, 'The horror! The horror!' It is another mystery. The siren sound comes in fact from a huge, iridescent, vermilion, metallic sphere that has fallen to earth in the jungle, a messenger from outer space that has been made the idol for blood sacrifices. 'It was as if God's Word had fallen into the muck mire of the abyss underlying the bottom of hell . . . as if the Sermon on the Mount had been preached in a roaring bedlam of lunatics.'⁹ As the explorer yields his head to the shaman at the sound of the Red One, he seems to gaze upon 'the serene face of the Medusa, Truth'. Yet what that truth was, the story does not tell – only that, in the total dichotomy between the hallucinatory message from the stars and the savagery of men, the boundaries of Jack London's split personality lay. But at the last, he had the courage to declare himself as he prepared for his own dying.

The stories of the South Seas, written toward the end of Jack London's life, show a writer moving away from a harsh vision of the shortcomings of mankind and society into a quest after psychological depth and truth. His untimely death cut off too soon a kind of genius reaching out toward the unknown and the best of his work among the cultures of the Pacific.

Andrew Sinclair

NOTES TO THE INTRODUCTION

1. Jack London, *The Cruise of the Snark* (New York, 1911), *foreword.*
2. Jack London to George Sterling, 24 November 1907, Huntington Library, San Marino, California.
3. Jack London, 'Shin-Bones', p. 214.
4. See Jack London Library Collection, Huntington Library.
5. Charmian London, *The Book of Jack London* (2 vols., New York, 1921), II, p. 323.
6. Jack London, Notes on night-pads, Huntington Library.
7. Charmian London, *The Book of Jack London*, II, pp. 343–4.
8. Jack London, Notes on 'Man', Utah State University Library at Logan.
9. Jack London, *The Red One* (New York, 1918), p. 49.

THE CHINAGO

> The coral waxes, the palm grows, but man departs.
> – Tahitian proverb

Ah Cho did not understand French. He sat in the crowded court room, very weary and bored, listening to the unceasing, explosive French that now one official and now another uttered. It was just so much gabble to Ah Cho, and he marvelled at the stupidity of the Frenchmen who took so long to find out the murderer of Chung Ga, and who did not find him at all. The five hundred coolies on the plantation knew that Ah San had done the killing, and here was Ah San not even arrested. It was true that all the coolies had agreed secretly not to testify against one another; but then, it was so simple, the Frenchmen should have been able to discover that Ah San was the man. They were very stupid, these Frenchmen.

Ah Cho had done nothing of which to be afraid. He had had no hand in the killing. It was true he had been present at it, and Schemmer, the overseer on the plantation, had rushed into the barracks immediately afterward and caught him there, along with four or five others; but what of that? Chung Ga had been stabbed only twice. It stood to reason that five or six men could not inflict two stab wounds. At the most, if a man had struck but once, only two men could have done it.

So it was that Ah Cho reasoned, when he, along with his four companions, had lied and blocked and obfuscated in their statements to the court concerning what had taken place. They had heard the sounds of the killing, and, like Schemmer, they had run to the spot. They had got there before Schemmer – that was all. True, Schemmer had testified that, attracted by the sound of quarrelling as he chanced to pass by, he had stood for at least five minutes outside; that then, when he entered, he found the prisoners already inside; and that they had not entered just before, because he had been standing by the one door to the barracks. But what of that? Ah Cho and his four fellow-prisoners had testified that Schemmer was mistaken. In the end they would be let go. They were all confident of that. Five men could not have their heads cut off for two stab wounds. Besides, no foreign devil had seen the killing. But these Frenchmen were so stupid. In China, as Ah Cho well knew, the magistrate would order all of them to the torture and learn the truth. The truth was very easy to learn under torture. But these Frenchmen did not torture – bigger fools they! Therefore they would never find out who killed Chung Ga.

But Ah Cho did not understand everything. The English Company that owned the plantation had imported into Tahiti, at great expense, the five hundred coolies. The stockholders were clamoring for dividends, and the Company had not yet paid any; wherefore the Company did not want its costly contract laborers to start the practice of killing one another. Also, there were the French, eager and willing to impose upon the Chinagos the virtues and excellences of French law. There was nothing like setting an example once in a while; and, besides, of what use was New Caledonia except to send men to live out their days in misery and pain in payment of the penalty for being frail and human?

Ah Cho did not understand all this. He sat in the court room and waited for the baffled judgment that would set him and his comrades free to go back to the plantation and work out the terms of their contracts. This judgment would soon be rendered. Proceedings were drawing to a close. He could see that. There was no more testifying, no more gabble of tongues. The French devils were tired, too, and evidently waiting for the judgment. And as he waited he remembered back in his life to the time when he had signed the contract and set sail in the ship for Tahiti. Times had been hard in his seacoast village, and when he indentured himself to labor for five years in the South Seas at fifty cents Mexican a day, he had thought himself fortunate. There were men in his village who toiled a whole year for ten dollars Mexican, and there were women who made nets all the year round for five dollars, while in the houses of shopkeepers there were maid-servants who received four dollars for a year of service. And here he was to receive fifty cents a day; for one day, only one day, he was to receive that princely sum! What if the work were hard? At the end of the five years he would return home – that was in the contract – and he would never have to work again. He would be a rich man for life, with a house of his own, a wife, and children growing up to venerate him. Yes, and back of the house he would have a small garden, a place of meditation and repose, with goldfish in a tiny lakelet, and wind bells tinkling in the several trees, and there would be a high wall all around so that his meditation and repose should be undisturbed.

Well, he had worked out three of those five years. He was already a wealthy man (in his own country), through his earnings, and only two years more intervened between the cotton plantation on Tahiti and the meditation and repose that awaited him. But just now he was losing money because of the unfortunate accident of being present at the killing of Chung Ga. He had lain three weeks in prison, and for each day of those three weeks he had lost fifty cents. But now judgment would soon be given, and he would go back to work.

Ah Cho was twenty-two years old. He was happy and good-natured, and it was easy for him to smile. While his body was slim in the Asiatic way, his face was rotund. It was round, like the moon, and it irradiated a gentle complacence and a sweet kindliness of spirit that was unusual among his countrymen. Nor did his looks belie him. He never caused trouble, never took part in wrangling. He did not gamble. His soul was not harsh enough for the soul that must belong to a gambler. He was content with little things and simple pleasures. The hush and quiet in the cool of the day after the blazing toil in the cotton field was to him an infinite satisfaction. He could sit for hours gazing at a solitary flower and philosophizing about the mysteries and riddles of being. A blue heron on a tiny crescent of sandy beach, a silvery splatter of flying fish, or a sunset of pearl and rose across the lagoon, could entrance him to all forgetfulness of the procession of wearisome days and of the heavy lash of Schemmer.

Schemmer, Karl Schemmer, was a brute, a brutish brute. But he earned his salary. He got the last particle of strength out of the five hundred slaves; for slaves they were until their term of years was up. Schemmer worked hard to extract the strength from those five hundred sweating bodies and to transmute it into bales of fluffy cotton ready for export. His dominant, iron-clad, primeval brutishness was what enabled him to effect the trans-mutation. Also, he was assisted by a thick leather belt, three inches wide and a yard in length, with which he always rode and which, on occasion, could come down on the naked back of a stooping coolie with a report like a pistol-shot. These reports were frequent when Schemmer rode down the furrowed field.

Once, at the beginning of the first year of contract labor, he had killed a coolie with a single blow of his fist. He had not exactly crushed the man's head like an egg-shell, but the blow had been sufficient to addle what was inside, and, after being sick for a week, the man had died. But the Chinese had not complained to the French devils that ruled over Tahiti. It was their own lookout. Schemmer was their problem. They must avoid his wrath as they avoided the venom of the centipedes that lurked in the grass or crept into the sleeping quarters on rainy nights. The Chinagos – such they were called by the indolent, brown-skinned island folk – saw to it that they did not displease Schemmer too greatly. This was equivalent to rendering up to him a full measure of efficient toil. That blow of Schemmer's fist had been worth thousands of dollars to the Company, and no trouble ever came of it to Schemmer.

The French, with no instinct for colonization, futile in their childish playgame of developing the resources of the island, were only too glad to see the English Company succeed. What matter of Schemmer and his redoubtable fist? The Chinago that died? Well, he was only a Chinago. Besides, he died of sunstroke, as the doctor's certificate attested. True, in all the history of Tahiti no one had ever died of sunstroke. But it was that, precisely that, which made the death of this Chinago unique. The doctor said as much in his report. He was very candid. Dividends must be paid, or else one more failure would be added to the long history of failure in Tahiti.

There was no understanding these white devils. Ah 'Cho pondered their inscrutableness as he sat in the court room waiting the judgment. There was no telling what went on at the back of their minds. He had seen a few of the white devils. They were all alike – the officers and sailors on the ship, the French officials, the several white men on the plantation, including Schemmer. Their minds all moved in mysterious ways there was no getting at. They grew angry without apparent cause, and their anger was always dangerous. They were like wild beasts at such times. They worried about little things, and on occasion could out-toil even a Chinago. They were not temperate as Chinagos were temperate; they were gluttons, eating prodigiously and drinking more prodigiously. A Chinago never knew when an act would please them or arouse a storm of wrath. A Chinago could never tell. What pleased one time, the very next time might provoke an outburst of anger. There was a curtain behind the eyes of the white devils that screened the backs of their minds from the Chinago's gaze. And then, on top of it all, was that terrible efficiency of the white devils, that ability to do things, to make things go, to work results, to bend to their wills all creeping, crawling things, and the powers of the very elements themselves. Yes, the white men were strange and wonderful, and they were devils. Look at Schemmer.

Ah Cho wondered why the judgment was so long in forming. Not a man on trial had laid hand on Chung Ga. Ah San alone had killed him. Ah San had done it, bending Chung Ga's head back with one hand by a grip of his queue, and with the other hand, from behind, reaching over and driving the knife into his body. Twice had he driven it in. There in the court room, with closed eyes, Ah Cho saw the killing acted over again – the squabble, the vile words bandied back and forth, the filth and insult flung upon venerable ancestors, the curses laid upon unbegotten generations, the leap of Ah San, the grip on the queue of Chung Ga, the knife that sank twice into his flesh, the bursting open of the door, the irruption of Schemmer, the dash for the door, the escape of Ah San, the flying belt of Schemmer that drove the rest into the corner, and the firing of the revolver as a signal that brought help to Schemmer. Ah Cho shivered as he lived it over. One blow of the belt had bruised his cheek, taking off some of the skin. Schemmer had pointed to the bruises when, on the witness-stand, he had identified Ah Cho. It was only just now that the marks had become no longer visible. That had been a blow. Half an inch nearer the centre and it would have taken out his eye. Then Ah Cho forgot the whole happening in a vision he caught of the garden of meditation and repose that would be his when he returned to his own land.

He sat with impassive face, while the magistrate rendered the judgment. Likewise were the faces of his four companions impassive. And they remained impassive when the interpreter explained that the five of them had been found guilty of the murder of Chung Ga, and that Ah Chow should have his head cut off, Ah Cho serve twenty years in prison in New Caledonia, Wong Li twelve years and Ah Tong ten years. There was no use in getting excited about it. Even Ah Chow remained expressionless as a mummy, though it was his head that was to be cut off. The magistrate added a few words, and the interpreter explained that Ah Chow's face having been most severely bruised by Schemmer's strap had made his identification so positive that, since one man must die, he might as well be that man. Also, the fact that Ah Cho's face likewise had been severely bruised, conclusively proving his presence at the murder and his undoubted participation, had merited him the twenty years of penal servitude. And down to the ten years of Ah Tong, the proportioned reason for each sentence was explained. Let the Chinagos take the lesson to heart, the Court said finally, for they must learn that the law would be fulfilled in Tahiti though the heavens fell.

The five Chinagos were taken back to jail. They were not shocked nor grieved. The sentences being unexpected was quite what they were accustomed to in their dealings with the white devils. From them a Chinago rarely expected more than the unexpected. The heavy punishment for a crime they had not committed was no stranger than the countless strange things that white devils did. In the weeks that followed, Ah Cho often contemplated Ah Chow with mild curiosity. His head was to be cut off by the guillotine that was being erected on the plantation. For him there would be no declining years, no gardens of tranquillity. Ah Cho philosophized and speculated about life and death. As for himself, he was not perturbed. Twenty years were merely twenty years. By that much was his garden removed from him – that was all. He was young, and the patience of Asia was in his bones. He could wait those twenty years, and by that time the heats of his blood would be assuaged and he would be better fitted for that garden of calm delight. He thought of a name for it; he would call it The Garden of the Morning Calm. He was made happy all day by the thought, and he was inspired to devise a moral maxim on the virtue of patience, which maxim proved a great comfort, especially to Wong Li and Ah Tong. Ah Chow, however, did not care for the maxim. His head was to be separated from his body in so short a time that he had no need for patience to wait for that event. He smoked well, ate well, slept well, and did not worry about the slow passage of time.

Cruchot was a gendarme. He had seen twenty years of service in the colonies, from Nigeria and Senegal to the South Seas, and those twenty years had not perceptibly brightened his dull mind. He was as slow-witted and stupid as in his peasant days in the south of France. He knew discipline and fear of authority, and from God down to the sergeant of gendarmes the only difference to him was the measure of slavish obedience which he rendered. In point of fact, the sergeant bulked bigger in his mind than God, except on Sundays when God's mouthpieces had their say. God was usually very remote, while the sergeant was ordinarily very close at hand.

Cruchot it was who received the order from the Chief Justice to the jailer commanding that functionary to deliver over to Cruchot the person of Ah Chow. Now, it happened that the Chief Justice had given a dinner the night before to the captain and officers of the French man-of-war. His hand was shaking when he wrote out the order, and his eyes were aching so dreadfully that he did not read over the order. It was only a Chinago's life he was signing away, anyway. So he did not notice that he had omitted the final letter in Ah Chow's name. The order read 'Ah Cho', and, when Cruchot presented the order, the jailer turned over to him the person of Ah Cho. Cruchot took that person beside him on the seat of a wagon, behind two mules, and drove away.

Ah Cho was glad to be out in the sunshine. He sat beside the gendarme and beamed. He beamed more ardently than ever when he noted the mules headed south toward Atimaono. Undoubtedly Schemmer had sent for him to be brought back. Schemmer wanted him to work. Very well, he would work well. Schemmer would never have cause to complain. It was a hot day. There had been a stoppage of the trades. The mules sweated, Cruchot sweated, and Ah Cho sweated. But it was Ah Cho that bore the heat with the least concern. He had toiled three years under that sun on the plantation. He beamed and beamed with such genial good nature that even Cruchot's heavy mind was stirred to wonderment.

'You are very funny,' he said at last.

Ah Cho nodded and beamed more ardently. Unlike the magistrate, Cruchot spoke to him in the Kanaka tongue, and this, like all Chinagos and all foreign devils, Ah Cho understood.

'You laugh too much,' Cruchot chided. 'One's heart should be full of tears on a day like this.'

'I am glad to get out of the jail.'

'Is that all?' The gendarme shrugged his shoulders.

'Is it not enough?' was the retort.

'Then you are not glad to have your head cut off?'

Ah Cho looked at him in abrupt perplexity and said:

'Why, I am going back to Atimaono to work on the plantation for Schemmer. Are you not taking me to Atimaono?'

Cruchot stroked his long mustaches reflectively. 'Well, well,' he said finally, with a flick of the whip at the off mule, 'so you don't know?'

'Know what?' Ah Cho was beginning to feel a vague alarm. 'Won't Schemmer let me work for him any more?'

'Not after to-day.' Cruchot laughed heartily. It was a good joke. 'You see, you won't be able to work after to-day. A man with his head off can't work, eh?' He poked the Chinago in the ribs, and chuckled.

Ah Cho maintained silence while the mules trotted a hot mile. Then he spoke: 'Is Schemmer going to cut off my head?'

Cruchot grinned as he nodded.

'It is a mistake,' said Ah Cho, gravely. 'I am not the Chinago that is to have his head cut off. I am Ah Cho. The honorable judge has determined that I am to stop twenty years in New Caledonia.'

The gendarme laughed. It was a good joke, this funny Chinago trying to cheat the guillotine. The mules trotted through a coconut grove and for half a mile beside the sparkling sea before Ah Cho spoke again.

'I tell you I am not Ah Chow. The honorable judge did not say that my head was to go off.'

'Don't be afraid,' said Cruchot, with the philanthropic intention of making it easier for his prisoner. 'It is not difficult to die that way.' He snapped his fingers. 'It is quick – like that. It is not like hanging on the end of a rope and kicking and making faces for five minutes. It is like killing a chicken with a hatchet. You cut its head off, that is all. And it is the same with a man. Pouf! – it is over. It doesn't hurt. You don't even think it hurts. You don't think. Your head is gone, so you cannot think. It is very good. That is the way I want to die – quick, ah, quick. You are lucky to die that way. You might get the leprosy and fall to pieces slowly, a finger at a time, and now and again a thumb, also the toes. I knew a man who was burned by hot water. It took him two days to die. You could hear him yelling a kilometre away. But you? Ah! so easy! Chck! – the knife cuts your neck like that. It is finished. The knife may even tickle. Who can say? Nobody who died that way ever came back to say.'

He considered this last an excruciating joke, and permitted himself to be convulsed with laughter for half a minute. Part of his mirth was assumed, but he considered it his humane duty to cheer up the Chinago.

'But I tell you I am Ah Cho,' the other persisted. 'I don't want my head cut off.'

Cruchot scowled. The Chinago was carrying the foolishness too far.

'I am not Ah Chow – ' Ah Cho began.

'That will do,' the gendarme interrupted. He puffed up his cheeks and strove to appear fierce.

'I tell you I am not – ' Ah Cho began again.

'Shut up!' bawled Cruchot.

After that they rode along in silence. It was twenty miles from Papeete to Atimaono, and over half the distance was covered by the time the Chinago again ventured into speech.

'I saw you in the court room, when the honorable judge sought after our guilt,' he began. 'Very good. And do you remember that Ah Chow, whose head is to be cut off – do you remember that he – Ah Chow – was a tall man? Look at me.'

He stood up suddenly, and Cruchot saw that he was a short man. And just as suddenly Cruchot caught a glimpse of a memory picture of Ah Chow, and in that picture Ah Chow was tall. To the gendarme all Chinagos looked alike. One face was like another. But between tallness and shortness he could differentiate, and he knew that he had the wrong man beside him on the seat. He pulled up the mules abruptly, so that the pole shot ahead of them, elevating their collars.

'You see, it was a mistake,' said Ah Cho, smiling pleasantly.

But Cruchot was thinking. Already he regretted that he had stopped the wagon. He was unaware of the error of the Chief Justice, and he had no way of working it out; but he did know that he had been given this Chinago to take to Atimaono and that it was his duty to take him to Atimaono. What if he was the wrong man and they cut his head off? It was only a Chinago when all was said, and what was a Chinago, anyway? Besides, it might not be a mistake. He did not know what went on in the minds of his superiors. They knew their business best. Who was he to do their thinking for them? Once, in the long ago, he had attempted to think for them, and the sergeant had said: 'Cruchot, you are a fool! The quicker you know that, the better you will get on. You are not to think; you are to obey and leave thinking to your betters.' He smarted under the recollection. Also, if he turned back to Papeete, he would delay the execution at Atimaono, and if he were wrong in turning back, he would get a reprimand from the sergeant who was waiting for the prisoner. And, furthermore, he would get a reprimand at Papeete as well.

He touched the mules with the whip and drove on. He looked at his watch. He would be half an hour late as it was, and the sergeant was bound to be angry. He put the mules into a faster trot. The more Ah Cho persisted in explaining the mistake, the more stubborn Cruchot became. The knowledge that he had the wrong man did not make his temper better. The knowledge that it was through no mistake of his confirmed him in the belief that the wrong he was doing was the right. And, rather than incur the displeasure of the sergeant, he would willingly have assisted a dozen wrong Chinagos to their doom.

As for Ah Cho, after the gendarme had struck him over the head with the butt of the whip and commanded him in a loud voice to shut up, there remained nothing for him to do but to shut up. The long ride continued in silence. Ah Cho pondered the strange ways of the foreign devils. There was no explaining them. What they were doing with him was of a piece with everything they did. First they found guilty five innocent men, and next they cut off the head of the man that even they, in their benighted ignorance, had deemed meritorious of no more than twenty years' imprisonment. And there was nothing he could do. He could only sit idly and take what these lords of life measured out to him. Once, he got in a panic, and the sweat upon his body turned cold; but he fought his way out of it. He endeavored to resign himself to his fate by remembering and repeating certain passages from the 'Yin Chih Wen' ('The Tract of the Quiet Way'); but, instead, he kept seeing his dream-garden of meditation and repose. This bothered him, until he abandoned himself to the dream and sat in his garden listening to the tinkling of the wind-bells in the several trees. And lo! sitting thus, in the dream, he was able to remember and repeat the passages from 'The Tract of the Quiet Way'.

So the time passed nicely until Atimaono was reached and the mules trotted up to the foot of the scaffold, in the shade of which stood the impatient sergeant. Ah Cho was hurried up the ladder of the scaffold. Beneath him on one side he saw assembled all the coolies of the plantation. Schemmer had decided that the event would be a good object-lesson, and so had called in the coolies from the fields and compelled them to be present. As they caught sight of Ah Cho they gabbled among themselves in low voices. They saw the mistake; but they kept it to themselves. The inexplicable white devils had doubtlessly changed their minds. Instead of taking the life of one innocent man, they were taking the life of another innocent man. Ah Chow or Ah Cho – what did it matter which? They could never understand the white dogs any more than could the white dogs understand them. Ah Cho was going to have his head cut off, but they, when their two remaining years of servitude were up, were going back to China.

Schemmer had made the guillotine himself. He was a handy man, and though he had never seen a guillotine, the French officials had explained the principle to him. It was on his suggestion that they had ordered the execution to take place at Atimaono instead of at Papeete. The scene of the crime, Schemmer had argued, was the best possible place for the punishment, and, in addition, it would have a salutary influence upon the half-thousand Chinagos on the plantation. Schemmer had also volunteered to act as executioner, and in that capacity he was now on the scaffold, experimenting with the instrument he had made. A banana tree, of the size and consistency of a man's neck, lay under the guillotine. Ah Cho watched with fascinated eyes. The German, turning a small crank, hoisted the blade to the top of the little derrick he had rigged. A jerk on a stout piece of cord loosed the blade and it dropped with a flash, neatly severing the banana trunk.

'How does it work?' The sergeant, coming out on top the scaffold, had asked the question.

'Beautifully,' was Schemmer's exultant answer. 'Let me show you.'

Again he turned the crank that hoisted the blade, jerked the cord, and sent the blade crashing down on the soft tree. But this time it went no more than two-thirds of the way through.

The sergeant scowled. 'That will not serve,' he said.

Schemmer wiped the sweat from his forehead. 'What it needs is more weight,' he announced. Walking up to the edge of the scaffold, he called his orders to the blacksmith for a twenty-five-pound piece of iron. As he stooped over to attach the iron to the broad top of the blade, Ah Cho glanced at the sergeant and saw his opportunity.

'The honorable judge said that Ah Chow was to have his head cut off,' he began.

The sergeant nodded impatiently. He was thinking of the fifteen-mile ride before him that afternoon, to the windward side of the island, and of Berthe, the pretty half-caste daughter of Lafière, the pearl-trader, who was waiting for him at the end of it.

'Well, I am not Ah Chow. I am Ah Cho. The honorable jailer has made a mistake. Ah Chow is a tall man, and you see I am short.'

The sergeant looked at him hastily and saw the mistake. 'Schemmer!' he called, imperatively. 'Come here.'

The German grunted, but remained bent over his task till the chunk of iron was lashed to his satisfaction. 'Is your Chinago ready?' he demanded.

'Look at him,' was the answer. 'Is he the Chinago?'

Schemmer was surprised. He swore tersely for a few seconds, and looked regretfully across at the thing he had made with his own hands and which he was eager to see work. 'Look here,' he said finally, 'we can't postpone this affair. I've lost three hours' work already out of those five hundred Chinagos. I can't afford to lose it all over again for the right man. Let's put the performance through just the same. It is only a Chinago.'

The sergeant remembered the long ride before him, and the pearl-trader's daughter, and debated with himself.

'They will blame it on Cruchot – if it is discovered,' the German urged. 'But there's little chance of its being discovered. Ah Chow won't give it away, at any rate.'

'The blame won't lie with Cruchot, anyway,' the sergeant said. 'It must have been the jailer's mistake.'

'Then let's go on with it. They can't blame us. Who can tell one Chinago from another? We can say that we merely carried out instructions with the Chinago that was turned over to us. Besides, I really can't take all those coolies a second time away from their labor.'

They spoke in French, and Ah Cho, who did not understand a word of it, nevertheless knew that they were determining his destiny. He knew, also, that the decision rested with the sergeant, and he hung upon that official's lips.

'All right,' announced the sergeant. 'Go ahead with it. He is only a Chinago.'

'I'm going to try it once more, just to make sure.' Schemmer moved the banana trunk forward under the knife, which he had hoisted to the top of the derrick.

Ah Cho tried to remember maxims from 'The Tract of the Quiet Way'. 'Live in concord', came to him; but it was not applicable. He was not going to live. He was about to die. No, that would not do. 'Forgive malice' – yes, but there was no malice to forgive. Schemmer and the rest were doing this thing without malice. It was to them merely a piece of work that had to be done, just as clearing the jungle, ditching the water, and planting cotton were pieces of work that had to be done. Schemmer jerked the cord, and Ah Cho forgot 'The Tract of the Quiet Way'. The knife shot down with a thud, making a clean slice of the tree.

'Beautiful!' exclaimed the sergeant, pausing in the act of lighting a cigarette. 'Beautiful, my friend.'

Schemmer was pleased at the praise.

'Come on, Ah Chow,' he said, in the Tahitian tongue.

'But I am not Ah Chow – ' Ah Cho began.

'Shut up!' was the answer. 'If you open your mouth again, I'll break your head.'

The overseer threatened him with a clenched fist, and he remained silent. What was the good of protesting? Those foreign devils always had their way. He allowed himself to be lashed to the vertical board that was the size of his body. Schemmer drew the buckles tight – so tight that the straps cut into his flesh and hurt. But he did not complain. The hurt would not last long. He felt the board tilting over in the air toward the horizontal, and closed his eyes. And in that moment he caught a last glimpse of his garden of meditation and repose. It seemed to him that he sat in the garden. A cool wind was blowing, and the bells in the several trees were tinkling softly. Also, birds were making sleepy noises, and from beyond the high wall came the subdued sound of village life.

Then he was aware that the board had come to rest, and from muscular pressures and tensions he knew that he was lying on his back. He opened his eyes. Straight above him he saw the suspended knife blazing in the sunshine. He saw the weight which had been added, and noted that one of Schemmer's knots had slipped. Then he heard the sergeant's voice in sharp command. Ah Cho closed his eyes hastily. He did not want to see that knife descend. But he felt it – for one great fleeting instant. And in that instant he remembered Cruchot and what Cruchot had said. But Cruchot was wrong. The knife did not tickle. That much he knew before he ceased to know.

THE HOUSE OF MAPUHI

Despite the heavy clumsiness of her lines, the *Aorai* handled easily in the light breeze, and her captain ran her well in before he hove to just outside the suck of the surf. The atoll of Hikueru lay low on the water, a circle of pounded coral sand a hundred yards wide, twenty miles in circumference, and from three to five feet above high-water mark. On the bottom of the huge and glassy lagoon was much pearl shell, and from the deck of the schooner, across the slender ring of the atoll, the divers could be seen at work. But the lagoon had no entrance for even a traditional schooner. With a favoring breeze cutters could win in through the tortuous and shallow channel, but the schooners lay off and on outside and sent in their small boats.

The *Aorai* swung out a boat smartly, into which sprang half a dozen brown-skinned sailors clad only in scarlet loin-cloths. They took the oars, while in the stern-sheets, at the steering sweep, stood a young man garbed in the tropic white that marks the European. But he was not all European. The golden strain of Polynesia betrayed itself in the sun-gilt of his fair skin and cast up golden sheens and lights through the glimmering blue of his eyes. Raoul he was, Alexandré Raoul, youngest son of Marie Raoul, the wealthy quarter-caste, who owned and managed half a dozen trading schooners similar to the *Aorai*. Across an eddy just outside the entrance, and in and through and over a boiling tide-rip, the boat fought its way to the mirrored calm of the lagoon. Young Raoul leaped out upon the white sand and shook hands with a tall native. The man's chest and shoulders were magnificent, but the stump of a right arm, beyond the flesh of which the age-whitened bone projected several inches, attested the encounter with a shark that had put an end to his diving days and made him a fawner and an intriguer for small favors.

'Have you heard, Alec?' were his first words. 'Mapuhi has

found a pearl – such a pearl. Never was there one like it ever fished up in Hikueru, nor in all the Paumotus, nor in all the world. Buy it from him. He has it now. And remember that I told you first. He is a fool and you can get it cheap. Have you any tobacco?'

Straight up the beach to a shack under a pandanus-tree Raoul headed. He was his mother's supercargo, and his business was to comb all the Paumotus for the wealth of copra, shell and pearls that they yielded up.

He was a young supercargo, it was his second voyage in such capacity, and he suffered much secret worry from his lack of experience in pricing pearls. But when Mapuhi exposed the pearl to his sight he managed to suppress the startle it gave him, and to maintain a careless, commercial expression on his face. For the pearl had struck him a blow. It was large as a pigeon egg, a perfect sphere, of a whiteness that reflected opalescent lights from all colors about it. It was alive. Never had he seen anything like it. When Mapuhi dropped it into his hand he was surprised by the weight of it. That showed that it was a good pearl. He examined it closely, through a pocket magnifying-glass. It was without flaw or blemish. The purity of it seemed almost to melt into the atmosphere out of his hand. In the shade it was softly luminous, gleaming like a tender moon. So translucently white was it, that when he dropped it into a glass of water he had difficulty in finding it. So straight and swiftly had it sunk to the bottom that he knew its weight was excellent.

'Well, what do you want for it?' he asked, with a fine assumption of nonchalance.

'I want – ' Mapuhi began, and behind him, framing his own dark face, the dark faces of two women and a girl nodded concurrence in what he wanted. Their heads were bent forward, they were animated by a suppressed eagerness, their eyes flashed avariciously.

'I want a house,' Mapuhi went on. 'It must have a roof of galvanized iron and an octagon-drop-clock. It must be six fathoms long with a porch all around. A big room must be in the centre, with a round table in the middle of it and the octagon-drop-clock on the wall. There must be four bedrooms, two on each side of the big room, and in each bedroom must be an iron bed, two chairs and a washstand. And back of the house must be a kitchen, a good kitchen, with pots and pans and a stove. And you must build the house on my island, which is Fakarava.'

'Is that all?' Raoul asked incredulously.

'There must be a sewing machine,' spoke up Tefara, Mapuhi's wife.

'Not forgetting the octagon-drop-clock,' added Nauri, Mapuhi's mother.

'Yes, that is all,' said Mapuhi.

Young Raoul laughed. He laughed long and heartily. But while he laughed he secretly performed problems in mental arithmetic. He had never built a house in his life, and his notions concerning house building were hazy. While he laughed he calculated the cost of the voyage to Tahiti for materials, of the materials themselves, of the voyage back again to Fakarava, and the cost of landing the materials and of building the house. It would come to four thousand French dollars, allowing a margin for safety – four thousand French dollars were equivalent to twenty thousand francs. It was impossible. How was he to know the value of such a pearl? Twenty thousand francs was a lot of money – and of his mother's money at that.

'Mapuhi,' he said, 'you are a big fool. Set a money price.'

But Mapuhi shook his head, and the three heads behind him shook with his.

'I want the house,' he said. 'It must be six fathoms long with a porch all around – '

'Yes, yes,' Raoul interrupted. 'I know all about your house, but it won't do. I'll give you a thousand Chili dollars.'

The four heads chorused a silent negative.

'And a hundred Chili dollars in trade.'

'I want the house,' Mapuhi began.

'What good will the house do you?' Raoul demanded. 'The first hurricane that comes along will wash it away. You ought to know. Captain Raffy says it looks like a hurricane right now.'

'Not on Fakarava,' said Mapuhi. 'The land is much higher there. On this island, yes. Any hurricane can sweep Hikueru. I will have the house on Fakarava. It must be six fathoms long with a porch all around – '

And Raoul listened again to the tale of the house. Several hours he spent in the endeavor to hammer the house-obsession out of Mapuhi's mind; but Mapuhi's mother and wife, and Ngakura, Mapuhi's daugher, bolstered him in his resolve for the house. Through the open doorway, while he listened for the twentieth time to the detailed description of the house that was wanted, Raoul saw his schooner's second boat draw up on the beach. The sailors rested on the oars, advertising haste to be gone. The first mate of the *Aorai* sprang ashore, exchanged a word with the one-armed native, then hurried toward Raoul. The day grew suddenly dark, as a squall obscured the face of the sun. Across the lagoon Raoul could see approaching the ominous line of the puff of wind.

'Captain Raffy says you've got to get to hell outa here,' was the mate's greeting. 'If there's any shell, we've got to run the risk of picking it up later on – so he says. The barometer's dropped to twenty-nine-seventy.'

The gust of wind struck the pandanus-tree overhead and tore through the palms beyond, flinging half a dozen ripe coconuts with heavy thuds to the ground. Then came the rain out of the distance, advancing with the roar of a gale of wind and causing the water of the lagoon to smoke in driven windrows. The sharp rattle of the first drops was on the leaves when Raoul sprang to his feet.

'A thousand Chili dollars, cash down, Mapuhi,' he said. 'And two hundred Chili dollars in trade.'

'I want a house – ' the other began.

'Mapuhi!' Raoul yelled, in order to make himself heard. 'You are a fool!'

He flung out of the house, and, side by side with the mate, fought his way down the beach toward the boat. They could not see the boat. The tropic rain sheeted about them so that they could see only the beach under their feet and the spiteful little waves from the lagoon that snapped and bit at the sand. A figure appeared through the deluge. It was Huru-Huru, the man with the one arm.

'Did you get the pearl?' he yelled in Raoul's ear.

'Mapuhi is a fool!' was the answering yell, and the next moment they were lost to each other in the descending water.

Half an hour later, Huru-Huru, watching from the seaward side of the atoll, saw the two boats hoisted in and the *Aorai* pointing her nose out to sea. And near her, just come in from the sea on the wings of the squall, he saw another schooner hove to and dropping a boat into the water. He knew her. It was the *Orohena*, owned by Toriki, the half-caste trader, who served as his own supercargo and who doubtlessly was even then in the stern-sheets of the boat. Huru-Huru chuckled. He knew that Mapuhi owed Toriki for trade-goods advanced the year before.

The squall had passed. The hot sun was blazing down, and the lagoon was once more a mirror. But the air was sticky like mucilage, and the weight of it seemed to burden the lungs and make breathing difficult.

'Have you heard the news, Toriki?' Huru-Huru asked. 'Mapuhi has found a pearl. Never was there a pearl like it ever fished up in Hikueru, nor anywhere in the Paumotus, nor anywhere in all the world. Mapuhi is a fool. Besides, he owes you money. Remember that I told you first. Have you any tobacco?'

And to the grass-shack of Mapuhi went Toriki. He was a masterful man, withal a fairly stupid one. Carelessly he glanced at the wonderful pearl – glanced for a moment only; and carelessly he dropped it into his pocket.

'You are lucky,' he said. 'It is a nice pearl. I will give you credit on the books.'

'I want a house,' Mapuhi began, in consternation. 'It must be six fathoms – '

'Six fathoms your grandmother!' was the trader's retort. 'You want to pay up your debts, that's what you want. You owed me twelve hundred dollars Chili. Very well; you owe them no longer. The amount is squared. Besides, I will give you credit for two hundred Chili. If, when I get to Tahiti, the pearl sells well, I will give you credit for another hundred – that will make three hundred. But mind, only if the pearl sells well. I may even lose money on it.'

Mapuhi folded his arms in sorrow and sat with bowed head. He had been robbed of his pearl. In place of his house, he had paid a debt. There was nothing to show for the pearl.

'You are a fool,' said Tefara.

'You are a fool,' said Nauri, his mother. 'Why did you let the pearl into his hand?'

'What was I to do?' Mapuhi protested. 'I owed him the money. He knew I had the pearl. You heard him yourself ask to see it. I had not told him. He knew. Somebody else told him. And I owed him the money.'

'Mapuhi is a fool,' mimicked Ngakura.

She was twelve years old and did not know any better. Mapuhi relieved his feelings by sending her reeling from a box on the ear; while Tefara and Nauri burst into tears and continued to upbraid him after the manner of women.

Huru-Huru, watching on the beach, saw a third schooner that he knew heave to outside the entrance and drop a boat. It was the *Hira*, well named, for she was owned by Levy, the German Jew, the greatest pearl buyer of them all, and, as was well known, Hira was the Tahitian god of fishermen and thieves.

'Have you heard the news?' Huru-Huru asked, as Levy, a fat man with massive asymmetrical features, stepped out upon the beach. 'Mapuhi has found a pearl. There was never a pearl like it in Hikueru, in all the Paumotus, in all the world. Mapuhi is a fool. He has sold it to Toriki for fourteen hundred Chili – I listened outside and heard. Toriki is likewise a fool. You can buy it from him cheap. Remember that I told you first. Have you any tobacco?'

'Where is Toriki?'

'In the house of Captain Lynch, drinking absinthe. He has been there an hour.'

And while Levy and Toriki drank absinthe and chaffered over the pearl, Huru-Huru listened and heard the stupendous price of twenty-five thousand francs agreed upon.

It was at this time that both the *Orohena* and the *Hira*, running in close to the shore, began firing guns and signalling frantically. The three men stepped outside in time to see the two schooners go hastily about and head off shore, dropping mainsails and flying-jibs on the run in the teeth of the squall that heeled them far over on the whitened water. Then the rain blotted them out.

'They'll be back after it's over,' said Toriki. 'We'd better be getting out of here.'

'I reckon the glass has fallen some more,' said Captain Lynch.

He was a white-bearded sea-captain, too old for service, who had learned that the only way to live on comfortable terms with his asthma was on Hikueru. He went inside to look at the barometer.

'Great God!' they heard him exclaim, and rushed in to join him at staring at a dial, which marked twenty-nine-twenty.

Again they came out, this time anxiously to consult sea and sky. The squall had cleared away, but the sky remained overcast. The two schooners, under all sail and joined by a third, could be seen making back. A veer in the wind induced them to slack off sheets, and five minutes afterward a sudden veer from the opposite quarter caught all three schooners aback, and those on shore could see the boom-tackles being slacked away or cast off on the jump. The sound of the surf was loud, hollow, and menacing, and a heavy swell was setting in. A terrible sheet of lightning burst before their eyes, illuminating the dark day, and the thunder rolled wildly about them.

Toriki and Levy broke into a run for their boats, the latter ambling along like a panic-stricken hippopotamus. As their two boats swept out the entrance, they passed the boat of the *Aorai* coming in. In the stern-sheets, encouraging the rowers, was Raoul. Unable to shake the vision of the pearl from his mind, he was returning to accept Mapuhi's price of a house.

He landed on the beach in the midst of a driving thunder squall that was so dense that he collided with Huru-Huru before he saw him.

'Too late,' yelled Huru-Huru. 'Mapuhi sold it to Toriki for fourteen hundred Chili, and Toriki sold it to Levy for twenty-five thousand francs. And Levy will sell it in France for a hundred thousand francs. Have you any tobacco?'

Raoul felt relieved. His troubles about the pearl were over. He need not worry any more, even if he had not got the pearl. But he did not believe Huru-Huru. Mapuhi might well have sold it for fourteen hundred Chili, but that Levy, who knew pearls, should have paid twenty-five thousand francs was too wide a stretch. Raoul decided to interview Captain Lynch on the subject, but when he arrived at that ancient mariner's house, he found him looking wide-eyed at the barometer.

'What do you read it?' Captain Lynch asked anxiously, rubbing his spectacles and staring again at the instrument.

'Twenty-nine-ten,' said Raoul. 'I have never seen it so low before.'

'I should say not!' snorted the captain. 'Fifty years boy and man on all the seas, and I've never seen it go down to that. Listen!'

They stood for a moment, while the surf rumbled and shook the house. Then they went outside. The squall had passed. They could see the *Aorai* lying becalmed a mile away and pitching and tossing madly in the tremendous seas that rolled in stately procession down out of the northeast and flung themselves furiously upon the coral shore. One of the sailors from the boat pointed at the mouth of the passage and shook his head. Raoul looked and saw a white anarchy of foam and surge.

'I guess I'll stay with you to-night, Captain,' he said; then turned to the sailor and told him to haul the boat out and to find shelter for himself and fellows.

'Twenty-nine flat,' Captain Lynch reported, coming out from another look at the barometer, a chair in his hand.

He sat down and stared at the spectacle of the sea. The sun came out, increasing the sultriness of the day, while the dead calm still held. The seas continued to increase in magnitude.

'What makes that sea is what gets me,' Raoul muttered petulantly. 'There is no wind, yet look at it, look at that fellow there!'

Miles in length, carrying tens of thousands of tons in weight, its impact shook the frail atoll like an earthquake. Captain Lynch was startled.

'Gracious!' he exclaimed, half-rising from his chair, then sinking back.

'But there is no wind,' Raoul persisted. 'I could understand it if there was wind along with it.'

'You'll get the wind soon enough without worryin' for it,' was the grim reply.

The two men sat on in silence. The sweat stood out on their skin in myriads of tiny drops that ran together, forming blotches of moisture, which, in turn, coalesced into rivulets that dripped to the ground. They panted for breath, the old man's efforts being especially painful. A sea swept up the beach, licking around the trunks of the coconuts and subsiding almost at their feet.

"Way past high-water mark,' Captain Lynch remarked, 'and I've been here eleven years.' He looked at his watch. 'It is three o'clock.'

A man and woman, at their heels a motley following of brats and curs, trailed disconsolately by. They came to a halt beyond the house, and, after much irresolution, sat down in the sand. A few minutes later another family trailed in from the opposite direction, the men and women carrying a heterogeneous assortment of possessions. And soon several hundred persons of all ages and sexes were congregated about the captain's dwelling. He called to one new arrival, a woman with a nursing babe in her arms, and in answer received the information that her house had just been swept into the lagoon.

This was the highest spot of land in miles, and already, in many places on either hand, the great seas were making a clean breach of the slender ring of the atoll and surging into the lagoon. Twenty miles around stretched the ring of the atoll, and in no place was it more than fifty fathoms wide. It was the height of the diving season, and from all the islands around, even as far as Tahiti, the natives had gathered.

'There are twelve hundred men, women and children here,' said Captain Lynch. 'I wonder how many will be here to-morrow morning.'

'But why don't it blow? – that's what I want to know,' Raoul demanded.

'Don't worry, young man, don't worry; you'll get your troubles fast enough.'

Even as Captain Lynch spoke, a great watery mass smote the atoll. The seawater churned about them three inches deep under their chairs. A low wail of fear went up from the many women. The children, with clasped hands, stared at the immense rollers and cried piteously. Chickens and cats, wading perturbedly in the water, as by common consent, with flight and scramble took refuge on the roof of the captain's house. A Paumotan, with a litter of new-born puppies in a basket, climbed into a coconut tree and twenty feet above the ground made the basket fast. The mother floundered about in the water beneath, whining and yelping.

And still the sun shone brightly and the dead calm continued. They sat and watched the seas and the insane pitching of the *Aorai*. Captain Lynch gazed at the huge mountains of water sweeping in until he could gaze no more. He covered his face with his hands to shut out the sight; then went into the house.

'Twenty-eight-sixty,' he said quietly when he returned.

In his arm was a coil of small rope. He cut it into two-fathom lengths, giving one to Raoul and, retaining one for himself, distributed the remainder among the women with the advice to pick out a tree and climb.

A light air began to blow out of the northeast, and the fan of it on his cheek seemed to cheer Raoul up. He could see the *Aorai* trimming her sheets and heading off shore, and he regretted that he was not on her. She would get away at any rate, but as for the atoll – A sea breached across, almost sweeping him off his feet, and he selected a tree. Then he remembered the barometer and ran back to the house. He encountered Captain Lynch on the same errand and together they went in.

'Twenty-eight-twenty,' said the old mariner. 'It's going to be fair hell around here – what was that?'

The air seemed filled with the rush of something. The house quivered and vibrated, and they heard the thrumming of a mighty note of sound. The windows rattled. Two panes crashed; a draught of wind tore in, striking them and making them stagger. The door opposite banged shut, shattering the latch. The white doorknob crumbled in fragments to the floor. The room's walls bulged like a gas balloon in the process of sudden inflation. Then came a new sound like the rattle of musketry, as the spray from a sea struck the wall of the house. Captain Lynch looked at his watch. It was four o'clock. He put on a coat of pilot cloth, unhooked the barometer, and stowed it away in a capacious pocket. Again a sea struck the house, with a heavy thud, and the light building tilted, twisted quarter-around on its foundation, and sank down, its floor at an angle of ten degrees.

Raoul went out first. The wind caught him and whirled him away. He noted that it had hauled around to the east. With a great effort he threw himself on the sand, crouching and holding his own. Captain Lynch, driven like a wisp of straw, sprawled over him. Two of the *Aorai*'s sailors, leaving a coconut tree to which they had been clinging, came to their aid, leaning against the wind at impossible angles and fighting and clawing every inch of the way.

The old man's joints were stiff and he could not climb, so the sailors, by means of short ends of rope tied together, hoisted him up the trunk, a few feet at a time, till they could make him fast, at the top of the tree, fifty feet from the ground. Raoul passed his length of rope around the base of an adjacent tree and stood looking on. The wind was frightful. He had never dreamed it could blow so hard. A sea breached across the atoll, wetting him to the knees ere it subsided into the lagoon. The sun had disappeared, and a lead-colored twilight settled down A few drops of rain, driving horizontally, struck him. The impact was like that of leaden pellets. A splash of salt spray struck his face. It was like the slap of a man's hand. His cheeks stung, and involuntary tears of pain were in his smarting eyes. Several hundred natives had taken to the trees, and he could have laughed at the bunches of human fruit clustering in the tops. Then, being Tahitian-born, he doubled his body at the waist, clasped the trunk of his tree with his hands, pressed the soles of his feet against the near surface of the trunk, and began to walk up the tree. At the top he found two women, two children and a man. One little girl clasped a house-cat in her arms.

From his eyrie he waved his hand to Captain Lynch, and that doughty patriarch waved back. Raoul was appalled at the sky. It had approached much nearer – in fact, it seemed just over his head; and it had turned from lead to black. Many people were still on the ground grouped about the bases of the trees and holding on. Several such clusters were praying, and in one the Mormon missionary was exhorting. A weird sound, rhythmical, faint as the faintest chirp of a far cricket, enduring but for a moment, but in that moment suggesting to him vaguely the thought of heaven and celestial music, came to his ear. He glanced about him and saw, at the base of another tree, a large cluster of people holding on by ropes and by one another. He could see their faces working and their lips moving in unison. No sound came to him, but he knew that they were singing hymns.

Still the wind continued to blow harder. By no conscious process could he measure it, for it had long since passed beyond all his experience of wind; but he knew somehow, nevertheless, that it was blowing harder. Not far away a tree was uprooted, flinging its load of human beings to the ground. A sea washed across the strip of sand, and they were gone. Things were happening quickly. He saw a brown shoulder and a black head silhouetted against the churning white of the lagoon. The next instant that, too, had vanished. Other trees were going, falling and criss-crossing like matches. He was amazed at the power of the wind. His own tree was swaying perilously, one woman was wailing and clutching the little girl, who in turn still hung on to the cat.

The man, holding the other child, touched Raoul's arm and pointed. He looked and saw the Mormon church careering drunkenly a hundred feet away. It had been torn from its foundations, and wind and sea were heaving and shoving it toward the lagoon. A frightful wall of water caught it, tilted it, and flung it against half a dozen coconut trees. The bunches of human fruit fell like ripe coconuts. The subsiding wave showed them on the ground, some lying motionless, others squirming and writhing. They reminded him strangely of ants. He was not shocked. He had risen above horror. Quite as a matter of course he noted the succeeding wave sweep the sand clean of the human wreckage. A third wave, more colossal than any he had yet seen, hurled the church into the lagoon, where it floated off into the obscurity to leeward, half-submerged, reminding him for all the world of a Noah's ark.

He looked for Captain Lynch's house, and was surprised to find it gone. Things certainly were happening quickly. He noticed that many of the people in the trees that still held had descended to the ground. The wind had yet again increased. His own tree showed that. It no longer swayed or bent over and back. Instead, it remained practically stationary, curved in a rigid angle from the wind and merely vibrating. But the vibration was sickening. It was like that of a tuning-fork or the tongue of a jew's-harp. It was the rapidity of the vibration that made it so bad. Even though its roots held, it could not stand the strain for long. Something would have to break.

Ah, there was one that had gone. He had not seen it go, but there it stood, the remnant, broken off half-way up the trunk. One did not know what happened unless he saw it. The mere crashing of trees and wails of human despair occupied no place in that mighty volume of sound. He chanced to be looking in Captain Lynch's direction when it happened. He saw the trunk of the tree, half-way up, splinter and part without noise. The head of the tree, with three sailors of the *Aorai* and the old captain, sailed off over the lagoon. It did not fall to the ground, but drove through the air like a piece of chaff. For a hundred yards he followed its flight, when it struck the water. He strained his eyes, and was sure that he saw Captain Lynch wave farewell.

Raoul did not wait for anything more. He touched the native and made signs to descend to the ground. The man was willing, but his women were paralyzed from terror, and he elected to remain with them. Raoul passed his rope around the tree and slid down. A rush of salt water went over his head. He held his breath and clung desperately to the rope. The water subsided,

and in the shelter of the trunk he breathed once more. He
fastened the rope more securely, and then was put under by
another sea. One of the women slid down and joined him, the
native remaining by the other woman, the two children and the
cat.

The supercargo had noticed how the groups clinging at the
bases of the other trees continually diminished. Now he saw the
process work out alongside him. It required all his strength to
hold on, and the woman who had joined him was growing
weaker. Each time he emerged from a sea he was surprised to
find himself still there, and next, surprised to find the woman
still there. At last he emerged to find himself alone. He looked
up. The top of the tree had gone as well. At half its original
height, a splintered end vibrated. He was safe. The roots still
held, while the tree had been shorn of its windage. He began to
climb up. He was so weak that he went slowly, and sea after sea
caught him before he was above them. Then he tied himself to
the trunk and stiffened his soul to face the night and he knew not
what.

He felt very lonely in the darkness. At times it seemed to him
that it was the end of the world and that he was the last one left
alive. Still the wind increased. Hour after hour it increased. By
what he calculated was eleven o'clock, the wind had become
unbelievable. It was a horrible, monstrous thing, a screaming
fury, a wall that smote and passed on but that continued to smite
and pass on – a wall without end. It seemed to him that he had
become light and ethereal; that it was he that was in motion;
that he was being driven with inconceivable velocity through
unending solidness. The wind was no longer air in motion. It
had become substantial as water or quicksilver. He had a feeling
that he could reach into it and tear it out in chunks as one might
do with the meat in the carcass of a steer; that he could seize
hold of the wind and hang on to it as a man might hang on to
the face of a cliff.

The wind strangled him. He could not face it and breathe, for
it rushed in through his mouth and nostrils, distending his lungs
like bladders. At such moments it seemed to him that his body

was being packed and swollen with solid earth. Only by pressing his lips to the trunk of the tree could he breathe. Also, the ceaseless impact of the wind exhausted him. Body and brain became wearied. He no longer observed, no longer thought, and was but semiconscious. One idea constituted his consciousnss: *So this was a hurricane.* That one idea persisted irregularly. It was like a feeble flame that flickered occasionally. From a state of stupor he would return to it – *So this was a hurricane.* Then he would go off into another stupor.

The height of the hurricane endured from eleven at night till three in the morning, and it was at eleven that the tree in which clung Mapuhi and his women snapped off. Mapuhi rose to the surface of the lagoon, still clutching his daughter Ngakura. Only a South Sea islander could have lived in such a driving smother. The pandanus-tree, to which he attached himself, turned over and over in the froth and churn; and it was only by holding on at times and waiting, and at other times shifting his grips rapidly, that he was able to get his head and Ngakura's to the surface at intervals sufficiently near together to keep the breath in them. But the air was mostly water, what with flying spray and sheeted rain that poured along at right angles to the perpendicular.

It was ten miles across the lagoon to the farther ring of sand. Here, tossing tree-trunks, timbers, wrecks of cutters, and wreckage of houses, killed nine out of ten of the miserable beings who survived the passage of the lagoon. Half-drowned, exhausted, they were hurled into this mad mortar of the elements and battered into formless flesh. But Mapuhi was fortunate. His chance was the one in ten; it fell to him by the freakage of fate. He emerged upon the sand, bleeding from a score of wounds. Ngakura's left arm was broken; the fingers of her right hand were crushed; and cheek and forehead were laid open to the bone. He clutched a tree that yet stood, and clung on, holding the girl and sobbing for air, while the waters of the lagoon washed by knee-high and at times waist-high.

At three in the morning the backbone of the hurricane broke. By five no more than a stiff breeze was blowing. And by six it was dead calm and the sun was shining. The sea had gone down.

On the yet restless edge of the lagoon, Mapuhi saw the broken
bodies of those that had failed in the landing. Undoubtedly
Tefara and Nauri were among them. He went along the beach
examining them, and came upon his wife, lying half in and half
out of the water. He sat down and wept, making harsh animal-
noises after the manner of primitive grief. Then she stirred
uneasily, and groaned. He looked more closely. Not only was she
alive, but she was uninjured. She was merely sleeping. Hers also
had been the one chance in ten.

Of the twelve hundred alive the night before but three hundred
remained. The Mormon missionary and a gendarme made the
census. The lagoon was cluttered with corpses. Not a house nor
a hut was standing. In the whole atoll not two stones remained
one upon another. One in fifty of the coconut palms still stood,
and they were wrecks, while on not one of them remained a
single nut. There was no fresh water. The shallow wells that
caught the surface seepage of the rain were filled with salt. Out
of the lagoon a few soaked bags of flour were recovered. The
survivors cut the hearts out of the fallen coconut trees and ate
them. Here and there they crawled into tiny hutches, made by
hollowing out the sand and covering over with fragments of
metal roofing. The missionary made a crude still, but he could
not distill water for three hundred persons. By the end of the
second day, Raoul, taking a bath in the lagoon, discovered that
his thirst was somewhat relieved. He cried out the news, and
thereupon three hundred men, women, and children could have
been seen, standing up to their necks in the lagoon and trying to
drink water in through their skins. Their dead floated about
them, or were stepped upon where they still lay upon the bottom.
On the third day the people buried their dead and sat down to
wait for the rescue steamers.

In the meantime, Nauri, torn from her family by the hurricane,
had been swept away on an adventure of her own. Clinging to a
rough plank that wounded and bruised her and that filled her
body with splinters, she was thrown clear over the atoll and
carried away to sea. Here, under the amazing buffets of mountains of water, she lost her plank. She was an old woman nearly

sixty; but she was Paumotan-born, and she had never been out of sight of the sea in her life. Swimming in the darkness, strangling, suffocating, fighting for air, she was struck a heavy blow on the shoulder by a coconut. On the instant her plan was formed, and she seized the nut. In the next hour she captured seven more. Tied together, they formed a life-buoy that preserved her life while at the same time it threatened to pound her to a jelly. She was a fat woman, and she bruised easily; but she had had experience of hurricanes, and, while she prayed to her shark god for protection from sharks, she waited for the wind to break. But at three o'clock she was in such a stupor that she did not know. Nor did she know at six o'clock when the dead calm settled down. She was shocked into consciousness when she was thrown upon the sand. She dug in with raw and bleeding hands and feet and clawed against the backwash until she was beyond the reach of the waves.

She knew where she was. This land could be no other than the tiny islet of Takokota. It had no lagoon. No one lived upon it. Hikueru was fifteen miles away. She could not see Hikueru, but she knew that it lay to the south. The days went by, and she lived on the coconuts that had kept her afloat. They supplied her with drinking water and with food. But she did not drink all she wanted, nor eat all she wanted. Rescue was problematical. She saw the smoke of the rescue steamers on the horizon, but what steamer could be expected to come to lonely, uninhabited Takokota?

From the first she was tormented by corpses. The sea persisted in flinging them upon her bit of sand, and she persisted, until her strength failed, in thrusting them back into the sea where the sharks tore at them and devoured them. When her strength failed, the bodies festooned her beach with ghastly horror, and she withdrew from them as far as she could, which was not far.

By the tenth day her last coconut was gone, and she was shrivelling from thirst. She dragged herself along the sand, looking for coconuts. It was strange that so many bodies floated up, and no nuts. Surely, there were more coconuts afloat than dead men! She gave up at last, and lay exhausted. The end had come. Nothing remained but to wait for death.

Coming out of a stupor, she became slowly aware that she was gazing at a patch of sandy-red hair on the head of a corpse. The sea flung the body toward her, then drew it back. It turned over, and she saw that it had no face. Yet there was something familiar about that patch of sandy-red hair. An hour passed. She did not exert herself to make the identification. She was waiting to die, and it mattered little to her what man that thing of horror once might have been.

But at the end of the hour she sat up slowly and stared at the corpse. An unusually large wave had thrown it beyond the reach of the lesser waves. Yes, she was right; that patch of red hair could belong to but one man in the Paumotus. It was Levy, the German Jew, the man who had bought the pearl and carried it away on the *Hira*. Well, one thing was evident: the *Hira* had been lost. The pearl-buyer's god of fishermen and thieves had gone back on him.

She crawled down to the dead man. His shirt had been torn away, and she could see the leather money-belt about his waist. She held her breath and tugged at the buckles. They gave easier than she had expected, and she crawled hurriedly away across the sand, dragging the belt after her. Pocket after pocket she unbuckled in the belt and found empty. Where could he have put it? In the last pocket of all she found it, the first and only pearl he had bought on the voyage. She crawled a few feet farther, to escape the pestilence of the belt, and examined the pearl. It was the one Mapuhi had found and been robbed of by Toriki. She weighed it in her hand and rolled it back and forth caressingly. But in it she saw no intrinsic beauty. What she did see was the house Mapuhi and Tefara and she had builded so carefully in their minds. Each time she looked at the pearl she saw the house in all its details, including the octagon-drop-clock on the wall. That was something to live for.

She tore a strip from her *ahu* and tied the pearl securely about her neck. Then she went along the beach, panting and groaning, but resolutely seeking for coconuts. Quickly she found one, and, as she glanced around, a second. She broke one, drinking its water, which was mildewy, and eating the last particle of the meat. A little later she found a shattered dugout. Its outrigger was gone, but she was hopeful, and, before the day was out, she found the outrigger. Every find was an augury. The pearl was a talisman. Late in the afternoon she saw a wooden box floating low in the water. When she dragged it out on the beach its contents rattled, and inside she found ten tins of salmon. She opened one by hammering it on the canoe. When a leak was started, she drained the tin. After that she spent several hours in extracting the salmon, hammering and squeezing it out a morsel at a time.

Eight days longer she waited for rescue. In the meantime she fastened the outrigger back on the canoe, using for lashings all the coconut-fiber she could find, and also what remained of her *ahu*. The canoe was badly cracked, and she could not make it water-tight; but a calabash made from a coconut she stored on board for a bailer. She was hard put for a paddle. With a piece of tin she sawed off all her hair close to the scalp. Out of the hair she braided a cord; and by means of the cord she lashed a three-foot piece of broom-handle to a board from the salmon case. She gnawed wedges with her teeth and with them wedged the lashing.

On the eighteenth day, at midnight, she launched the canoe through the surf and started back for Hikueru. She was an old woman. Hardship had stripped her fat from her till scarcely more than bones and skin and a few stringy muscles remained. The canoe was large and should have been paddled by three strong men. But she did it alone, with a make-shift paddle. Also, the canoe leaked badly, and one-third of her time was devoted to bailing. By clear daylight she looked vainly for Hikueru. Astern, Takokota had sunk beneath the sea-rim. The sun blazed down on her nakedness, compelling her body to surrender its moisture. Two tins of salmon were left, and in the course of the day she battered holes in them and drained the liquid. She had no time to waste in extracting the meat. A current was setting to the westward, she made westing whether she made southing or not.

In the early afternoon, standing upright in the canoe, she

sighted Hikueru. Its wealth of coconut palms was gone. Only here and there, at wide intervals, could she see the ragged remnants of trees. The sight cheered her. She was nearer than she had thought. The current was setting her to the westward. She bore up against it and paddled on. The wedges in the paddle-lashing worked loose, and she lost much time, at frequent intervals, in driving them tight. Then there was the bailing. One hour in three she had to cease paddling in order to bail. And all the time she drifted to the westward.

By sunset Hikueru bore southeast from her, three miles away. There was a full moon, and by eight o'clock the land was due east and two miles away. She struggled on for another hour, but the land was as far away as ever. She was in the main grip of the current; the canoe was too large; the paddle was too inadequate; and too much of her time and strength was wasted in bailing. Besides, she was very weak and growing weaker. Despite her efforts, the canoe was drifting off to the westward.

She breathed a prayer to her shark god, slipped over the side, and began to swim. She was actually refreshed by the water, and quickly left the canoe astern. At the end of an hour the land was perceptibly nearer. Then came her fright. Right before her eyes, not twenty feet away, a large fin cut the water. She swam steadily toward it, and slowly it glided away, curving off toward the right and circling around her. She kept her eyes on the fin and swam on. When the fin disappeared, she lay face downward on the water and watched. When the fin reappeared she resumed her swimming. The monster was lazy – she could see that. Without doubt he had been well fed since the hurricane. Had he been very hungry, she knew he would not have hesitated from making a dash for her. He was fifteen feet long, and one bite, she knew, could cut her in half.

But she did not have any time to waste on him. Whether she swam or not, the current drew away from the land just the same. A half-hour went by, and the shark began to grow bolder. Seeing no harm in her he drew closer, in narrowing circles, cocking his eyes at her impudently as he slid past. Sooner or later, she knew well enough, he would get up sufficient courage to dash at her.

She resolved to play first. It was a desperate act she meditated. She was an old woman, alone in the sea and weak from starvation and hardship; and yet she, in the face of this sea-tiger, must anticipate his dash by herself dashing at him. She swam on, waiting her chance. At last he passed languidly by, barely eight feet away. She rushed at him suddenly, feigning that she was attacking him. He gave a wild flirt of his tail as he fled away, and his sandpaper hide, striking her, took off her skin from elbow to shoulder. He swam rapidly in a widening circle, and at last disappeared.

In the hole in the sand, covered over by fragments of metal roofing, Mapuhi and Tefara lay disputing.

'If you had done as I said,' charged Tefara, for the thousandth time, 'and hidden the pearl and told no one, you would have it now.'

'But Huru-Huru was with me when I opened the shell – have I not told you so times and times and times without end?'

'And now we shall have no house. Raoul told me to-day that if you had not sold the pearl to Toriki – '

'I did not sell it. Toriki robbed me.'

' – that if you had not sold the pearl, he would give you five thousand French dollars, which is ten thousand Chili.'

'He has been talking to his mother,' Mapuhi explained. 'She has an eye for a pearl.'

'And now the pearl is lost,' Tefara complained.

'It paid my debt with Toriki. That is twelve hundred I have made, anyway.'

'Toriki is dead,' she cried. 'They have heard no word of his schooner. She was lost along with the *Aorai* and the *Hira*. Will Toriki pay you the three hundred credit he promised? No, because Toriki is dead. And had you found no pearl, would you to-day owe Toriki the twelve hundred? No, because Toriki is dead, and you cannot pay dead men.'

'But Levy did not pay Toriki,' Mapuhi said. 'He gave him a piece of paper that was good for the money in Papeete; and now Levy is dead and cannot pay; and Toriki is dead and the paper lost with him, and the pearl is lost with Levy. You are right,

Tefara. I have lost the pearl, and got nothing for it. Now let us sleep.'

He held up his hand suddenly and listened. From without came a noise, as of one who breathed heavily and with pain. A hand fumbled against the mat that served for a door.

'Who is there?' Mapuhi cried.

'Nauri,' came the answer. 'Can you tell me where is my son, Mapuhi?'

Tefara screamed and gripped her husband's arm.

'A ghost!' she chattered. 'A ghost!'

Mapuhi's face was a ghastly yellow. He clung weakly to his wife.

'Good woman,' he said in faltering tones, striving to disguise his voice, 'I know your son well. He is living on the east side of the lagoon.'

From without came the sound of a sigh. Mapuhi began to feel elated. He had fooled the ghost.

'But where do you come from, old woman?' he asked.

'From the sea,' was the dejected answer.

'I knew it! I knew it!' screamed Tefara, rocking to and fro.

'Since when has Tefara bedded in a strange house?' came Nauri's voice through the matting.

Mapuhi looked fear and reproach at his wife. It was her voice that had betrayed them.

'And since when has Mapuhi, my son, denied his old mother?' the voice went on.

'No, no, I have not – Mapuhi has not denied you,' he cried. 'I am not Mapuhi. He is on the east end of the lagoon, I tell you.'

Ngakura sat up in bed and began to cry. The matting started to shake.

'What are you doing?' Mapuhi demanded.

'I am coming in,' said the voice of Nauri.

One end of the matting lifted. Tefara tried to dive under the blankets, but Mapuhi held on to her. He had to hold on to something. Together, struggling with each other, with shivering bodies and chattering teeth, they gazed with protruding eyes at the lifting mat. They saw Nauri, dripping with sea-water, without her *ahu*, creep in. They rolled over backward from her and fought for Ngakura's blanket with which to cover their heads.

'You might give your old mother a drink of water,' the ghost said plaintively.

'Give her a drink of water,' Tefara commanded in a shaking voice.

'Give her a drink of water,' Mapuhi passed on the command to Ngakura.

And together they kicked out Ngakura from under the blanket. A minute later, peeping, Mapuhi saw the ghost drinking. When it reached out a shaking hand and laid it on his, he felt the weight of it and was convinced that it was no ghost. Then he emerged, dragging Tefara after him, and in a few minutes all were listening to Nauri's tale. And when she told of Levy, and dropped the pearl into Tefara's hand, even she was reconciled to the reality of her mother-in-law.

'In the morning,' said Tefara, 'you will sell the pearl to Raoul for five thousand French.'

'The house?' objected Nauri.

'He will build the house,' Tefara answered. 'He says it will cost four thousand French. Also will he give one thousand French in credit, which is two thousand Chili.'

'And it will be six fathoms long?' Nauri queried.

'Ay,' answered Mapuhi, 'six fathoms.'

'And in the middle room will be the octagon-drop-clock?'

'Ay, and the round table as well.'

'Then give me something to eat, for I am hungry,' said Nauri, complacently. 'And after that we will sleep, for I am weary. And to-morrow we will have more talk about the house before we sell the pearl. It will be better if we take the thousand French in cash. Money is ever better than credit in buying goods from the traders.'

THE WHALE TOOTH

It was in the early days in Fiji, when John Starhurst arose in the mission-house at Rewa Village and announced his intention of carrying the Gospel throughout all Viti Levu. Now Viti Levu means the 'Great Land', it being the largest island in a group composed of many large islands, to say nothing of hundreds of small ones. Here and there on the coasts, living by most precarious tenure, was a sprinkling of missionaries, traders, bêche-de-mer fishers, and whaleship deserters. The smoke of the hot ovens arose under their windows, and the bodies of the slain were dragged by their doors on the way to the feasting.

The Lotu, or the Worship, was progressing slowly, and, often, in crablike fashion. Chiefs, who announced themselves Christians and were welcomed into the body of the chapel, had a distressing habit of backsliding in order to partake of the flesh of some favorite enemy. Eat or be eaten had been the law of the land; and eat or be eaten promised to remain the law of the land for a long time to come. There were chiefs, such as Tanoa, Tuiveikoso, and Tuikilakila, who had literally eaten hundreds of their fellow-men. But among these gluttons Ra Undreundre ranked highest. Ra Undreundre lived at Takiraki. He kept a register of his gustatory exploits. A row of stones outside his house marked the bodies he had eaten. This row was two hundred and thirty paces long, and the stones in it numbered eight hundred and seventy-two. Each stone represented a body. The row of stones might have been longer, had not Ra Undreundre unfortunately received a spear in the small of his back in a bush skirmish on Somo Somo and been served up on the table of Naungavuli, whose mediocre string of stones numbered only forty-eight.

The hard-worked, fever-stricken missionaries stuck doggedly to their task, at times despairing, and looking forward for some special manifestation, some outburst of Pentecostal fire that would bring a glorious harvest of souls. But cannibal Fiji had remained obdurate. The frizzle-headed man-eaters were loath to leave their fleshpots so long as the harvest of human carcasses was plentiful. Sometimes, when the harvest was too plentiful, they imposed on the missionaries by letting the word slip out that on such a day there would be a killing and a barbecue. Promptly the missionaries would buy the lives of the victims with stick tobacco, fathoms of calico and quarts of trade-beads. Natheless the chiefs drove a handsome trade in thus disposing of their surplus live meat. Also, they could always go out and catch more.

It was at this juncture the John Starhurst proclaimed that he would carry the Gospel from coast to coast of the Great Land, and that he would begin by penetrating the mountain fastnesses of the head-waters of the Rewa River. His words were received with consternation.

The native teachers wept softly. His two fellow-missionaries strove to dissuade him. The King of Rewa warned him that the mountain dwellers would surely kai-kai him – kai-kai meaning 'to eat' – and that he, the King of Rewa, having become Lotu, would be put to the necessity of going to war with the mountain dwellers. That he could not conquer them he was perfectly aware. That they might come down the river and sack Rewa Village he was likewise perfectly aware. But what was he to do? If John Starhurst persisted in going out and being eaten, there would be a war that would cost hundreds of lives.

Later in the day a deputation of Rewa chiefs waited upon John Starhurst. He heard them patiently, and argued patiently with them, though he abated not a whit from his purpose. To his fellow-missionaries he explained that he was not bent upon martyrdom; that the call had come for him to carry the Gospel into Viti Levu, and that he was merely obeying the Lord's wish.

To the traders, who came and objected most strenuously of all, he said: 'Your objections are valueless. They consist merely of the damage that may be done your businesses. You are interested in making money, but I am interested in saving souls. The heathen of this dark land must be saved.'

John Starhurst was not a fanatic. He would have been the first man to deny the imputation. He was eminently sane and practical. He was sure that his mission would result in good, and he had private visions of igniting the Pentecostal spark in the souls of the mountaineers and of inaugurating a revival that would sweep down out of the mountains and across the length and breadth of the Great Land from sea to sea and to the isles in the midst of the sea. There were no wild lights in his mild gray eyes, but only calm resolution and an unfaltering trust in the Higher Power that was guiding him.

One man only he found who approved of his project, and that was Ra Vatu, who secretly encouraged him and offered to lend him guides to the first foothills. John Starhurst, in turn, was greatly pleased by Ra Vatu's conduct. From an incorrigible heathen, with a heart as black as his practices, Ra Vatu was beginning to emanate light. He even spoke of becoming Lotu. True, three years before he had expressed a similar intention, and would have entered the church had not John Starhurst entered objection to his bringing his four wives along with him. Ra Vatu had had economic and ethical objections to monogamy. Besides, the missionary's hair-splitting objection had offended him; and, to prove that he was a free agent and a man of honor, he had swung his huge war-club over Starhurst's head. Starhurst had escaped by rushing in under the club and holding on to him until help arrived. But all that was now forgiven and forgotten. Ra Vatu was coming into the church, not merely as a converted heathen, but as a converted polygamist as well. He was only waiting, he assured Starhurst, until his oldest wife, who was very sick, should die.

John Starhurst journeyed up the sluggish Rewa in one of Ra Vatu's canoes. This canoe was to carry him for two days, when, the head of navigation reached, it would return. Far in the distance, lifted into the sky, could be seen the great smoky mountains that marked the backbone of the Great Land. All day John Starhurst gazed at them with eager yearning.

Sometimes he prayed silently. At other times he was joined in prayer by Narau, a native teacher, who for seven years had been Lotu, ever since the day he had been saved from the hot oven by Dr James Ellery Brown at the trifling expense of one hundred sticks of tobacco, two cotton blankets and a large bottle of painkiller. At the last moment, after twenty hours of solitary supplication and prayer, Narau's ears had heard the call to go forth with John Starhurst on the mission to the mountains.

'Master, I will surely go with thee,' he had announced.

John Starhurst had hailed him with sober delight. Truly, the Lord was with him thus to spur on so broken-spirited a creature as Narau.

'I am indeed without spirit, the weakest of the Lord's vessels,' Narau explained, the first day in the canoe.

'You should have faith, stronger faith,' the missionary chided him.

Another canoe journeyed up the Rewa that day. But it journeyed an hour astern, and it took care not to be seen. This canoe was also the property of Ra Vatu. In it was Erirola, Ra Vatu's first cousin and trusted henchman; and in the small basket that never left his hand was a whale tooth. It was a magnificent tooth, fully six inches long, beautifully proportioned, the ivory turned yellow and purple with age. This tooth was likewise the property of Ra Vatu; and in Fiji, when such a tooth goes forth, things usually happen. For this is the virtue of the whale tooth: Whoever accepts it cannot refuse the request that may accompany it or follow it. The request may be anything from a human life to a tribal alliance, and no Fijian is so dead to honor as to deny the request when once the tooth has been accepted. Sometimes the request hangs fire, or the fulfilment is delayed, with untoward consequences.

High up the Rewa, at the village of a chief, Mongondro by name, John Starhurst rested at the end of the second day of the journey. In the morning, attended by Narau, he expected to start on foot for the smoky mountains that were now green and velvety with nearness. Mongondro was a sweet-tempered, mild-mannered little old chief, short-sighted and afflicted with elephantiasis, and no longer inclined toward the turbulence of war. He received the missionary with warm hospitality, gave him food from his own table, and even discussed religious matters with him. Mongondro was of an inquiring bent of mind, and pleased John Starhurst greatly by asking him to account for the existence and beginning of things. When the missionary had finished his summary of the Creation according to Genesis, he saw that Mongondro was deeply affected. The little old chief smoked silently for some time. Then he took the pipe from his mouth and shook his head sadly.

'It cannot be,' he said. 'I, Mongondro, in my youth, was a good workman with the adze. Yet three months did it take me to make a canoe – a small canoe, a very small canoe. And you say that all this land and water was made by one man – '

'Nay, was made by one God, the only true God,' the missionary interrupted.

'It is the same thing,' Mongondro went on, 'that all the land and all the water, the trees, the fish, and bush and mountains, the sun, the moon and the stars, were made in six days! No, no. I tell you that in my youth I was an able man, yet did it require me three months for one small canoe. It is a story to frighten children with; but no man can believe it.'

'I am a man,' the missionary said.

'True, you are a man. But it is not given to my dark understanding to know what you believe.'

'I tell you, I do believe that everything was made in six days.'

'So you say, so you say,' the old cannibal murmured soothingly.

It was not until after John Starhurst and Narau had gone off to bed that Erirola crept into the chief's house, and, after diplomatic speech, handed the whale tooth to Mongondro.

The old chief held the tooth in his hands for a long time. It was a beautiful tooth, and he yearned for it. Also, he divined the request that must accompany it. 'No, no; whale teeth were beautiful,' and his mouth watered for it, but he passed it back to Erirola with many apologies.

*

In the early dawn John Starhurst was afoot, striding along the bush trail in his big leather boots, at his heels the faithful Narau, himself at the heels of a naked guide lent him by Mongondro to show the way to the next village, which was reached by midday. Here a new guide showed the way. A mile in the rear plodded Erirola, the whale tooth in the basket slung on his shoulder. For two days more he brought up the missionary's rear, offering the tooth to the village chiefs. But village after village refused the tooth. It followed so quickly the missionary's advent that they divined the request that would be made, and would have none of it.

They were getting deep into the mountains, and Erirola took a secret trail, cut in ahead of the missionary, and reached the stronghold of the Buli of Gatoka. Now the Buli was unaware of John Starhurst's imminent arrival. Also, the tooth was beautiful – an extraordinary specimen, while the coloring of it was of the rarest order. The tooth was presented publicly. The Buli of Gatoka, seated on his best mat, surrounded by his chief men, three busy fly-brushers at his back, deigned to receive from the hand of his herald the whale tooth presented by Ra Vatu and carried into the mountains by his cousin, Erirola. A clapping of hands went up at the acceptation of the present, the assembled headmen, heralds and fly-brushers crying aloud in chorus:

'A! woi! woi! woi! A! woi! woi! woi! A tabua levu! woi! woi! A mudua, mudua, mudua!'

'Soon will come a man, a white man,' Erirola began, after the proper pause. 'He is a missionary man, and he will come to-day. Ra Vatu is pleased to desire his boots. He wishes to present them to his good friend, Mongondro, and it is in his mind to send them with the feet along in them, for Mongondro is an old man and his teeth are not good. Be sure, O Buli, that the feet go along in the boots. As for the rest of him, it may stop here.'

The delight in the whale tooth faded out of the Buli's eyes, and he glanced about him dubiously. Yet had he already accepted the tooth.

'A little thing like a missionary does not matter,' Erirola prompted.

'No, a little thing like a missionary does not matter,' the Buli answered, himself again. 'Mongondro shall have the boots. Go, you young men, some three or four of you, and meet the missionary on the trail. Be sure you bring back the boots as well.'

'It is too late,' said Erirola. 'Listen! He comes now.'

Breaking through the thicket of brush, John Starhurst, with Narau close on his heels, strode upon the scene. The famous boots, having filled in wading the stream, squirted fine jets of water at every step. Starhurst looked about him with flashing eyes. Upborne by an unwavering trust, untouched by doubt or fear, he exulted in all he saw. He knew that since the beginning of time he was the first white man ever to tread the mountain stronghold of Gatoka.

The grass houses clung to the steep mountain side or overhung the rushing Rewa. On either side towered a mighty precipice. At the best, three hours of sunlight penetrated that narrow gorge. No coconuts nor bananas were to be seen, though dense, tropic vegetation overran everything, dripping in airy festoons from the sheer lips of the precipices and running riot in all the crannied ledges. At the far end of the gorge the Rewa leaped eight hundred feet in a single span, while the atmosphere of the rock fortress pulsed to the rhythmic thunder of the fall.

From the Buli's house John Starhurst saw emerging the Buli and his followers.

'I bring you good tidings,' was the missionary's greeting.

'Who has sent you?' the Buli rejoined quietly.

'God.'

'It is a new name in Viti Levu,' the Buli grinned. 'Of what islands, villages or passes may he be chief?'

'He is the chief over all islands, all villages, all passes,' John Starhurst answered solemnly. 'He is the Lord over heaven and earth, and I am come to bring His word to you.'

'Has he sent whale teeth?' was the insolent query.

'No, but more precious than whale teeth is the – '

'It is the custom, between chiefs, to send whale teeth,' the Buli interrupted. 'Your chief is either a niggard, or you are a fool, to

come empty-handed into the mountains. Behold, a more generous than you is before you.'

So saying, he showed the whale tooth he had received from
Erirola.

Narau groaned.

'It is the whale tooth of Ra Vatu,' he whispered to Starhurst.
'I know it well. Now are we undone.'

'A gracious thing,' the missionary answered, passing his hand
through his long beard and adjusting his glasses. 'Ra Vatu has
arranged that we should be well received.'

But Narau groaned again, and backed away from the heels he
had dogged so faithfully.

'Ra Vatu is soon to become Lotu,' Starhurst explained, 'and I
have come bringing the Lotu to you.'

'I want none of your Lotu,' said the Buli, proudly. 'And it is
in my mind that you will be clubbed this day.'

The Buli nodded to one of his big mountaineers, who stepped
forward, swinging a club. Narau bolted into the nearest house,
seeking to hide among the women and mats; but John Starhurst
sprang in under the club and threw his arms around his
executioner's neck. From this point of vantage he proceeded to
argue. He was arguing for his life, and he knew it; but he was
neither excited nor afraid.

'It would be an evil thing for you to kill me,' he told the man.
'I have done you no wrong, nor have I done the Buli wrong.'

So well did he cling to the neck of the one man that they dared
not strike with their clubs. And he continued to cling and to
dispute for his life with those who clamored for his death.

'I am John Starhurst,' he went on calmly. 'I have labored in
Fiji for three years, and I have done it for no profit. I am here
among you for good. Why should any man kill me? To kill me
will not profit any man.'

The Buli stole a look at the whale tooth. He was well paid for
the deed.

The missionary was surrounded by a mass of naked savages,
all struggling to get at him. The death song, which is the song of
the oven, was raised, and his expostulations could no longer be

heard. But so cunningly did he twine and wreathe his body about his captor's that the death-blow could not be struck. Erirola smiled, and the Buli grew angry.

'Away with you!' he cried. 'A nice story to go back to the coast – a dozen of you and one missionary, without weapons, weak as a woman, overcoming all of you.'

'Wait, O Buli,' John Starhurst called out from the thick of the scuffle, 'and I will overcome even you. For my weapons are Truth and Right, and no man can withstand them.'

'Come to me, then,' the Buli answered, 'for my weapon is only a poor miserable club, and, as you say, it cannot withstand you.'

The group separated from him, and John Starhurst stood alone, facing the Buli, who was leaning on an enormous, knotted war-club.

'Come to me, missionary man, and overcome me,' the Buli challenged.

'Even so will I come to you and overcome you,' John Starhurst made answer, first wiping his spectacles and settling them properly, then beginning his advance.

The Buli raised the club and waited.

'In the first place, my death will profit you nothing,' began the argument.

'I leave the answer to my club,' was the Buli's reply.

And to every point he made the same reply, at the same time watching the missionary closely in order to forestall that cunning run-in under the lifted club. Then, and for the first time, John Starhurst knew that his death was at hand. He made no attempt to run in. Bareheaded, he stood in the sun and prayed aloud – the mysterious figure of the inevitable white man, who, with Bible, bullet or rum bottle, has confronted the amazed savage in his every stronghold. Even so stood John Starhurst in the rock fortress of the Buli of Gatoka.

'Forgive them, for they know not what they do,' he prayed. 'O Lord! have mercy upon Fiji. Have compassion for Fiji. O Jehovah, hear us for His sake, Thy Son, whom Thou didst give that through Him all men might also become Thy children. From Thee we came, and our mind is that to Thee we may return. The land is dark, O Lord, the land is dark. But Thou art mighty to save. Reach out Thy hand, O Lord, and save Fiji, poor cannibal Fiji.'

The Buli grew impatient.

'Now will I answer thee,' he muttered, at the same time swinging his club with both hands.

Narau, hiding among the women and the mats, heard the impact of the blow and shuddered. Then the death song arose, and he knew his beloved missionary's body was being dragged to the oven as he heard the words:

'Drag me gently. Drag me gently.'

'For I am the champion of my land.'

'Give thanks! Give thanks! Give thanks!'

Next, a single voice arose out of the din, asking:

'Where is the brave man?'

A hundred voices bellowed the answer:

'Gone to be dragged into the oven and cooked.'

'Where is the coward?' the single voice demanded.

'Gone to report!' the hundred voices bellowed back. 'Gone to report! Gone to report!'

Narau groaned in anguish of spirit. The words of the old song were true. He was the coward, and nothing remained to him but to go and report.

MAUKI

He weighed one hundred and ten pounds. His hair was kinky and negroid, and he was black. He was peculiarly black. He was neither blue-black nor purple-black, but plum-black. His name was Mauki, and he was the son of a chief. He had three *tambos*. *Tambo* is Melanesian for *taboo*, and is first cousin to that Polynesian word. Mauki's three *tambos* were as follows: first, he must never shake hands with a woman, nor have a woman's hand touch him or any of his personal belongings; secondly, he must never eat clams nor any food from a fire in which clams had been cooked; thirdly, he must never touch a crocodile, nor travel in a canoe that carried any part of a crocodile even if as large as a tooth.

Of a different black were his teeth, which were deep black, or, perhaps better, *lamp*-black. They had been made so in a single night, by his mother, who had compressed about them a powdered mineral which was dug from the landslide back of Port Adams. Port Adams is a salt-water village on Malaita, and Malaita is the most savage island in the Solomons – so savage that no traders nor planters have yet gained a foothold on it; while, from the time of the earliest *bêche-de-mer* fishers and sandalwood traders down to the latest labor recruiters equipped with automatic rifles and gasolene engines, scores of white adventurers have been passed out by tomahawks and soft-nosed Snider bullets. So Malaita remains to-day, in the twentieth century, the stamping ground of the labor recruiters, who farm its coasts for laborers who engage and contract themselves to toil on the plantations of the neighboring and more civilized islands for a wage of thirty dollars a year. The natives of those neighboring and more civilized islands have themselves become too civilized to work on plantations.

Mauki's ears were pierced, not in one place, nor two places, but in a couple of dozen places. In one of the smaller holes he carried a clay pipe. The larger holes were too large for such use. The bowl of the pipe would have fallen through. In fact, in the largest hole in each ear he habitually wore round wooden plugs that were an even four inches in diameter. Roughly speaking, the circumference of said holes was twelve and one-half inches. Mauki was catholic in his tastes. In the various smaller holes he carried such things as empty rifle cartridges, horseshoe nails, copper screws, pieces of string, braids of sennit, strips of green leaf and, in the cool of the day, scarlet hibiscus flowers. From which it will be seen that pockets were not necessary to his well-being. Besides, pockets were impossible, for his only wearing apparel consisted of a piece of calico several inches wide. A pocket knife he wore in his hair, the blade snapped down on a kinky lock. His most prized possession was the handle of a china cup, which he suspended from a ring of turtle-shell, which, in turn, was passed through the partition-cartilage of his nose.

But in spite of embellishments, Mauki had a nice face. It was really a pretty face, viewed by any standard, and for a Melanesian it was a remarkably good-looking face. Its one fault was its lack of strength. It was softly effeminate, almost girlish. The features were small, regular and delicate. The chin was weak, and the mouth was weak. There was no strength nor character in the jaws, forehead and nose. In the eyes only could be caught any hint of the unknown quantities that were so large a part of his make-up and that other persons could not understand. These unknown quantities were pluck, pertinacity, fearlessness, imagination and cunning; and when they found expression in some consistent and striking action, those about him were astounded.

Mauki's father was chief over the village at Port Adams, and thus, by birth a salt-water man, Mauki was half amphibian. He knew the way of the fishes and oysters, and the reef was an open book to him. Canoes, also, he knew. He learned to swim when he was a year old. At seven years he could hold his breath a full minute and swim straight down to bottom through thirty feet of water. And at seven years he was stolen by the bushmen, who cannot even swim and who are afraid of salt water. Thereafter

Mauki saw the sea only from a distance, through rifts in the jungle and from open spaces on the high mountain sides. He became the slave of old Fanfoa, head chief over a score of scattered bush-villages on the range-lips of Malaita, the smoke of which, on calm mornings, is about the only evidence the seafaring white men have of the teeming interior population. For the whites do not penetrate Malaita. They tried it once, in the days when the search was on for gold, but they always left their heads behind to grin from the smoky rafters of the bushmen's huts.

When Mauki was a young man of seventeen, Fanfoa got out of tobacco. He got dreadfully out of tobacco. It was hard times in all his villages. He had been guilty of a mistake. Suo was a harbor so small that a large schooner could not swing at anchor in it. It was surrounded by mangroves that overhung the deep water. It was a trap, and into the trap sailed two white men in a small ketch. They were after recruits, and they possessed much tobacco and trade-goods, to say nothing of three rifles and plenty of ammunition. Now there were no salt-water men living at Suo, and it was there that the bushmen could come down to the sea. The ketch did a splendid traffic. It signed on twenty recruits the first day. Even old Fanfoa signed on. And that same day the score of new recruits chopped off the two white men's heads, killed the boat's crew and burned the ketch. Thereafter, and for three months, there was tobacco and trade-goods in plenty and to spare in all the bush-villages. Then came the man-of-war that threw shells for miles into the hills, frightening the people out of their villages and into the deeper bush. Next the man-of-war sent landing parties ashore. The villages were all burned, along with the tobacco and trade-stuff. The coconuts and bananas were chopped down, the taro gardens uprooted, and the pigs and chickens killed.

It taught Fanfoa a lesson, but in the meantime he was out of tobacco. Also, his young men were too frightened to sign on with the recruiting vessels. That was why Fanfoa ordered his slave, Mauki, to be carried down and signed on for half a case of tobacco advance, along with knives, axes, calico and beads, which he would pay for with his toil on the plantations. Mauki was sorely frightened when they brought him on board the schooner. He was a lamb led to the slaughter. White men were ferocious creatures. They had to be, or else they would not make a practice of venturing along the Malaita coast and into all harbors, two on a schooner, when each schooner carried from fifteen to twenty blacks as boat's crew, and often as high as sixty or seventy black recruits. In addition to this, there was always the danger of the shore population, the sudden attack and the cutting off of the schooner and all hands. Truly, white men must be terrible. Besides, they were possessed of such devil-devils – rifles that shot very rapidly many times, things of iron and brass that made the schooners go when there was no wind, and boxes that talked and laughed just as men talked and laughed. Ay, and he had heard of one white man whose particular devil-devil was so powerful that he could take out all his teeth and put them back at will.

Down into the cabin they took Mauki. On deck, the one white man kept guard with two revolvers in his belt. In the cabin the other white man sat with a book before him, in which he inscribed strange marks and lines. He looked at Mauki as though he had been a pig or a fowl, glanced under the hollows of his arms, and wrote in the book. Then he held out the writing stick and Mauki just barely touched it with his hand, in so doing pledging himself to toil for three years on the plantations of the Moongleam Soap Company. It was not explained to him that the will of the ferocious white men would be used to enforce the pledge, and that, behind all, for the same use, was all the power and all the warships of Great Britain.

Other blacks there were on board, from unheard-of far places, and when the white man spoke to them, they tore the long feather from Mauki's hair, cut that same hair short, and wrapped about his waist a lava-lava of bright yellow calico.

After many days on the schooner, and after beholding more land and islands than he had ever dreamed of, he was landed on New Georgia, and put to work in the field clearing jungle and cutting cane grass. For the first time he knew what work was. Even as a slave to Fanfoa he had not worked like this. And he did not like work. It was up at dawn and in at dark, on two meals a day. And the food was tiresome. For weeks at a time they were given nothing but sweet potatoes to eat, and for weeks at a time it would be nothing but rice. He cut out the coconut from the shells day after day; and for long days and weeks he fed the fires that smoked the copra, till his eyes got sore and he was set to felling trees. He was a good axe-man, and later he was put in the bridge-building gang. Once, he was punished by being put in the road-building gang. At times he served as boat's crew in the whale-boats, when they brought in copra from distant beaches or when the white men went out to dynamite fish.

Among other things he learned *bêche-de-mer* English, with which he could talk with all white men, and with all recruits who otherwise would have talked in a thousand different dialects. Also, he learned certain things about the white men, principally that they kept their word. If they told a boy he was going to receive a stick of tobacco, he got it. If they told a boy they would knock seven bells out of him if he did a certain thing, when he did that thing seven bells invariably were knocked out of him. Mauki did not know what seven bells were, but they occurred in *bêche-de-mer*, and he imagined them to be the blood and teeth that sometimes accompanied the process of knocking out seven bells. One other thing he learned: no boy was struck or punished unless he did wrong. Even when the white men were drunk, as they were frequently, they never struck unless a rule had been broken.

Mauki did not like the plantation. He hated work, and he was the son of a chief. Furthermore, it was ten years since he had been stolen from Port Adams by Fanfoa, and he was homesick. He was even homesick for the slavery under Fanfoa. So he ran away. He struck back into the bush, with the idea of working southward to the beach and stealing a canoe in which to go home to Port Adams. But the fever got him, and he was captured and brought back more dead than alive.

A second time he ran away, in the company of two Malaita boys. They got down the coast twenty miles, and were hidden in the hut of a Malaita freeman, who dwelt in that village. But in the dead of night two white men came, who were not afraid of all the village people and who knocked seven bells out of the three runaways, tied them like pigs and tossed them into the whale-boat. But the man in whose house they had hidden – seven times seven bells must have been knocked out of him from the way the hair, skin and teeth flew, and he was discouraged for the rest of his natural life from harboring runaway laborers.

For a year Mauki toiled on. Then he was made a house-boy, and had good food and easy times, with light work in keeping the house clean and serving the white men with whiskey and beer at all hours of the day and most hours of the night. He liked it, but he liked Port Adams more. He had two years longer to serve, but two years were too long for him in the throes of homesickness. He had grown wiser with his year of service, and, being now a house-boy, he had opportunity. He had the cleaning of the rifles, and he knew where the key to the store-room was hung. He planned the escape, and one night ten Malaita boys and one boy from San Cristoval sneaked from the barracks and dragged one of the whale-boats down to the beach. It was Mauki who supplied the key that opened the padlock on the boat, and it was Mauki who equipped the boat with a dozen Winchesters, an immense amount of ammunition, a case of dynamite with detonators and fuse, and ten cases of tobacco.

The northwest monsoon was blowing, and they fled south in the night-time, hiding by day on detached and uninhabited islets, or dragging their whale-boat into the bush on the large islands. Thus they gained Guadalcanar, skirted halfway along it, and crossed the Indispensable Straits to Florida Island. It was here that they killed the San Cristoval boy, saving his head and cooking and eating the rest of him. The Malaita coast was only twenty miles away, but the last night a strong current and baffling winds prevented them from gaining across. Daylight found them still several miles from their goal. But daylight brought a cutter, in which were two white men, who were not afraid of eleven Malaita men armed with twelve rifles. Mauki and his companions were carried back to Tulagi, where lived the great white master of all the white men. And the great white

master held a court, after which, one by one, the runaways were
tied up and given twenty lashes each, and sentenced to a fine of
fifteen dollars. Then they were sent back to New Georgia, where
the white men knocked seven bells out of them all around and
put them to work. But Mauki was no longer house-boy. He was
put in the road-making gang. The fine of fifteen dollars had been
paid by the men from whom he had run away, and he was told
that he would have to work it out, which meant six months'
additional toil. Further, his share of the stolen tobacco earned
him another year of toil.

Port Adams was now three years and a half away, so he stole
a canoe one night, hid on the islets in Manning Straits, passed
through the Straits, and began working along the eastern coast
of Ysabel, only to be captured, two-thirds of the way along, by
the white men on Meringe Lagoon. After a week, he escaped
from them and took to the bush. There were no bush natives on
Ysabel, only salt-water men, who were all Christians. The white
men put up a reward of five hundred sticks of tobacco, and every
time Mauki ventured down to the sea to steal a canoe he was
chased by the salt-water men. Four months of this passed when,
the reward having been raised to a thousand sticks, he was
caught and sent back to New Georgia and the road-building
gang. Now a thousand sticks are worth fifty dollars, and Mauki
had to pay the reward himself, which required a year and eight
months' labor. So Port Adams was now five years away.

His homesickness was greater than ever, and it did not appeal
to him to settle down and be good, work out his four years, and
go home. The next time, he was caught in the very act of running
away. His case was brought before Mr Haveby, the island
manager of the Moongleam Soap Company, who adjudged him
an incorrigible. The Company had plantations on the Santa
Cruz Islands, hundreds of miles across the sea, and there it sent
its Solomon Islands' incorrigibles. And there Mauki was sent,
though he never arrived. The schooner stopped at Santa Anna,
and in the night Mauki swam ashore, where he stole two rifles
and a case of tobacco from the trader and got away in a canoe to
Cristoval. Malaita was now to the north, fifty or sixty miles

away. But when he attempted the passage, he was caught by a light gale and driven back to Santa Anna, where the trader clapped him in irons and held him against the return of the schooner from Santa Cruz. The two rifles the trader recovered, but the case of tobacco was charged up to Mauki at the rate of another year. The sum of years he now owed the Company was six.

On the way back to New Georgia, the schooner dropped anchor in Marau Sound, which lies at the southeastern extremity of Guadalcanar. Mauki swam ashore with handcuffs on his wrists and got away to the bush. The schooner went on, but the Moongleam trader ashore offered a thousand sticks, and to him Mauki was brought by the bushmen with a year and eight months tacked on to his account. Again, and before the schooner called in, he got away, this time in a whale-boat accompanied by a case of the trader's tobacco. But a northwest gale wrecked him upon Ugi, where the Christian natives stole his tobacco and turned him over to the Moongleam trader who resided there. The tobacco the natives stole meant another year for him, and the tale was now eight years and a half.

'We'll send him to Lord Howe,' said Mr Haveby. 'Bunster is there, and we'll let them settle it between them. It will be a case, I imagine, of Mauki getting Bunster, or Bunster getting Mauki, and good riddance in either event.'

If one leaves Meringe Lagoon, on Ysabel, and steers a course due north, magnetic, at the end of one hundred and fifty miles he will lift the pounded coral beaches of Lord Howe above the sea. Lord Howe is a ring of land some one hundred and fifty miles in circumference, several hundred yards wide at its widest, and towering in places to a height of ten feet above sea-level. Inside this ring of sand is a mighty lagoon studded with coral patches. Lord Howe belongs to the Solomons neither geographically nor ethnologically. It is an atoll, while the Solomons are high islands; and its people and language are Polynesian, while the inhabitants of the Solomons are Melanesian. Lord Howe has been populated by the westward Polynesian drift which continues to this day, big outrigger canoes being washed upon its beaches by the southeast trade. That there has been a slight Melanesian drift in the period of the northwest monsoon, is also evident.

Nobody ever comes to Lord Howe, or Ontong-Java as it is sometimes called. Thomas Cook & Son do not sell tickets to it, and tourists do not dream of its existence. Not even a white missionary has landed on its shore. Its five thousand natives are as peaceable as they are primitive. Yet they were not always peaceable. The *Sailing Directions* speak of them as hostile and treacherous. But the men who compile the *Sailing Directions* have never heard of the change that was worked in the hearts of the inhabitants, who, not many years ago, cut off a big bark and killed all hands with the exception of the second mate. This survivor carried the news to his brothers. The captains of three trading schooners returned with him to Lord Howe. They sailed their vessels right into the lagoon and proceeded to preach the white man's gospel that only white men shall kill white men and that the lesser breeds must keep hands off. The schooners sailed up and down the lagoon, harrying and destroying. There was no escape from the narrow sand-circle, no bush to which to flee. The men were shot down at sight, and there was no avoiding being sighted. The villages were burned, the canoes smashed, the chickens and pigs killed, and the precious coconut-trees chopped down. For a month this continued, when the schooners sailed away; but the fear of the white man had been seared into the souls of the islanders and never again were they rash enough to harm one.

Max Bunster was the one white man on Lord Howe, trading in the pay of the ubiquitous Moongleam Soap Company. And the Company billeted him on Lord Howe, because, next to getting rid of him, it was the most out-of-the-way place to be found. That the Company did not get rid of him was due to the difficulty of finding another man to take his place. He was a strapping big German, with something wrong in his brain. Semimadness would be a charitable statement of his condition. He was a bully and a coward, and a thrice-bigger savage than any savage on the island. Being a coward, his brutality was of the cowardly order. When he first went into the Company's employ, he was stationed on Savo. When a consumptive colonial was sent to take his place, he beat him up with his fists and sent him off a wreck in the schooner that brought him.

Mr Haveby next selected a young Yorkshire giant to relieve Bunster. The Yorkshire man had a reputation as a bruiser and preferred fighting to eating. But Bunster wouldn't fight. He was a regular little lamb – for ten days, at the end of which time the Yorkshire man was prostrated by a combined attack of dysentery and fever. Then Bunster went for him, among other things getting him down and jumping on him a score or so of times. Afraid of what would happen when his victim recovered, Bunster fled away in a cutter to Guvutu, where he signalized himself by beating up a young Englishman already crippled by a Boer bullet through both hips.

Then it was that Mr Haveby sent Bunster to Lord Howe, the falling-off place. He celebrated his landing by mopping up half a case of gin and by thrashing the elderly and wheezy mate of the schooner which had brought him. When the schooner departed, he called the kanakas down to the beach and challenged them to throw him in a wrestling bout, promising a case of tobacco to the one who succeeded. Three kanakas he threw, but was promptly thrown by a fourth, who, instead of receiving the tobacco, got a bullet through his lungs.

And so began Bunster's reign on Lord Howe. Three thousand people lived in the principal village; but it was deserted, even in broad day, when he passed through. Men, women and children fled before him. Even the dogs and pigs got out of the way, while the king was not above hiding under a mat. The two prime ministers lived in terror of Bunster, who never discussed any moot subject, but struck out with his fists instead.

And to Lord Howe came Mauki, to toil for Bunster for eight long years and a half. There was no escaping from Lord Howe. For better or worse, Bunster and he were tied together. Bunster weighed two hundred pounds. Mauki weighed one hundred and ten. Bunster was a degenerate brute. But Mauki was a primitive savage. While both had wills and ways of their own.

Mauki had no idea of the sort of master he was to work for.

He had had no warnings, and he had concluded as a matter of course that Bunster would be like other white men, a drinker of much whiskey, a ruler and a lawgiver who always kept his word and who never struck a boy undeserved. Bunster had the advantage. He knew all about Mauki, and gloated over the coming into possession of him. The last cook was suffering from a broken arm and a dislocated shoulder, so Bunster made Mauki cook and general house-boy.

And Mauki soon learned that there were white men and white men. On the very day the schooner departed he was ordered to buy a chicken from Samisee, the native Tongan missionary. But Samisee had sailed across the lagoon and would not be back for three days. Mauki returned with the information. He climbed the steep stairway (the house stood on piles twelve feet above the sand), and entered the living-room to report. The trader demanded the chicken. Mauki opened his mouth to explain the missionary's absence. But Bunster did not care for explanations. He struck out with his fist. The blow caught Mauki on the mouth and lifted him into the air. Clear through the doorway he flew, across the narrow veranda, breaking the top railing, and down to the ground. His lips were a contused, shapeless mass, and his mouth was full of blood and broken teeth.

'That'll teach you that back talk don't go with me,' the trader shouted, purple with rage, peering down at him over the broken railing.

Mauki had never met a white man like this, and he resolved to walk small and never offend. He saw the boat-boys knocked about, and one of them put in irons for three days with nothing to eat for the crime of breaking a rowlock while pulling. Then, too, he heard the gossip of the village and learned why Bunster had taken a third wife – by force, as was well known. The first and second wives lay in the graveyard, under the white coral sand, with slabs of coral rock at head and feet. They had died, it was said, from beatings he had given them. The third wife was certainly ill-used, as Mauki could see for himself.

But there was no way by which to avoid offending the white man, who seemed offended with life. When Mauki kept silent, he was struck and called a sullen brute. When he spoke, he was struck for giving back talk. When he was grave, Bunster accused him of plotting and gave him a thrashing in advance; and when he strove to be cheerful and to smile, he was charged with sneering at his lord and master and given a taste of stick. Bunster was a devil. The village would have done for him, had it not remembered the lesson of the three schooners. It might have done for him anyway, if there had been a bush to which to flee. As it was, the murder of the white man, of any white man, would bring a man-of-war that would kill the offenders and chop down the precious coconut-trees. Then there were the boat-boys, with minds fully made up to drown him by accident at the first opportunity to capsize the cutter. Only Bunster saw to it that the boat did not capsize.

Mauki was of a different breed, and, escape being impossible while Bunster lived, he was resolved to get the white man. The trouble was that he could never find a chance. Bunster was always on guard. Day and night his revolvers were ready to hand. He permitted nobody to pass behind his back, as Mauki learned after having been knocked down several times. Bunster knew that he had more to fear from the good-natured, even sweet-faced, Malaita boy than from the entire population of Lord Howe; and it gave added zest to the programme of torment he was carrying out. And Mauki walked small, accepted his punishments and waited.

All other white men had respected his *tambos*, but not so Bunster. Mauki's weekly allowance of tobacco was two sticks. Bunster passed them to his woman and ordered Mauki to receive them from her hand. But this could not be, and Mauki went without his tobacco. In the same way he was made to miss many a meal, and to go hungry many a day. He was ordered to make chowder out of the big clams that grew in the lagoon. This he could not do, for clams were *tambo*. Six times in succession he refused to touch the clams, and six times he was knocked senseless. Bunster knew that the boy would die first, but called his refusal mutiny, and would have killed him had there been another cook to take his place.

One of the trader's favorite tricks was to catch Mauki's kinky locks and bat his head against the wall. Another trick was to catch Mauki unawares and thrust the live end of a cigar against his flesh. This Bunster called vaccination, and Mauki was vaccinated a number of times a week. Once, in a rage, Bunster ripped the cup handle from Mauki's nose, tearing the hole clear out of the cartilage.

'Oh, what a mug!' was his comment, when he surveyed the damage he had wrought.

The skin of a shark is like sandpaper, but the skin of a ray fish is like a rasp. In the South Seas the natives use it as a wood file in smoothing down canoes and paddles. Bunster had a mitten made of ray fish skin. The first time he tried it on Mauki, with one sweep of the hand it fetched the skin off his back from neck to armpit. Bunster was delighted. He gave his wife a taste of the mitten, and tried it out thoroughly on the boat-boys. The prime ministers came in for a stroke each, and they had to grin and take it for a joke.

'Laugh, damn you, laugh!' was the cue he gave.

Mauki came in for the largest share of the mitten. Never a day passed without a caress from it. There were times when the loss of so much cuticle kept him awake at night, and often the half-healed surface was raked raw afresh by the facetious Mr Bunster. Mauki continued his patient wait, secure in the knowledge that sooner or later his time would come. And he knew just what he was going to do, down to the smallest detail, when the time did come.

One morning Bunster got up in a mood for knocking seven bells out of the universe. He began on Mauki, and wound up on Mauki, in the interval knocking down his wife and hammering all the boat-boys. At breakfast he called the coffee slops and threw the scalding contents of the cup into Mauki's face. By ten o'clock Bunster was shivering with ague, and half an hour later he was burning with fever. It was no ordinary attack. It quickly became pernicious, and developed into black-water fever. The days passed, and he grew weaker and weaker, never leaving his bed. Mauki waited and watched, the while his skin grew intact once more. He ordered the boys to beach the cutter, scrub her bottom, and give her a general overhauling. They thought the order emanated from Bunster, and they obeyed. But Bunster at the time was lying unconscious and giving no orders. This was Mauki's chance, but still he waited.

When the worst was past, and Bunster lay convalescent and conscious, but weak as a baby, Mauki packed his few trinkets, including the china cup handle, into his trade box. Then he went over to the village and interviewed the king and his two prime ministers.

'This fella Bunster, him good fella you like too much?' he asked.

They explained in one voice that they liked the trader not at all. The ministers poured forth a recital of all the indignities and wrongs that had been heaped upon them. The king broke down and wept. Mauki interrupted rudely.

'You savve me – me big fella marster my country. You no like 'm this fella white marster. Me no like 'm. Plenty good you put hundred coconut, two hundred coconut, three hundred coconut along cutter. Him finish, you go sleep 'm good fella. Altogether kanaka sleep 'm good fella. Bime by big fella noise along house, you no savve hear 'm that fella noise. You altogether sleep strong fella too much.'

In like manner Mauki interviewed the boat-boys. Then he ordered Bunster's wife to return to her family house. Had she refused, he would have been in a quandary, for his *tambo* would not have permitted him to lay hands on her.

The house deserted, he entered the sleeping-room, where the trader lay in a doze. Mauki first removed the revolvers, then placed the ray fish mitten on his hand. Bunster's first warning was a stroke of the mitten that removed the skin the full length of his nose.

'Good fella, eh?' Mauki grinned, between two strokes, one of which swept the forehead bare and the other of which cleaned off one side of his face. 'Laugh, damn you, laugh.'

Mauki did his work thoroughly, and the kanakas, hiding in

their houses, heard the 'big fella noise' that Bunster made and continued to make for an hour or more.

When Mauki was done, he carried the boat compass and all the rifles and ammunition down to the cutter, which he proceeded to ballast with cases of tobacco. It was while engaged in this that a hideous, skinless thing came out of the house and ran screaming down the beach till it fell in the sand and mowed and gibbered under the scorching sun. Mauki looked toward it and hesitated. Then he went over and removed the head, which he wrapped in a mat and stowed in the stern-locker of the cutter.

So soundly did the kanakas sleep through that long hot day that they did not see the cutter run out through the passage and head south, close-hauled on the southeast trade. Nor was the cutter ever sighted on that long tack to the shores of Ysabel, and during the tedious head-beat from there to Malaita. He landed at Port Adams with a wealth of rifles and tobacco such as no one man had ever possessed before. But he did not stop there. He had taken a white man's head, and only the bush could shelter him. So back he went to the bush-villages, where he shot old Fanfoa and half a dozen of the chief men, and made himself the chief over all the villages. When his father died, Mauki's brother ruled in Port Adams, and, joined together, salt-water men and bushmen, the resulting combination was the strongest of the ten score fighting tribes in Malaita.

More than his fear of the British government was Mauki's fear of the all-powerful Moongleam Soap Company; and one day a message came up to him in the bush, reminding him that he owed the Company eight and one-half years of labor. He sent back a favorable answer, and then appeared the inevitable white man, the captain of the schooner, the only white man during Mauki's reign who ventured the bush and came out alive. This man not only came out, but he brought with him seven hundred and fifty dollars in gold sovereigns – the money price of eight years and a half of labor plus the cost price of certain rifles and cases of tobacco.

Mauki no longer weighs one hundred and ten pounds. His stomach is three times its former girth, and he has four wives.

He has many other things – rifles and revolvers, the handle of a china cup, and an excellent collection of bushmen's heads. But more precious than the entire collection is another head, perfectly dried and cured, with sandy hair and a yellowish beard, which is kept wrapped in the finest of fibre lava-lavas. When Mauki goes to war with villages beyond his realm, he invariably gets out this head, and, alone in his grass palace, contemplates it long and solemnly. At such times the hush of death falls on the village, and not even a pickaninny dares make a noise. The head is esteemed the most powerful devil-devil on Malaita, and to the possession of it is ascribed all of Mauki's greatness.

THE SEED OF McCOY

The *Pyrenees*, her iron sides pressed low in the water by her cargo of wheat, rolled sluggishly, and made it easy for the man who was climbing aboard from out a tiny outrigger canoe. As his eyes came level with the rail, so that he could see inboard, it seemed to him that he saw a dim, almost indiscernible haze. It was more like an illusion, like a blurring film that had spread abruptly over his eyes. He felt an inclination to brush it away, and the same instant he thought that he was growing old and that it was time to send to San Francisco for a pair of spectacles.

As he came over the rail he cast a glance aloft at the tall masts, and, next, at the pumps. They were not working. There seemed nothing the matter with the big ship, and he wondered why she had hoisted the signal of distress. He thought of his happy islanders, and hoped it was not disease. Perhaps the ship was short of water or provisions. He shook hands with the captain whose gaunt face and care-worn eyes made no secret of the trouble, whatever it was. At the same moment the new-comer was aware of a faint, indefinable smell. It seemed like that of burnt bread, but different.

He glanced curiously about him. Twenty feet away a weary-faced sailor was calking the deck. As his eyes lingered on the man, he saw suddenly arise from under his hands a faint spiral of haze that curled and twisted and was gone. By now he had reached the deck. His bare feet were pervaded by a dull warmth that quickly penetrated the thick calluses. He knew now the nature of the ship's distress. His eyes roved swiftly forward, where the full crew of weary-faced sailors regarded him eagerly. The glance from his liquid brown eyes swept over them like a benediction, soothing them, wrapping them about as in the mantle of a great peace. 'How long has she been afire, Captain?'

he asked in a voice so gentle and unperturbed that it was as the cooing of a dove.

At first the captain felt the peace and content of it stealing in upon him; then the consciousness of all that he had gone through and was going through smote him, and he was resentful. By what right did this ragged beach-comber, in dungaree trousers and a cotton shirt, suggest such a thing as peace and content to him and his overwrought, exhausted soul? The captain did not reason this; it was the unconscious process of emotion that caused his resentment.

'Fifteen days,' he answered shortly. 'Who are you?'

'My name is McCoy,' came the answer in tones that breathed tenderness and compassion.

'I mean, are you the pilot?'

McCoy passed the benediction of his gaze over the tall, heavy-shouldered man with the haggard, unshaven face who had joined the captain.

'I am as much a pilot as anybody,' was McCoy's answer. 'We are all pilots here, Captain, and I know every inch of these waters.'

But the captain was impatient.

'What I want is some of the authorities. I want to talk with them, and blame quick.'

'Then I'll do just as well.'

Again that insidious suggestion of peace, and his ship a raging furnace beneath his feet! The captain's eyebrows lifted impatiently and nervously, and his fist clenched as if he were about to strike a blow with it.

'Who in hell are you?' he demanded.

'I am the chief magistrate,' was the reply in a voice that was still the softest and gentlest imaginable.

The tall, heavy-shouldered man broke out in a harsh laugh that was partly amusement, but mostly hysterical. Both he and the captain regarded McCoy with incredulity and amazement. That this barefooted beach-comber should possess such high-sounding dignity was inconceivable. His cotton shirt, unbuttoned, exposed a grizzled chest and the fact that there was no undershirt beneath. A worn straw hat failed to hide the ragged gray hair. Halfway down his chest descended an untrimmed patriarchal beard. In any slop-shop, two shillings would have outfitted him complete as he stood before them.

'Any relation to the McCoy of the *Bounty*?' the captain asked.

'He was my great-grandfather.'

'Oh,' the captain said, then bethought himself. 'My name is Davenport, and this is my first mate, Mr Konig.'

They shook hands.

'And now to business.' The captain spoke quickly, the urgency of a great haste pressing his speech. 'We've been on fire for over two weeks. She's ready to break all hell loose any moment. That's why I held for Pitcairn. I want to beach her, or scuttle her, and save the hull.'

'Then you made a mistake, Captain,' said McCoy. 'You should have slacked away for Mangareva. There's a beautiful beach there, in a lagoon where the water is like a mill-pond.'

'But we're here, ain't we?' the first mate demanded. 'That's the point. We're here, and we've got to do something.'

McCoy shook his head kindly.

'You can do nothing here. There is no beach. There isn't even anchorage.'

'Gammon!' said the mate. 'Gammon!' he repeated loudly, as the captain signalled him to be more soft-spoken. 'You can't tell me that sort of stuff. Where d'ye keep your own boats, hey – your schooner, or cutter, or whatever you have? Hey? Answer me that.'

McCoy smiled as gently as he spoke. His smile was a caress, an embrace that surrounded the tired mate and sought to draw him into the quietude and rest of McCoy's tranquil soul.

'We have no schooner or cutter,' he replied. 'And we carry our canoes to the top of the cliff.'

'You've got to show me,' snorted the mate. 'How d'ye get around to the other islands, heh? Tell me that.'

'We don't get around. As governor of Pitcairn, I sometimes go. When I was younger, I was away a great deal – sometimes on the trading schooners, but mostly on the missionary brig. But she's gone now, and we depend on passing vessels. Sometimes we have had as high as six calls in one year. At other times, a year, and even longer, has gone by without one passing ship. Yours is the first in seven months.'

'And you mean to tell me – ' the mate began.

But Captain Davenport interfered.

'Enough of this. We're losing time. What is to be done, Mr McCoy?'

The old man turned his brown eyes, sweet as a woman's, shoreward, and both captain and mate followed his gaze around from the lonely rock of Pitcairn to the crew clustering forward and waiting anxiously for the announcement of a decision. McCoy did not hurry. He thought smoothly and slowly, step by step, with the certitude of a mind that was never vexed or outraged by life.

'The wind is light now,' he said finally. 'There is a heavy current setting to the westward.'

'That's what made us fetch to leeward,' the captain interrupted, desiring to vindicate his seamanship.

'Yes, that is what fetched you to leeward,' McCoy went on. 'Well, you can't work up against this current to-day. And if you did, there is no beach. Your ship will be a total loss.'

He paused, and captain and mate looked despair at each other.

'But I will tell you what you can do. The breeze will freshen to-night around midnight – see those tails of clouds and that thickness to windward, beyond the point there? That's where she'll come from, out of the southeast, hard. It is three hundred miles to Mangareva. Square away for it. There is a beautiful bed for your ship there.'

The mate shook his head.

'Come in to the cabin, and we'll look at the chart,' said the captain.

McCoy found a stifling, poisonous atmosphere in the pent cabin. Stray waftures of invisible gases bit his eyes and made them sting. The deck was hotter, almost unbearably hot to his bare feet. The sweat poured out of his body. He looked almost with apprehension about him. This malignant, internal heat was astounding. It was a marvel that the cabin did not burst into flames. He had a feeling as if of being in a huge bake-oven where the heat might at any moment increase tremendously and shrivel him up like a blade of grass.

As he lifted one foot and rubbed the hot sole against the leg of his trousers, the mate laughed in a savage, snarling fashion.

'The anteroom of hell,' he said. 'Hell herself is right down there under your feet.'

'It's hot!' McCoy cried involuntarily, mopping his face with a bandana handkerchief.

'Here's Mangareva,' the captain said, bending over the table and pointing to a black speck in the midst of the white blankness of the chart. 'And here, in between, is another island. Why not run for that?'

McCoy did not look at the chart.

'That's Crescent Island,' he answered. 'It is uninhabited, and it is only two or three feet above water. Lagoon, but no entrance. No, Mangareva is the nearest place for your purpose.'

'Mangareva it is, then,' said Captain Davenport, interrupting the mate's growling objection. 'Call the crew aft, Mr Konig.'

The sailors obeyed, shuffling wearily along the deck and painfully endeavoring to make haste. Exhaustion was evident in every movement. The cook came out of his galley to hear, and the cabin-boy hung about near him.

When Captain Davenport had explained the situation and announced his intention of running for Mangareva, an uproar broke out. Against a background of throaty rumbling arose inarticulate cries of rage, with here and there a distinct curse, or word, or phrase. A shrill Cockney voice soared and dominated for a moment, crying: 'Gawd! After bein' in 'ell for fifteen days – an' now 'e wants us to sail this floatin' 'ell to sea again!'

The captain could not control them, but McCoy's gentle presence seemed to rebuke and calm them, and the muttering and cursing died away, until the full crew, save here and there an anxious face directed at the captain, yearned dumbly toward the green-clad peaks and beetling coast of Pitcairn.

Soft as a spring zephyr was the voice of McCoy:

'Captain, I thought I heard some of them say they were starving.'

'Ay,' was the answer, 'and so we are. I've had a sea-biscuit and a spoonful of salmon in the last two days. We're on whack. You see, when we discovered the fire, we battened down immediately to suffocate the fire. And then we found how little food there was in the pantry. But it was too late. We didn't dare break out the lazarette. Hungry? I'm just as hungry as they are.'

He spoke to the men again, and again the throat-rumbling and cursing arose, their faces convulsed and animal-like with rage. The second and third mates had joined the captain, standing behind him at the break of the poop. Their faces were set and expressionless; they seemed bored, more than anything else, by this mutiny of the crew. Captain Davenport glanced questioningly at his first mate, and that person merely shrugged his shoulders in token of his helplessness.

'You see,' the captain said to McCoy, 'you can't compel sailors to leave the safe land and go to sea on a burning vessel. She has been their floating coffin for over two weeks now. They are worked out, and starved out, and they've got enough of her. We'll beat up for Pitcairn.'

But the wind was light, the *Pyrenees'* bottom was foul, and she could not beat up against the strong westerly current. At the end of two hours she had lost three miles. The sailors worked eagerly, as if by main strength they could compel the *Pyrenees* against the adverse elements. But steadily, port tack and starboard tack, she sagged off to the westward. The captain paced restlessly up and down, pausing occasionally to survey the vagrant smoke-wisps and to trace them back to the portions of the deck from which they sprang. The carpenter was engaged constantly in attempting to locate such places, and, when he succeeded, in calking them tighter and tighter.

'Well, what do you think?' the captain finally asked McCoy, who was watching the carpenter with all a child's interest and curiosity in his eyes.

McCoy looked shoreward, where the land was disappearing in the thickening haze.

'I think it would be better to square away for Mangareva. With that breeze that is coming, you'll be there to-morrow evening.'

'But what if the fire breaks out? It is liable to do it any moment.'

'Have your boats ready in the falls. The same breeze will carry your boats to Mangareva if the ship burns out from under.'

Captain Davenport debated for a moment, and then McCoy heard the question he had not wanted to hear, but which he knew was surely coming.

'I have no chart of Mangareva. On the general chart it is only a fly-speck. I would not know where to look for the entrance into the lagoon. Will you come along and pilot her in for me?'

McCoy's serenity was unbroken.

'Yes, Captain,' he said, with the same quiet unconcern with which he would have accepted an invitation to dinner; 'I'll go with you to Mangareva.'

Again the crew was called aft, and the captain spoke to them from the break of the poop.

'We've tried to work her up, but you see how we've lost ground. She's setting off in a two-knot current. This gentleman is the Honorable McCoy, Chief Magistrate and Governor of Pitcairn Island. He will come along with us to Mangareva. So you see the situation is not so dangerous. He would not make such an offer if he thought he was going to lose his life. Besides, whatever risk there is, if he of his own free will come on board and take it, we can do no less. What do you say for Mangareva?'

This time there was no uproar. McCoy's presence, the surety and calm that seemed to radiate from him, had had its effect. They conferred with one another in low voices. There was little urging. They were virtually unanimous, and they shoved the Cockney out as their spokesman. That worthy was overwhelmed with consciousnes of the heroism of himself and his mates, and with flashing eyes he cried:

'By Gawd! if 'e will, we will!'

The crew mumbled its assent and started forward.

'One moment, Captain,' McCoy said, as the other was turning to give orders to the mate. 'I must go ashore first.'

Mr Konig was thunderstruck, staring at McCoy as if he were a madman.

'Go ashore!' the captain cried. 'What for? It will take you three hours to get there in your canoe.'

McCoy measured the distance of the land away, and nodded.

'Yes, it is six now. I won't get ashore till nine. The people cannot be assembled earlier than ten. As the breeze freshens up to-night, you can begin to work up against it, and pick me up at daylight to-morrow morning.'

'In the name of reason and common-sense,' the captain burst forth, 'what do you want to assemble the people for? Don't you realize that my ship is burning beneath me?'

McCoy was as placid as a summer sea, and the other's anger produced not the slightest ripple upon it.

'Yes, Captain,' he cooed in his dove-like voice, 'I do realize that your ship is burning. That is why I am going with you to Mangareva. But I must get permission to go with you. It is our custom. It is an important matter when the governor leaves the island. The people's interests are at stake, and so they have the right to vote their permission or refusal. But they will give it, I know that.'

'Are you sure?'

'Quite sure.'

'Then if you know they will give it, why bother with getting it? Think of the delay – a whole night.'

'It is our custom,' was the imperturbable reply. 'Also, I am the governor, and I must make arrangements for the conduct of the island during my absence.'

'But it is only a twenty-four-hour run to Mangareva,' the captain objected. 'Suppose it took you six times that long to return to windward; that would bring you back by the end of a week.'

McCoy smiled his large, benevolent smile.

'Very few vessels come to Pitcairn, and when they do, they are usually from San Francisco or from around the Horn. I shall be

fortunate if I get back in six months. I may be away a year, and
I may have to go to San Francisco in order to find a vessel that
will bring me back. My father once left Pitcairn to be gone three
months, and two years passed before he could get back. Then,
too, you are short of food. If you have to take to the boats, and
the weather comes up bad, you may be days in reaching land. I
can bring off two canoe loads of food in the morning. Dried
bananas will be best. As the breeze freshens, you beat up against
it. The nearer you are, the bigger loads I can bring off. Good-
by.'

He held out his hand. The captain shook it, and was reluctant
to let go. He seemed to cling to it as a drowning sailor clings to a
life-buoy.

'How do I know you will come back in the morning?' he asked.

'Yes, that's it!' cried the mate. 'How do we know but what
he's skinning out to save his own hide?'

McCoy did not speak. He looked at them sweetly and benig-
nantly, and it seemed to them that they received a message from
his tremendous certitude of soul.

The captain released his hand, and, with a last sweeping
glance that embraced the crew in its benediction, McCoy went
over the rail and descended into his canoe.

The wind freshened, and the *Pyrenees*, despite the foulness of
her bottom, won half a dozen miles away from the westerly
current. At daylight, with Pitcairn three miles to windward,
Captain Davenport made out two canoes coming off to him.
Again McCoy clambered up the side and dropped over the rail
to the hot deck. He was followed by many packages of dried
bananas, each package wrapped in dry leaves.

'Now, Captain,' he said, 'swing the yards and drive for dear
life. You see, I am no navigator,' he explained a few minutes
later, as he stood by the captain aft, the latter with gaze
wandering from aloft to overside as he estimated the *Pyrenees'*
speed. 'You must fetch her to Mangareva. When you have picked
up the land, then I will pilot her in. What do you think she is
making?'

'Eleven,' Captain Davenport answered, with a final glance at the water rushing past.

'Eleven. Let me see, if she keeps up that gait, we'll sight Mangareva between eight and nine o'clock to-morrow morning. I'll have her on the beach by ten, or by eleven at latest. And then your troubles will be all over.'

It almost seemed to the captain that the blissful moment had already arrived, such was the persuasive convincingness of McCoy. Captain Davenport had been under the fearful strain of navigating his burning ship for over two weeks, and he was beginning to feel that he had had enough.

A heavier flaw of wind struck the back of his neck and whistled by his ears. He measured the weight of it, and looked quickly overside.

'The wind is making all the time,' he announced. 'The old girl's doing nearer twelve than eleven right now. If this keeps up, we'll be shortening down to-night.'

All day the *Pyrenees*, carrying her load of living fire, tore across the foaming sea. By nightfall, royals and topgallantsails were in, and she flew on into the darkness, with great, crested seas roaring after her. The auspicious wind had had its effect, and fore and aft a visible brightening was apparent. In the second dog-watch some careless soul started a song, and by eight bells the whole crew was singing.

Captain Davenport had his blankets brought up and spread on top the house.

'I've forgotten what sleep is,' he explained to McCoy. 'I'm all in. But give me a call at any time you think necessary.'

At three in the morning he was aroused by a gentle tugging at his arm. He sat up quickly, bracing himself against the skylight, stupid yet from his heavy sleep. The wind was thrumming its war-song in the rigging, and a wild sea was buffeting the *Pyrenees*. Amidships she was wallowing first one rail under and then the other, flooding the waist more often than not. McCoy was shouting something he could not hear. He reached out, clutched the other by the shoulder, and drew him close so that his own ear was close to the other's lips.

'It's three o'clock,' came McCoy's voice, still retaining its dovelike quality, but curiously muffled, as if from a long way off. 'We've run two hundred and fifty. Crescent Island is only thirty miles away, somewhere there dead ahead. There's no lights on it. If we keep running, we'll pile up, and lose ourselves as well as the ship.'

'What d' ye think – heave to?'

'Yes; heave to till daylight. It will only put us back four hours.'

So the *Pyrenees*, with her cargo of fire, was hove to, bitting the teeth of the gale and fighting and smashing the pounding seas. She was a shell, filled with a conflagration, and on the outside of the shell, clinging precariously, the little motes of men, by pull and haul, helped her in the battle.

'It is most unusual, this gale,' McCoy told the captain, in the lee of the cabin. 'By rights there should be no gale at this time of the year. But everything about the weather has been unusual. There has been a stoppage of the trades, and now it's howling right out of the trade quarter.' He waved his hand into the darkness, as if his vision could dimly penetrate for hundreds of miles. 'It is off to the westward. There is something big making off there somewhere – a hurricane or something. We're lucky to be so far to the eastward. But this is only a little blow,' he added. 'It can't last. I can tell you that much.'

By daylight the gale had eased down to normal. But daylight revealed a new danger. It had come on thick. The sea was covered by a fog, or, rather, by a pearly mist that was fog-like in density, in so far as it obstructed vision, but that was no more than a film on the sea, for the sun shot it through and filled it with a glowing radiance.

The deck of the *Pyrenees* was making more smoke than on the preceding day, and the cheerfulness of officers and crew had vanished. In the lee of the galley the cabin-boy could be heard whimpering. It was his first voyage, and the fear of death was at his heart. The captain wandered about like a lost soul, nervously chewing his mustache, scowling, unable to make up his mind what to do.

'What do you think?' he asked, pausing by the side of McCoy, who was making a breakfast off fried bananas and a mug of water.

McCoy finished the last banana, drained the mug, and looked slowly around. In his eyes was a smile of tenderness as he said:

'Well, Captain, we might as well drive as burn. Your decks are not going to hold out forever. They are hotter this morning. You haven't a pair of shoes I can wear? It is getting uncomfortable for my bare feet.'

The *Pyrenees* shipped two heavy seas as she was swung off and put once more before it, and the first mate expressed a desire to have all that water down in the hold, if only it could be introduced without taking off the hatches. McCoy ducked his head into the binnacle and watched the course set.

'I'd hold her up some more, Captain,' he said. 'She's been making drift when hove to.'

'I've set it to a point higher already,' was the answer. 'Isn't that enough?'

'I'd make it two points, Captain. This bit of a blow kicked that westerly current ahead faster than you imagine.'

Captain Davenport compromised on a point and a half, and then went aloft, accompanied by McCoy and the first mate, to keep a lookout for land. Sail had been made, so that the *Pyrenees* was doing ten knots. The following sea was dying down rapidly. There was no break in the pearly fog, and by ten o'clock Captain Davenport was growing nervous. All hands were at their stations, ready, at the first warning of land ahead, to spring like fiends to the task of bringing the *Pyrenees* up on the wind. That land ahead, a surf-washed outer reef, would be perilously close when it revealed itself in such a fog.

Another hour passed. The three watchers aloft stared intently into the pearly radiance.

'What if we miss Mangareva?' Captain Davenport asked abruptly.

McCoy, without shifting his gaze, answered softly:

'Why, let her drive, Captain. That is all we can do. All the

Paumotus are before us. We can drive for a thousand miles through reefs and atolls. We are bound to fetch up somewhere.'

'Then drive it is.' Captain Davenport evidenced his intention of descending to the deck. 'We've missed Mangareva. God knows where the next land is. I wish I'd held her up that other half-point,' he confessed a moment later. 'This cursed current plays the devil with a navigator.'

'The old navigators called the Paumotus the Dangerous Archipelago,' McCoy said, when they had regained the poop. 'This very current was partly responsible for that name.'

'I was talking with a sailor chap in Sydney, once,' said Mr Konig. 'He'd been trading in the Paumotus. He told me insurance was eighteen per cent. Is that right?'

McCoy smiled and nodded.

'Except that they don't insure,' he explained. 'The owners write off twenty per cent of the cost of their schooners each year.'

'My God!' Captain Davenport groaned. 'That makes the life of a schooner only five years!' He shook his head sadly, murmuring, 'Bad waters! bad waters!'

Again they went into the cabin to consult the big general chart; but the poisonous vapors drove them coughing and gasping on deck.

'Here is Moerenhout Island.' Captain Davenport pointed it out on the chart, which he had spread on the house. 'It can't be more than a hundred miles to leeward.'

'A hundred and ten.' McCoy shook his head doubtfully. 'It might be done, but it is very difficult. I might beach her, and then again I might put her on the reef. A bad place, a very bad place.'

'We'll take the chance,' was Captain Davenport's decision, as he set about working out the course.

Sail was shortened early in the afternoon, to avoid running past in the night; and in the second dog-watch the crew manifested its regained cheerfulness. Land was so very near, and their troubles would be over in the morning.

But morning broke clear, with a blazing tropic sun. The southeast trade had swung around to the eastward, and was driving the *Pyrenees* through the water at an eight-knot clip. Captain Davenport worked up his dead reckoning, allowing generously for drift, and announced Moerenhout Island to be not more than ten miles off. The *Pyrenees* sailed the ten miles; she sailed ten miles more; and the lookouts at the three mastheads saw naught but the naked, sun-washed sea.

'But the land is there, I tell you,' Captain Davenport shouted to them from the poop.

McCoy smiled soothingly, but the captain glared about him like a madman, fetched his sextant, and took a chronometer sight.

'I knew I was right,' he almost shouted, when he had worked up the observation. 'Twenty-one, fifty-five, south; one-thirty-six, two, west. There you are. We're eight miles to windward yet. What did you make it out, Mr Konig?'

The first mate glanced at his own figures, and said in a low voice:

'Twenty-one, fifty-five all right; but my longitude's one-thirty-six, forty-eight. That puts us considerably to leeward – '

But Captain Davenport ignored his figures with so contemptuous a silence as to make Mr Konig grit his teeth and curse savagely under his breath.

'Keep her off,' the captain ordered the man at the wheel. 'Three points – steady there, as she goes!'

Then he returned to his figures and worked them over. The sweat poured from his face. He chewed his mustache, his lips, and his pencil, staring at the figures as a man might at a ghost. Suddenly, with a fierce, muscular outburst, he crumpled the scribbled paper in his fist and crushed it under a foot. Mr Konig grinned vindictively and turned away, while Captain Davenport leaned against the cabin and for half an hour spoke no word, contenting himself with gazing to leeward with an expression of musing hopelessness on his face.

'Mr McCoy,' he broke silence abruptly. 'The chart indicates a group of islands, but not how many, off there to the north'ard, or nor'-nor'westward, about forty miles – the Acteon Islands. What about them?'

'There are four, all low,' McCoy answered. 'First to the southeast is Matuerui – no people, no entrance to the lagoon. Then comes Tenarunga. There used to be about a dozen people there, but they may be all gone now. Anyway, there is no entrance for a ship – only a boat entrance, with a fathom of water. Vehauga and Teua-raro are the other two. No entrances, no people, very low. There is no bed for the *Pyrenees* in that group. She would be a total wreck.'

'Listen to that!' Captain Davenport was frantic. 'No people! No entrances! What in the devil are islands good for?

'Well, then,' he barked suddenly, like an excited terrier, 'the chart gives a whole mess of islands off to the nor'west. What about them? What one has an entrance where I can lay my ship?'

McCoy calmly considered. He did not refer to the chart. All these islands, reefs, shoals, lagoons, entrances and distances were marked on the chart of his memory. He knew them as the city dweller knows his buildings, streets and alleys.

'Papakena and Vanavana are off there to the westward, or west-nor'westward a hundred miles and a bit more,' he said. 'One is uninhabited, and I heard that the people on the other had gone off to Cadmus Island. Anyway, neither lagoon has an entrance. Ahunui is another hundred miles on to the nor'west. No entrance, no people.'

'Well, forty miles beyond them are two islands?' Captain Davenport queried, raising his head from the chart.

McCoy shook his head.

'Paros and Manuhungi – no entrances, no people. Nengo-Nengo is forty miles beyond them, in turn, and it has no people and no entrance. But there is Hao Island. It is just the place. The lagoon is thirty miles long and five miles wide. There are plenty of people. You can usually find water. And any ship in the world can go through the entrance.'

He ceased and gazed solicitously at Captain Davenport, who, bending over the chart with a pair of dividers in hand, had just emitted a low groan.

'Is there any lagoon with an entrance anywhere nearer than Hao Island?' he asked.

'No, Captain; that is the nearest.'

'Well, it's three hundred and forty miles.' Captain Davenport was speaking very slowly, with decision. 'I won't risk the responsibility of all these lives. I'll wreck her on the Acteons. And she's a good ship, too,' he added regretfully, after altering the course, this time making more allowance than ever for the westerly current.

An hour later the sky was overcast. The southeast trade still held, but the ocean was a checker-board of squalls.

'We'll be there by one o'clock,' Captain Davenport announced confidently. 'By two o'clock at the outside. McCoy, you put her ashore on the one where the people are.'

The sun did not appear again, nor, at one o'clock, was any land to be seen. Captain Davenport looked astern at the *Pyrenees'* canting wake.

'Good Lord!' he cried. 'An easterly current! Look at that!'

Mr Konig was incredulous. McCoy was noncommittal, though he said that in the Paumotus there was no reason why it should not be an easterly current. A few minutes later a squall robbed the *Pyrenees* temporarily of all her wind, and she was left rolling heavily in the trough.

'Where's that deep lead? Over with it, you there!' Captain Davenport held the lead-line and watched it sag off to the northeast. 'There, look at that! Take hold of it for yourself.'

McCoy and the mate tried it, and felt the line thrumming and vibrating savagely to the grip of the tidal stream.

'A four-knot current,' said Mr Konig.

'An easterly current instead of a westerly,' said Captain Davenport, glaring accusingly at McCoy, as if to cast the blame for it upon him.

'That is one of the reasons, Captain, for insurance being eighteen per cent in these waters,' McCoy answered cheerfully. 'You never can tell. The currents are always changing. There was a man who wrote books, I forget his name, in the yacht *Casco*. He missed Takaroa by thirty miles and fetched Tikei, all because of the shifting currents. You are up to windward now, and you'd better keep off a few points.'

'But how much has this current set me?' the captain demanded irately. 'How am I to know how much to keep off?'

'I don't know, Captain,' McCoy said with great gentleness.

The wind returned, and the *Pyrenees*, her deck smoking and shimmering in the bright gray light, ran off dead to leeward. Then she worked back, port tack and starboard tack, crisscrossing her track, combing the sea for the Acteon Islands, which the masthead lookouts failed to sight.

Captain Davenport was beside himself. His rage took the form of sullen silence, and he spent the afternoon in pacing the poop or leaning against the weather-shrouds. At nightfall, without even consulting McCoy, he squared away and headed into the northwest. Mr Konig, surreptitiously consulting chart and binnacle, and McCoy, openly and innocently consulting the binnacle, knew that they were running for Hao Island. By midnight the squalls ceased, and the stars came out. Captain Davenport was cheered by the promise of a clear day.

'I'll get an observation in the morning,' he told McCoy, 'though what my latitude is, is a puzzler. But I'll use the Sumner method, and settle that. Do you know the Sumner line?'

And thereupon he explained it in detail to McCoy.

The day proved clear, the trade blew steadily out of the east, and the *Pyrenees* just as steadily logged her nine knots. Both the captain and mate worked out the position on a Sumner line, and agreed, and at noon agreed again, and verified the morning sights by the noon sights.

'Another twenty-four hours and we'll be there,' Captain Davenport assured McCoy. 'It's a miracle the way the old girl's decks hold out. But they can't last. They can't last. Look at them smoke, more and more every day. Yet it was a tight deck to begin with, fresh-calked in 'Frisco. I was surprised when the fire first broke out and we battened down. Look at that!'

He broke off to gaze with dropped jaw at a spiral of smoke that coiled and twisted in the lee of the mizzenmast twenty feet above the deck.

'Now, how did that get there?' he demanded indignantly.

Beneath it there was no smoke. Crawling up from the deck,

sheltered from the wind by the mast, by some freak it took form and visibility at that height. It writhed away from the mast, and for a moment overhung the captain like some threatening portent. The next moment the wind whisked it away, and the captain's jaw returned to place.

'As I was saying, when we first battened down, I was surprised. It was a tight deck, yet it leaked smoke like a sieve. And we've calked and calked ever since. There must be tremendous pressure underneath to drive so much smoke through.'

That afternoon the sky became overcast again, and squally, drizzly weather set in. The wind shifted back and forth between southeast and northeast, and at midnight the *Pyrenees* was caught aback by a sharp squall from the southwest, from which point the wind continued to blow intermittently.

'We won't make Hao until ten or eleven,' Captain Davenport complained at seven in the morning, when the fleeting promise of the sun had been erased by hazy cloud masses in the eastern sky. And the next moment he was plaintively demanding, 'And what are the currents doing?'

Lookouts at the mastheads could report no land, and the day passed in drizzling calms and violent squalls. By nightfall a heavy sea began to make from the west. The barometer had fallen to 29.50. There was no wind, and still the ominous sea continued to increase. Soon the *Pyrenees* was rolling madly in the huge waves that marched in an unending procession from out of the darkness of the west. Sail was shortened as fast as both watches could work, and, when the tired crew had finished, its grumbling and complaining voices, peculiarly animal-like and manacing, could be heard in the darkness. Once the starboard watch was called aft to lash down and make secure, and the men openly advertised their sullenness and unwillingness. Every slow movement was a protest and a threat. The atmosphere was moist and sticky like mucilage, and in the absence of wind all hands seemed to pant and gasp for air. The sweat stood out on faces and bare arms, and Captain Davenport for one, his face more gaunt and care-worn than ever, and his eyes troubled and staring, was oppressed by a feeling of impending calamity.

'It's off to the westward,' McCoy said encouragingly. 'At worst, we'll be only on the edge of it.'

But Captain Davenport refused to be comforted, and by the light of a lantern read up the chapter in his *Epitome* that related to the strategy of shipmasters in cyclonic storms. From somewhere amidships the silence was broken by a low whimpering from the cabin-boy.

'Oh, shut up!' Captain Davenport yelled suddenly and with such force as to startle every man on board and to frighten the offender into a wild wail of terror.

'Mr Konig,' the captain said in a voice that trembled with rage and nerves, 'will you kindly step for'ard and stop that brat's mouth with a deck mop?'

But it was McCoy who went forward, and in a few minutes had the boy comforted and asleep.

Shortly before daybreak the first breath of air began to move from out the southeast, increasing swiftly to a stiff and stiffer breeze. All hands were on deck waiting for what might be behind it.

'We're all right now, Captain,' said McCoy, standing close to his shoulder. 'The hurricane is to the west'ard, and we are south of it. This breeze is the in-suck. It won't blow any harder. You can begin to put sail on her.'

'But what's the good? Where shall I sail? This is the second day without observations, and we should have sighted Hao Island yesterday morning. Which way does it bear, north, south, east or what? Tell me that, and I'll make sail in a jiffy.'

'I am no navigator, Captain,' McCoy said in his mild way.

'I used to think I was one,' was the retort, 'before I got into these Paumotus.'

At mid-day the cry of 'Breakers ahead!' was heard from the lookout. The *Pyrenees* was kept off, and sail after sail was loosed and sheeted home. The *Pyrenees* was sliding through the water and fighting a current that threatened to set her down upon the breakers. Officers and men were working like mad, cook and cabin-boy, Captain Davenport himself, and McCoy all lending a hand. It was a close shave. It was a low shoal, a bleak and perilous place over which the seas broke unceasingly, where no man could live, and on which not even sea-birds could rest. The *Pyrenees* was swept within a hundred yards of it before the wind carried her clear, and at this moment the panting crew, its work done, burst out in a torrent of curses upon the head of McCoy – of McCoy who had come on board, and proposed the run to Mangareva, and lured them all away from the safety of Pitcairn Island to certain destruction in this baffling and terrible stretch of sea. But McCoy's tranquil soul was undisturbed. He smiled at them with simple and gracious benevolence, and, somehow, the exalted goodness of him seemed to penetrate to their dark and sombre souls, shaming them, and from very shame stilling the curses vibrating in their throats.

'Bad waters! bad waters!' Captain Davenport was murmuring as his ship forged clear; but he broke off abruptly to gaze at the shoal which should have been dead astern, but which was already on the *Pyrenees*' weather-quarter and working up rapidly to windward.

He sat down and buried his face in his hands. And the first mate saw, and McCoy saw, and the crew saw, what he had seen. South of the shoal an easterly current had set them down upon it; north of the shoal an equally swift westerly current had clutched the ship and was sweeping her away.

'I've heard of these Paumotus before,' the captain groaned, lifting his blanched face from his hands. 'Captain Moyendale told me about them after losing his ship on them. And I laughed at him behind his back. God forgive me, I laughed at him. What shoal is that?' he broke off, to ask McCoy.

'I don't know, Captain.'

'Why don't you know?'

'Because I never saw it before, and because I have never heard of it. I do know that it is not charted. These waters have never been thoroughly surveyed.'

'Then you don't know where we are?'

'No more than you do,' McCoy said gently.

At four in the afternoon coconut-trees were sighted, apparently growing out of the water. A little later the low land of an atoll was raised above the sea.

'I know where we are now, Captain.' McCoy lowered the glasses from his eyes. 'That's Resolution Island. We are forty miles beyond Hao Island, and the wind is in our teeth.'

'Get ready to beach her then. Where's the entrance?'

'There's only a canoe passage. But now that we know where we are, we can run for Barclay de Tolley. It is only one hundred and twenty miles from here, due nor'-nor'west. With this breeze we can be there by nine o'clock to-morrow morning.'

Captain Davenport consulted the chart and debated with himself.

'If we wreck her here,' McCoy added, 'we'd have to make the run to Barclay de Tolley in the boats just the same.'

The captain gave his orders, and once more the *Pyrenees* swung off for another run across the inhospitable sea.

And the middle of the next afternoon saw despair and mutiny on her smoking deck. The current had accelerated, the wind had slackened, and the *Pyrenees* had sagged off to the west. The lookout sighted Barclay de Tolley to the eastward, barely visible from the masthead, and vainly and for hours the *Pyrenees* tried to beat up to it. Ever, like a mirage, the coconut-trees hovered on the horizon, visible only from the masthead. From the deck they were hidden by the bulge of the world.

Again Captain Davenport consulted McCoy and the chart. Makemo lay seventy-five miles to the southwest. Its lagoon was thirty miles long, and its entrance was excellent. When Captain Davenport gave his orders, the crew refused duty. They announced that they had had enough of hell-fire under their feet. There was the land. What if the ship could not make it? They could make it in the boats. Let her burn, then. Their lives amounted to something to them. They had served faithfully the ship, now they were going to serve themselves.

They sprang to the boats, brushing the second and third mates out of the way, and proceeded to swing the boats out and to prepare to lower away. Captain Davenport and the first mate, revolvers in hand, were advancing to the break of the poop, when McCoy, who had climbed on top of the cabin, began to speak.

He spoke to the sailors, and at the first sound of his dovelike, cooing voice they paused to hear. He extended to them his own ineffable serenity and peace. His soft voice and simple thoughts flowed out to them in a magic stream, soothing them against their wills. Long forgotten things came back to them, and some remembered lullaby songs of childhood and the content and rest of the mother's arm at the end of the day. There was no more trouble, no more danger, no more irk, in all the world. Everything was as it should be, and it was only a matter of course that they should turn their backs upon the land and put to sea once more with hell-fire hot beneath their feet.

McCoy spoke simply; but it was not what he spoke. It was his personality that spoke more eloquently than any word he could utter. It was an alchemy of soul occultly subtle and profoundly deep – a mysterious emanation of the spirit, seductive, sweetly humble, and terribly imperious. It was illumination in the dark crypts of their souls, a compulsion of purity and gentleness vastly greater than that which resided in the shining, death-spitting revolvers of the officers.

The men wavered reluctantly where they stood, and those who had loosed the turns made them fast again. Then one, and then another, and then all of them, began to sidle awkwardly away.

McCoy's face was beaming with childlike pleasure as he descended from the top of the cabin. There was no trouble. For that matter there had been no trouble averted. There never had been any trouble, for there was no place for such in the blissful world in which he lived.

'You hypnotized 'em,' Mr Konig grinned at him, speaking in a low voice.

'Those boys are good,' was the answer. 'Their hearts are good. They have had a hard time, and they have worked hard, and they will work hard to the end.'

Mr Konig had no time to reply. His voice was ringing out orders, the sailors were springing to obey, and the *Pyrenees* was paying slowly off from the wind until her bow should point in the direction of Makemo.

The wind was very light, and after sun-down almost ceased. It was insufferably warm, and fore and aft men sought vainly to sleep. The deck was too hot to lie upon, and poisonous vapors, oozing through the seams, crept like evil spirits over the ship, stealing into the nostrils and windpipes of the unwary and causing fits of sneezing and coughing. The stars blinked lazily in the dim vault overhead; and the full moon, rising in the east, touched with its light the myriads of wisps and threads and spidery films of smoke that intertwined and writhed and twisted along the deck, over the rails, and up the masts and shrouds.

'Tell me,' Captain Davenport said, rubbing his smarting eyes, 'what happened with that *Bounty* crowd after they reached Pitcairn? The account I read said they burnt the *Bounty*, and that they were not discovered until many years later. But what happened in the meantime? I've always been curious to know. They were men with their necks in the rope. There were some native men, too. And then there were women. That made it look like trouble right from the jump.'

'There was trouble,' McCoy answered. 'They were bad men. They quarreled about the women right away. One of the mutineers, Williams, lost his wife. All the women were Tahitian women. His wife fell from the cliffs when hunting sea-birds. Then he took the wife of one of the native men away from him. All the native men were made very angry by this, and they killed off nearly all the mutineers. Then the mutineers that escaped killed off all the native men. The women helped. And the natives killed each other. Everybody killed everybody. They were terrible men.

'Timiti was killed by two other natives while they were combing his hair in friendship. The white men had sent them to do it. Then the white men killed them. The wife of Tullaloo killed him in a cave because she wanted a white man for husband. They were very wicked. God had hidden His face from them. At the end of two years all the native men were murdered, and all the white men except four. They were Young, John Adams, McCoy, who was my great-grandfather, and Quintal. He was a very bad man, too. Once, just because his wife did not catch enough fish for him, he bit off her ear.'

'They were a bad lot!' Mr Konig exclaimed.

'Yes, they were very bad,' McCoy agreed and went on serenely cooing of the blood and lust of his iniquitous ancestry. 'My great-grandfather escaped murder in order to die by his own hand. He made a still and manufactured alcohol from the roots of the ti-plant. Quintal was his chum, and they got drunk together all the time. At last McCoy got delirium tremens, tied a rock to his neck and jumped into the sea.

'Quintal's wife, the one whose ear he bit off, also got killed by falling from the cliffs. Then Quintal went to Young and demanded his wife, and went to Adams and demanded his wife. Adams and Young were afraid of Quintal. They knew he would kill them. So they killed him, the two of them together, with a hatchet. Then Young died. And that was about all the trouble they had.'

'I should say so,' Captain Davenport snorted. 'There was nobody left to kill.'

'You see, God had hidden His face,' McCoy said.

By morning no more than a faint air was blowing from the eastward, and, unable to make appreciable southing by it, Captain Davenport hauled up full-and-by on the port tack. He was afraid of that terrible westerly current which had cheated him out of so many ports of refuge. All day the calm continued, and all night, while the sailors, on a short ration of dried banana, were grumbling. Also, they were growing weak and complaining of stomach pains caused by the straight banana diet. All day the current swept the *Pyrenees* to the westward, while there was no wind to bear her south. In the middle of the first dog-watch, coconut-trees were sighted due south, their tufted heads rising above the water and marking the low-lying atoll beneath.

'That is Taenga Island,' McCoy said. 'We need a breeze to-night, or else we'll miss Makemo.'

'What's become of the southeast trade?' the captain demanded. 'Why don't it blow? What's the matter?'

'It is the evaporation from the big lagoons – there are so many of them,' McCoy explained. 'The evaporation upsets the whole system of trades. It even causes the wind to back up and blow gales from the southwest. This is the Dangerous Archipelago, Captain.'

Captain Davenport faced the old man, opened his mouth, and was about to curse, but paused and refrained. McCoy's presence was a rebuke to the blasphemies that stirred in his brain and trembled in his larynx. McCoy's influence had been growing during the many days they had been together. Captain Davenport was an autocrat of the sea, fearing no man, never bridling his tongue, and now he found himself unable to curse in the presence of this old man with the feminine brown eyes and the voice of a dove. When he realized this, Captain Davenport experienced a distinct shock. This old man was merely the seed of McCoy, of McCoy of the *Bounty*, the mutineer fleeing from the hemp that waited him in England, the McCoy who was a power for evil in the early days of blood and lust and violent death on Pitcairn Island.

Captain Davenport was not religious, yet in that moment he felt a mad impulse to cast himself at the other's feet – and to say he knew not what. It was an emotion that so deeply stirred him, rather than a coherent thought, and he was aware in some vague way of his own unworthiness and smallness in the presence of this other man who possessed the simplicity of a child and the gentleness of a woman.

Of course he could not so humble himself before the eyes of his officers and men. And yet the anger that had prompted the blasphemy still raged in him. He suddenly smote the cabin with his clenched hand and cried:

'Look here, old man, I won't be beaten. These Paumotus have cheated and tricked me and made a fool of me. I refuse to be beaten. I am going to drive this ship, and drive and drive and drive clear through the Paumotus to China but what I find a bed for her. If every man deserts, I'll stay by her. I'll show the Paumotus. They can't fool me. She's a good girl, and I'll stick by her as long as there's a plank to stand on. You hear me?'

'And I'll stay with you, Captain,' McCoy said.

During the night, light, baffling airs blew out of the south, and the frantic captain, with his cargo of fire, watched and measured his westward drift and went off by himself at times to curse softly so that McCoy should not hear.

Daylight showed more palms growing out of the water to the south.

'That's the leeward point of Makemo,' McCoy said. 'Katiu is only a few miles to the west. We may make that.'

But the current, sucking between the two islands, swept them to the northwest, and at one in the afternoon they saw the palms of Katiu rise above the sea and sink back into the sea again.

A few minutes later, just as the captain had discovered that a new current from the northeast had gripped the *Pyrenees*, the masthead lookouts raised coconut palms in the northwest.

'It is Raraka,' said McCoy. 'We won't make it without wind. The current is drawing us down to the southwest. But we must watch out. A few miles farther on a current flows north and turns in a circle to the northwest. This will sweep us away from Fakarava, and Fakarava is the place for the *Pyrenees* to find her bed.'

'They can sweep all they da – all they well please,' Captain Davenport remarked with heat. 'We'll find a bed for her somewhere just the same.'

But the situation on the *Pyrenees* was reaching a culmination. The deck was so hot it seemed an increase of a few degrees would cause it to burst into flames. In many places even the heavy-soled shoes of the men were no protection, and they were compelled to step lively to avoid scorching their feet. The smoke had increased and grown more acrid. Every man on board was suffering from inflamed eyes, and they coughed and strangled like a crew of tuberculosis patients. In the afternoon the boats were swung out and equipped. The last several packages of dried bananas were stored in them, as well as the instruments of the officers. Captain Davenport even put the chronometer into the long-boat, fearing the blowing up of the deck at any moment.

All night this apprehension weighed heavily on all, and in the first morning light, with hollow eyes and ghastly faces, they stared at one another as if in surprise that the *Pyrenees* still held together and that they still were alive.

Walking rapidly at times, and even occasionally breaking into an undignified hop-skip-and-run, Captain Davenport inspected his ship's deck.

'It is a matter of hours now, if not of minutes,' he announced on his return to the poop.

The cry of land came down from the masthead. From the deck the land was invisible, and McCoy went aloft, while the captain took advantage of the opportunity to curse some of the bitterness out of his heart. But the cursing was suddenly stopped by a dark line on the water which he sighted to the northeast. It was not a squall, but a regular breeze – the disrupted trade-wind, eight points out of its direction but resuming business once more.

'Hold her up, Captain,' McCoy said as soon as he reached the poop. 'That's the easterly point of Fakarava, and we'll go in through the passage full-tilt, the wind abeam and every sail drawing.'

At the end of an hour, the coconut-trees and the low-lying land were visible from the deck. The feeling that the end of the *Pyrenees'* resistance was imminent weighed heavily on everybody. Captain Davenport had the three boats lowered and dropped short astern, a man in each to keep them apart. The *Pyrenees* closely skirted the shore, the surf-whitened atoll a bare two cable-lengths away.

'Get ready to wear her, Captain,' McCoy warned.

And a minute later the land parted, exposing a narrow passage and the lagoon beyond, a great mirror, thirty miles in length and a third as broad.

'Now, Captain.'

For the last time the yards of the *Pyrenees* swung around as she obeyed the wheel and headed into the passage. The turns had scarcely been made, and nothing had been coiled down, when the men and mates swept back to the poop in panic terror. Nothing had happened, yet they averred that something was going to happen. They could not tell why. They merely knew that it was about to happen. McCoy started forward to take up his position on the bow in order to con the vessel in; but the captain gripped his arm and whirled him around.

'Do it from here,' he said. 'That deck's not safe. What's the matter?' he demanded the next instant. 'We're standing still.'

McCoy smiled.

'You are bucking a seven-knot current, Captain,' he said. 'That is the way the full ebb runs out of this passage.'

At the end of another hour the *Pyrenees* had scarcely gained her length, but the wind freshened and she began to forge ahead.

'Better get into the boats, some of you,' Captain Davenport commanded.

His voice was still ringing, and the men were just beginning to move in obedience, when the amidship deck of the *Pyrenees*, in a mass of flame and smoke, was flung upward into the sails and rigging, part of it remaining there and the rest falling into the sea. The wind being abeam, was what had saved the men crowded aft. They made a blind rush to gain the boats, but McCoy's voice, carrying its convincing message of vast calm and endless time, stopped them.

'Take it easy,' he was saying. 'Everything is all right. Pass that boy down somebody, please.'

The man at the wheel had forsaken it in a funk, and Captain Davenport had leaped and caught the spokes in time to prevent the ship from yawing in the current and going ashore.

'Better take charge of the boats,' he said to Mr Konig. 'Tow one of them short, right under the quarter . . . When I go over, it'll be on the jump.'

Mr Konig hesitated, then went over the rail and lowered himself into the boat.

'Keep her off half a point, Captain.'

Captain Davenport gave a start. He had thought he had the ship to himself.

'Ay, ay; half a point it is,' he answered.

Amidships the *Pyrenees* was an open, flaming furnace, out of which poured an immense volume of smoke which rose high above the masts and completely hid the forward part of the ship. McCoy, in the shelter of the mizzen-shrouds, continued his difficult task of conning the ship through the intricate channel. The fire was working aft along the deck from the seat of explosion, while the soaring tower of canvas on the mainmast went up and vanished in a sheet of flame. Forward, though they could not see them, they knew that the head-sails were still drawing.

'If only she don't burn all her canvas off before she makes inside,' the captain groaned.

'She'll make it,' McCoy assured him with supreme confidence. 'There is plenty of time. She is bound to make it. And once inside, we'll put her before it; that will keep the smoke away from us and hold back the fire from working aft.'

A tongue of flame sprang up the mizzen, reached hungrily for the lowest tier of canvas, missed it, and vanished. From aloft a burning shred of rope-stuff fell square on the back of Captain Davenport's neck. He acted with the celerity of one stung by a bee as he reached up and brushed the offending fire from his skin.

'How is she heading, Captain?'

'Nor'west by west.'

'Keep her west-nor'west.'

Captain Davenport put the wheel up and steadied her.

'West by north, Captain.'

'West by north she is.'

'And now west.'

Slowly, point by point, as she entered the lagoon, the *Pyrenees* described the circle that put her before the wind; and point by point, with all the calm certitude of a thousand years of time to spare, McCoy chanted the changing course.

'Another point, Captain.'

'A point it is.'

Captain Davenport whirled several spokes over, suddenly reversing and coming back one to check her.

'Steady.'

'Steady she is – right on it.'

Despite the fact that the wind was now astern, the heat was so intense that Captain Davenport was compelled to steal sidelong glances into the binnacle, letting go the wheel, now with one hand, now with the other, to rub or shield his blistering cheeks.

McCoy's beard was crinkling and shrivelling and the smell of it, strong in the other's nostrils, compelled him to look toward McCoy with sudden solicitude. Captain Davenport was letting go the spokes alternately with his hands in order to rub their blistering backs against his trousers. Every sail on the mizzen-mast vanished in a rush of flame, compelling the two men to crouch and shield their faces.

'Now,' said McCoy, stealing a glance ahead at the low shore, 'four points up, Captain, and let her drive.'

Shreds and patches of burning rope and canvas were falling about them and upon them. The tarry smoke from a smouldering piece of rope at the captain's feet set him off into a violent coughing fit, during which he still clung to the spokes.

The *Pyrenees* struck, her bow lifted, and she ground ahead gently to a stop. A shower of burning fragments, dislodged by the shock, fell about them. The ship moved ahead again and struck a second time. She crushed the fragile coral under her keel, drove on, and struck a third time.

'Hard over,' said McCoy. 'Hard over?' he questioned gently, a minute later.

'She won't answer,' was the reply.

'All right. She is swinging around.' McCoy peered over the side. 'Soft, white sand. Couldn't ask better. A beautiful bed.'

As the *Pyrenees* swung around her stern away from the wind, a fearful blast of smoke and flame poured aft. Captain Davenport deserted the wheel in blistering agony. He reached the painter of the boat that lay under the quarter, then looked for McCoy, who was standing aside to let him go down.

'You first,' the captain cried, gripping him by the shoulder and almost throwing him over the rail. But the flame and smoke were too terrible, and he followed hard after McCoy, both men wriggling on the rope and sliding down into the boat together. A sailor in the bow, without waiting for orders, slashed the painter through with his sheath-knife. The oars, poised in readiness, bit into the water, and the boat shot away.

'A beautiful bed, Captain,' McCoy murmured, looking back.

'Ay, a beautiful bed, and all thanks to you,' was the answer.

The three boats pulled away for the white beach of pounded coral, beyond which, on the edge of a coconut grove, could be seen a half-dozen grass-houses, and a score or more of excited natives, gazing wide-eyed at the conflagration that had come to land.

The boats grounded and they stepped out on the white beach.

'And now,' said McCoy, 'I must see about getting back to Pitcairn.'

GOOD-BY, JACK

Hawaii is a queer place. Everything socially is what I may call topsy-turvy. Not but what things are correct. They are almost too much so. But still things are sort of upside down. The most ultra-exclusive set there is the 'Missionary Crowd'. It comes with rather a shock to learn that in Hawaii the obscure, martyrdom-seeking missionary sits at the head of the table of the moneyed aristocracy. But it is true. The humble New Englanders who came out in the third decade of the nineteenth century, came for the lofty purpose of teaching the kanakas the true religion, the worship of the one only genuine and undeniable God. So well did they succeed in this, and also in civilizing the kanaka, that by the second or third generation he was practically extinct. This being the fruit of the seed of the Gospel, the fruit of the seed of the missionaries (the sons and the grandsons) was the possession of the islands themselves – of the land, the ports, the town sites and the sugar plantations. The missionary who came to give the bread of life remained to gobble up the whole heathen feast.

But that is not the Hawaiian queerness I started out to tell. Only one cannot speak of things Hawaiian without mentioning the missionaries. There is Jack Kersdale, the man I wanted to tell about; he came of missionary stock. That is, on his grandmother's side. His grandfather was old Benjamin Kersdale, a Yankee trader, who got his start for a million in the old days by selling cheap whiskey and square-face gin. There's another queer thing. The old missionaries and old traders were mortal enemies. You see, their interests conflicted. But their children made it up by inter-marrying and dividing the islands between them.

Life in Hawaii is a song. That's the way Stoddard put it in his 'Hawaii Noi':

> 'Thy life is music – Fate the notes prolong!
> Each isle a stanza, and the whole a song.'

And he was right. Flesh is golden there. The native women are sun-ripe Junos, the native men bronzed Apollos. They sing, and dance, and all are flower-bejewelled and flower-crowned. And, outside the rigid 'Missionary Crowd', the white men yield to the climate and the sun, and no matter how busy they may be, are prone to dance and sing and wear flowers behind their ears and in their hair. Jack Kersdale was one of these fellows. He was one of the busiest men I ever met. He was a several-times millionaire. He was a sugar king, a coffee planter, a rubber pioneer, a cattle rancher and a promoter of three out of every four new enterprises launched in the islands. He was a society man, a club man, a yachtsman, a bachelor, and withal as handsome a man as was ever doted upon by mamas with marriageable daughters. Incidentally, he had finished his education at Yale, and his head was crammed fuller with vital statistics and scholarly information concerning Hawaii Nei than any other islander I ever encountered. He turned off an immense amount of work, and he sang and danced and put flowers in his hair as immensely as any of the idlers.

He had grit, and had fought two duels – both political – when he was no more than a raw youth essaying his first adventures in politics. In fact, he played a most creditable and courageous part in the last revolution, when the native dynasty was overthrown; and he could not have been over sixteen at the time. I am pointing out that he was no coward, in order that you may appreciate what happens later on. I've seen him in the breaking yard at the Haleakala Ranch, conquering a four-year-old brute that for two years had defied the pick of Von Tempsky's cowboys. And I must tell of one other thing. It was down in Kona – or up, rather, for the Kona people scorn to live at less than a thousand feet elevation. We were all on the *lanai* of Doctor Goodhue's bungalow. I was talking with Dottie Fairchild when it happened. A big centipede – it was seven inches, for we measured it afterward – fell from the rafters overhead squarely into her coiffure. I confess, the hideousness of it paralyzed me. I couldn't move. My mind refused to work. There, within two feet of me, the ugly venomous devil was writhing in her hair. It threatened at any moment to fall down upon her exposed shoulders – we had just come out from dinner.

'What is it?' she asked, starting to raise her hand to her head.

'Don't!' I cried. 'Don't!'

'But what is it?' she insisted, growing frightened by the fright she read in my eyes and on my stammering lips.

My exclamation attracted Kersdale's attention. He glanced our way carelessly, but in that glance took in everything. He came over to us, but without haste.

'Please don't move, Dottie,' he said quietly.

He never hesitated, nor did he hurry and make a bungle of it.

'Allow me,' he said.

And with one hand he caught her scarf and drew it tightly around her shoulders so that the centipede could not fall inside her bodice. With the other hand – the right – he reached into her hair, caught the repulsive abomination as near as he was able by the nape of the neck, and held it tightly between thumb and forefinger as he withdrew it from her hair. It was as horrible and heroic a sight as man could wish to see. It made my flesh crawl. The centipede, seven inches of squirming legs, writhed and twisted and dashed itself about his hand, the body twining around the fingers and the legs digging into the skin and scratching as the beast endeavored to free itself. It bit him twice – I saw it – though he assured the ladies that he was not harmed as he dropped it upon the walk and stamped it into the gravel. But I saw him in the surgery five minutes afterward, with Doctor Goodhue scarifying the wounds and injecting permanganate of potash. The next morning Kersdale's arm was as big as a barrel, and it was three weeks before the swelling went down.

All of which has nothing to do with my story, but which I could not avoid giving in order to show that Jack Kersdale was anything but a coward. It was the cleanest exhibition of grit I have ever seen. He never turned a hair. The smile never left his lips. And he dived with thumb and forefinger into Dottie Fairchild's hair as gayly as if it had been a box of salted almonds. Yet that was the man I was destined to see stricken with fear a thousand times more hideous even than the fear that was mine when I saw that writhing abomination in Dottie Fairchild's hair, dangling over her eyes and the trap of her bodice.

I was interested in leprosy, and upon that, as upon every other island subject, Kersdale had encyclopedic knowledge. In fact, leprosy was one of his hobbies. He was an ardent defender of the settlement at Molokai, where all the island lepers were segregated. There was much talk and feeling among the natives, fanned by the demagogues, concerning the cruelties of Molokai, where men and women, not alone banished from friends and family, were compelled to live in perpetual imprisonment until they died. There were no reprieves, no commutations of sentences. 'Abandon hope' was written over the portal of Molokai.

'I tell you they are happy there,' Kersdale insisted. 'And they are infinitely better off than their friends and relatives outside who have nothing the matter with them. The horrors of Molokai are all poppycock. I can take you through any hospital or any slum in any of the great cities of the world and show you a thousand times worse horrors. The living death! The creatures that once were men! Bosh! You ought to see those living deaths racing horses on the Fourth of July. Some of them own boats. One has a gasolene launch. They have nothing to do but have a good time. Food, shelter, clothes, medical attendance, everything is theirs. They are the wards of the Territory. They have a much finer climate than Honolulu, and the scenery is magnificent. I shouldn't mind going down there myself for the rest of my days. It is a lovely spot.'

So Kersdale on the joyous leper. He was not afraid of leprosy. He said so himself, and that there wasn't one chance in a million for him or any other white man to catch it, though he confessed afterward that one of his school chums, Alfred Starter, had contracted it, gone to Molokai, and there died.

'You know, in the old days,' Kersdale explained, 'there was no certain test for leprosy. Anything unusual or abnormal was sufficient to send a fellow to Molokai. The result was that dozens were sent there who were no more lepers than you or I. But they don't make that mistake now. The Board of Health tests are infallible. The funny thing is that when the test was discovered they immediately went down to Molokai and applied it, and they found a number who were not lepers. They were immediately deported. Happy to get away? They wailed harder at leaving the settlement than when they left Honolulu to go to it. Some refused to leave, and really had to be forced out. One of them even married a leper woman in the last stages and then wrote pathetic letters to the Board of Health, protesting against his expulsion on the ground that no one was so well able as he to take care of his poor old wife.'

'What is this infallible test?' I demanded.

'The bacteriological test. There is no getting away from it. Doctor Hervey – he's our expert, you know – was the first man to apply it here. He is a wizard. He knows more about leprosy than any living man, and if a cure is ever discovered, he'll be that discoverer. As for the test, it is very simple. They have succeeded in isolating the *bacillus deprae* and studying it. They know it now when they see it. All they do is to snip a bit of skin from the suspect and subject it to the bacteriological test. A man without any visible symptoms may be chock full of the leprosy bacilli.'

'Then you or I, for all we know,' I suggested, 'may be full of it now.'

Kersdale shrugged his shoulders and laughed.

'Who can say? It takes seven years for it to incubate. If you have any doubts go and see Doctor Hervey. He'll just snip out a piece of your skin and let you know in a jiffy.'

Later on he introduced me to Dr Hervey, who loaded me down with Board of Health reports and pamphlets on the subject, and took me out to Kalihi, the Honolulu receiving station, where suspects were examined and confirmed lepers were held for deportation to Molokai. These deportations occurred about once a month, when, the last good-bys said, the lepers were marched on board the little steamer, the *Noeau*, and carried down to the settlement.

One afternoon, writing letters at the club, Jack Kersdale dropped in on me.

'Just the man I want to see,' was his greeting. 'I'll show you the saddest aspect of the whole situation – the lepers wailing as they depart for Molokai. The *Noeau* will be taking them on board in a few minutes. But let me warn you not to let your feelings be harrowed. Real as their grief is, they'd wail a whole sight harder a year hence if the Board of Health tried to take them away from Molokai. We've just time for a whiskey and soda. I've a carriage outside. It won't take us five minutes to get down to the wharf.'

To the wharf we drove. Some forty sad wretches, amid their mats, blankets and luggage of various sorts, were squatting on the stringer piece. The *Noeau* had just arrived and was making fast to a lighter that lay between her and the wharf. A Mr McVeigh, the superintendent of the settlement, was overseeing the embarkation, and to him I was introduced, also to Dr Georges, one of the Board of Health physicians whom I had already met at Kalihi. The lepers were a woebegone lot. The faces of the majority were hideous – too horrible for me to describe. But here and there I noticed fairly good-looking persons, with no apparent signs of the fell disease upon them. One, I noticed, a little white girl, not more than twelve, with blue eyes and golden hair. One cheek, however, showed the leprous bloat. On my remarking upon the sadness of her alien situation among the brown-skinned afflicted ones, Doctor Georges replied:

'Oh, I don't know. It's a happy day in her life. She comes from Kauai. Her father is a brute. And now that she has developed the disease she is going to join her mother at the settlement. Her mother was sent down three years ago – a very bad case.'

'You can't always tell from appearances,' Mr McVeigh explained. 'That man there, that big chap, who looks the pink of condition, with nothing the matter with him, I happen to know has a perforating ulcer in his foot and another in his shoulder blade. Then there are others – there, see that girl's hand, the one who is smoking the cigarette. See her twisted fingers. That's the anaesthetic form. It attacks the nerves. You could cut her fingers off with a dull knife, or rub them off on a nutmeg-grater, and she would not experience the slightest sensation.'

'Yes, but that fine-looking woman, there,' I persisted; 'surely,

surely, there can't be anything the matter with her. She is too glorious and gorgeous altogether.'

'A sad case,' Mr McVeigh answered over his shoulder, already turning away to walk down the wharf with Kersdale.

She was a beautiful woman, and she was pure Polynesian. From my meagre knowledge of the race and its types I could not but conclude that she had descended from old chief stock. She could not have been more than twenty-three or four. Her lines and proportions were magnificent, and she was just beginning to show the amplitude of the women of her race.

'It was a blow to all of us,' Dr Georges volunteered. 'She gave herself up voluntarily, too. No one suspected. But somehow she had contracted the disease. It broke us all up, I assure you. We've kept it out of the papers, though. Nobody but us and her family knows what has become of her. In fact, if you were to ask any man in Honolulu, he'd tell you it was his impression that she was somewhere in Europe. It was at her request that we've been so quiet about it. Poor girl, she has a lot of pride.'

'But who is she?' I asked. 'Certainly, from the way you talk about her, she must be somebody.'

'Did you ever hear of Lucy Mokunui?' he asked.

'Lucy Mokunui?' I repeated, haunted by some familiar association. I shook my head. 'It seems to me I've heard the name, but I've forgotten it.'

'Never heard of Lucy Mokunui! The Hawaiian nightingale! I beg your pardon. Of course you are a *malahini*,* and could not be expected to know. Well, Lucy Mokunui was the best beloved of Honolulu – of all Hawaii, for that matter.'

'You say was,' I interrupted.

'And I mean it. She is finished.' He shrugged his shoulders pityingly. 'A dozen *haoles* – I beg your pardon, white men – have lost their hearts to her at one time or another. And I'm not counting in the ruck. The dozen I refer to were *haoles* of position and prominence.

'She could have married the son of the Chief Justice if she'd

* *Malahini* – newcomer.

wanted to. You think she's beautiful, eh? But you should hear
her sing. Finest native woman singer in Hawaii Nei. Her throat
is pure silver and melted sunshine. We adored her. She toured
America first with the Royal Hawaiian Band. After that she
made two more trips on her own – concert work.'

'Oh!' I cried. 'I remember now. I heard her two years ago at
the Boston Symphony. So that is she. I recognize her now.'

I was oppressed by a heavy sadness. Life was a futile thing at
best. A short two years and this magnificent creature, at the
summit of her magnificent success, was one of the leper squad
awaiting deportation to Molokai. Henley's lines came into my
mind:

> 'The poor old tramp explains his poor old ulcers;
> Life is, I think, a blunder and a shame.'

I recoiled from my own future. If this awful fate fell to Lucy
Mokunui, what might not my lot be? – or anybody's lot? I was
thoroughly aware that in life we are in the midst of death – but
to be in the midst of living death, to die and not be dead, to be
one of that draft of creatures that once were men, ay, and women,
like Lucy Mokunui, the epitome of all Polynesian charms, an
artist as well, and well beloved of men – I am afraid I must have
betrayed my perturbation, for Doctor Georges hastened to assure
me that they were very happy down in the settlement.

It was all too inconceivably monstrous. I could not bear to
look at her. A short distance away, behind a stretched rope
guarded by a policeman, were the lepers' relatives and friends.
They were not allowed to come near. There were no last
embraces, no kisses of farewell. They called back and forth to
one another – last messages, last words of love, last reiterated
instructions. And those behind the rope looked with terrible
intensity. It was the last time they would behold the faces of their
loved ones, for they were the living dead, being carted away in
the funeral ship to the graveyard of Molokai.

Doctor Georges gave the command, and the unhappy wretches
dragged themselves to their feet and under their burdens of
luggage began to stagger across the lighter and aboard the

steamer. It was the funeral procession. At once the wailing started from those behind the rope. It was blood-curdling; it was heart-rending. I never heard such woe, and I hope never to again. Kersdale and McVeigh were still at the other end of the wharf, talking earnestly – politics, of course, for both were head-over-heels in that particular game. When Lucy Mokunui passed me, I stole a look at her. She *was* beautiful. She was beautiful by our standards as well – one of those rare blossoms that occur but once in generations. And she, of all women, was doomed to Molokai. She walked like a queen, across the lighter, straight on board, and aft on the open deck where the lepers huddled by the rail, wailing, now, to their dear ones on shore.

The lines were cast off, and the *Noeau* began to move away from the wharf. The wailing increased. Such grief and despair! I was just resolving that never again would I be a witness to the sailing of the *Noeau*, when McVeigh and Kersdale returned. The latter's eyes were sparkling, and his lips could not quite hide the smile of delight that was his. Evidently the politics they had talked had been satisfactory. The rope had been flung aside, and the lamenting relatives now crowded the stringer piece on either side of us.

'That's her mother,' Doctor Georges whispered, indicating an old woman next to me, who was rocking back and forth and gazing at the steamer rail out of tear-blinded eyes. I noticed that Lucy Mokunui was also wailing. She stopped abruptly and gazed at Kersdale. Then she stretched forth her arms in that adorable, sensuous way that Olga Nethersole has of embracing an audience. And with arms outspread, she cried:

'Good-by, Jack! Good-by!'

He heard the cry, and looked. Never was a man overtaken by more crushing fear. He reeled on the stringer piece, his face went white to the roots of his hair, and he seemed to shrink and wither away inside his clothes. He threw up his hands and groaned, 'My God! My God!' Then he controlled himself by a great effort.

'Good-by, Lucy! Good-by!' he called.

And he stood there on the wharf, waving his hands to her till the *Noeau* was clear away and the faces lining her after-rail were vague and indistinct.

'I thought you knew,' said McVeigh, who had been regarding him curiously. 'You, of all men, should have known. I thought that was why you were here.'

'I know now,' Kersdale answered with immense gravity. 'Where's the carriage?'

He walked rapidly – half-ran – to it. I had to half-run myself to keep up with him.

'Drive to Doctor Hervey's,' he told the driver. 'Drive as fast as you can.'

He sank down in the seat, panting and gasping. The pallor of his face had increased. His lips were compressed and the sweat was standing out on his forehead and upper lip. He seemed in some horrible agony.

'For God's sake, Martin, make those horses go!' he broke out suddenly. 'Lay the whip into them! – do you hear? – lay the whip into them!'

'They'll break, sir,' the driver remonstrated.

'Let them break,' Kersdale answered. 'I'll pay your fine and square you with the police. Put it to them. That's right. Faster! Faster!

'And I never knew, I never knew,' he muttered, sinking back in the seat and with trembling hands wiping the sweat away.

The carriage was bouncing, swaying and lurching around corners at such a wild pace as to make conversation impossible. Besides, there was nothing to say. But I could hear him muttering over and over, 'And I never knew. I never knew.'

THE SHERIFF OF KONA

'You cannot escape liking the climate,' Cudworth said, in reply to my panegyric on the Kona coast. 'I was a young fellow, just out of college, when I came here eighteen years ago. I never went back, except, of course, to visit. And I warn you, if you have some spot dear to you on earth, not to linger here too long, else you will find this dearer.'

We had finished dinner, which had been served on the big *lanai*, the one with a northerly exposure, though *exposure* is indeed a misnomer in so delectable a climate.

The candles had been put out, and a slim, white-clad Japanese slipped like a ghost through the silvery moonlight, presented us with cigars, and faded away into the darkness of the bungalow. I looked through a screen of banana and lehua trees, and down across the guava scrub to the quiet sea a thousand feet beneath. For a week, ever since I had landed from the tiny coasting-steamer, I had been stopping with Cudworth, and during that time no wind had ruffled that unvexed sea. True, there had been breezes, but they were the gentlest zephyrs that ever blew through summer isles. They were not winds; they were sighs – long, balmy sighs of a world at rest.

'A lotus land,' I said.

'Where each day is like every day, and every day is a paradise of days,' he answered. 'Nothing ever happens. It is not too hot. It it not too cold. It is always just right. Have you noticed how the land and the sea breathe turn and turn about?'

Indeed I had noticed that delicious, rhythmic, breathing. Each morning I had watched the sea-breeze begin at the shore and slowly extend seaward as it blew the mildest, softest whiff of ozone to the land. It played over the sea, just faintly darkening its surface, with here and there and everywhere long lanes of calm, shifting, changing, drifting, according to the capricious kisses of the breeze. And each evening I had watched the sea breath die away to heavenly calm, and heard the land breath softly make its way through the coffee trees and monkey-pods.

'It is a land of perpetual calm,' I said. 'Does it ever blow here? – ever really blow? You know what I mean.'

Cudworth shook his head and pointed eastward.

'How can it blow, with a barrier like that to stop it?'

Far above towered the huge bulks of Mauna Kea and Mauna Loa, seeming to blot out half the starry sky. Two miles and a half above our heads they reared their own heads, white with snow that the tropic sun had failed to melt.

'Thirty miles away, right now, I'll wager, it is blowing forty miles an hour.'

I smiled incredulously.

Cudworth stepped to the *lanai* telephone. He called up, in succession, Waimea, Kohala and Hamakua. Snatches of his conversation told me that the wind was blowing: 'Rip-snorting and back-jumping, eh? . . . How long? . . . Only a week? . . . Hello, Abe, is that you? . . . Yes, yes . . . You *will* plant coffee on the Hamakua coast . . . Hang your wind-breaks! You should see *my* trees.'

'Blowing a gale,' he said to me, turning from hanging up the receiver. 'I always have to joke Abe on his coffee. He has five hundred acres, and he's done marvels in wind-breaking, but how he keeps the roots in the ground is beyond me. Blow? It always blows on the Hamakua side. Kohala reports a schooner under double reefs beating up the channel between Hawaii and Maui, and making heavy weather of it.'

'It is hard to realize,' I said lamely. 'Doesn't a little whiff of it ever eddy around somehow, and get down here?'

'Not a whiff. Our land-breeze is absolutely of no kin, for it begins this side of Mauna Kea and Mauna Loa. You see, the land radiates its heat quicker than the sea, and so, at night, the land breathes over the sea. In the day the land becomes warmer than the sea, and the sea breathes over the land . . . Listen! Here comes the land-breath now, the mountain wind.'

I could hear it coming, rustling softly through the coffee trees, stirring the monkey-pods, and sighing through the sugar-cane. On the *lanai* the hush still reigned. Then it came, the first feel of the mountain wind, faintly balmy, fragrant and spicy, and cool, deliciously cool, a silken coolness, a wine-like coolness – cool as only the mountain wind of Kona can be cool.

'Do you wonder that I lost my heart to Kona eighteen years ago?' he demanded. 'I could never leave it now. I think I should die. It would be terrible. There was another man who loved it, even as I. I think he loved it more, for he was born here on the Kona coast. He was a great man, my best friend, my more than brother. But he left it, and he did not die.'

'Love?' I queried. 'A woman?'

Cudworth shook his head.

'Nor will he ever come back, though his heart will be here until he dies.'

He paused and gazed down upon the beachlights of Kailua. I smoked silently and waited.

'He was already in love . . . with his wife. Also, he had three children, and he loved them. They are in Honolulu now. The boy is going to college.'

'Some rash act?' I questioned, after a time, impatiently.

He shook his head. 'Neither guilty of anything criminal, nor charged with anything criminal. He was the Sheriff of Kona.'

'You choose to be paradoxical,' I said.

'I suppose it does sound that way,' he admitted, 'and that is the perfect hell of it.'

He looked at me searchingly for a moment, and then abruptly took up the tale.

'He was a leper. No, he was not born with it – no one is born with it; it came upon him. This man – what does it matter? Lyte Gregory was his name. Every *kamaina* knows the story. He was straight American stock, but he was built like the chieftains of old Hawaii. He stood six feet three. His stripped weight was two hundred and twenty pounds, not an ounce of which was not clean muscle or bone. He was the strongest man I have ever seen. He was an athlete and a giant. He was a god. He was my friend. And his heart and his soul were as big and as fine as his body.

'I wonder what you would do if you saw your friend, your brother, on the slippery lip of a precipice, slipping, slipping, and you were able to do nothing. That was just it. I could do nothing. I saw it coming, and I could do nothing. My God, man! what could I do? There it was, malignant and incontestable, the mark of the thing on his brow. No one else saw it. It was because I loved him so, I do believe, that I alone saw it. I could not credit the testimony of my senses. It was too incredibly horrible. Yet there it was, on his brow, on his ears: I had seen it, the slight puff of the earlobes – oh, so imperceptibly slight. I watched it for months. Then, next, hoping against hope, the darkening of the skin above both eyebrows – oh, so faint, just like the dimmest touch of sunburn. I should have thought it sunburn but that there was a shine to it, such an invisible shine, like a little highlight seen for a moment and gone the next. I tried to believe it was sunburn, only I could not. I knew better. No one noticed it but me. No one ever noticed it except Stephen Kaluna, and I did not know that till afterward. But I saw it coming, the whole damnable, unnamable awfulness of it; but I refused to think about the future. I was afraid. I could not. And of nights I cried over it.

'He was my friend. We fished sharks on Niihau together. We hunted wild cattle on Mauna Kea and Mauna Loa. We broke horses and branded steers on the Carter Ranch. We hunted goats through Haleakala. He taught me diving and surfing until I was nearly as clever as he, and he was cleverer than the average Kanaka. I have seen him dive in fifteen fathoms, and he could stay down two minutes. He was an amphibian and a mountaineer. He could climb wherever a goat dared climb. He was afraid of nothing. He was on the wrecked *Luga*, and he swam thirty miles in thirty-six hours in a heavy sea. He could fight his way out through breaking combers that would batter you and me to a jelly. He was a great, glorious man-god. We went though the Revolution together. We were both romantic loyalists. He was shot twice and sentenced to death. But he was too great a man for the republicans to kill. He laughed at them. Later, they gave him honor and made him Sheriff of Kona. He was a simple man, a boy that never grew up. His was no intricate brain pattern. He had no twists nor quirks in his mental processes. He went straight to the point, and his points were always simple.

'And he was sanguine. Never have I known so confident a man, nor a man so satisfied and happy. He did not ask anything from life. There was nothing left to be desired. For him life had no arrears. He had been paid in full, cash down, and in advance. What more could he possibly desire than that magnificent body, that iron constitution, that immunity from all ordinary ills, and that lowly wholesomeness of soul? Physically he was perfect. He had never been sick in his life. He did not know what a headache was. When I was so afflicted he used to look at me in wonder, and make me laugh with his clumsy attempts at sympathy. He did not understand such a thing as a headache. He could not understand. Sanguine? No wonder. How could he be otherwise with that tremendous vitality and incredible health?

'Just to show you what faith he had in his glorious star, and, also, what sanction he had for that faith. He was a youngster at the time – I had just met him – when he went into a poker game at Wailuku. There was a big German in it, Schultz his name was, and he played a brutal, domineering game. He had had a run of luck as well, and he was quite insufferable, when Lyte Gregory dropped in and took a hand. The very first hand it was Schultz's blind. Lyte came in, as well as the others, and Schultz raised them out – all except Lyte. He did not like the German's tone, and he raised him back. Schultz raised in turn, and in turn Lyte raised Schultz. So they went, back and forth. The stakes were big. And do you know what Lyte held? A pair of kings and three little clubs. It wasn't poker. Lyte wasn't playing poker. He was playing his optimism. He didn't know what Schultz held, but he raised and raised until he made Schultz squeal, and Schultz held three aces all the time. Think of it! A man with a pair of kings compelling three aces to see before the draw!

'Well, Schultz called for two cards. Another German was dealing, Schultz's friend at that. Lyte knew then that he was up against three of a kind. Now what did he do? What would you have done? Drawn three cards and held up the kings, of course. Not Lyte, he was playing optimism. He threw the kings away, held up the three little clubs and drew two cards. He never looked at them. He looked across at Schultz to bet, and Schultz did bet, big. Since he himself held three aces, he knew he had Lyte, because he played Lyte for threes, and, necessarily, they would have to be smaller threes. Poor Schultz! He was perfectly correct under the premises. His mistake was that he thought Lyte was playing poker. They bet back and forth for five minutes, until Schultz's certainty began to ooze out. And all the time Lyte had never looked at his two cards, and Schultz knew it. I could see Schultz think, and revive, and splurge with his bets again. But the strain was too much for him.

'"Hold on, Gregory," he said at last. "I've got you beaten from the start. I don't want any of your money. I've got – "

'"Never mind what you've got," Lyte interrupted. "You don't know what I've got. I guess I'll take a look."

'He looked, and raised the German a hundred dollars. Then they went at it again, back and forth and back and forth, until Schultz weakened and called, and laid down his three aces. Lyte faced his five cards. They were all black. He had drawn two more clubs. Do you know, he just about broke Schultz's nerve as a poker player. He never played in the same form again. He lacked confidence after that, and was a bit wobbly.

'"But how could you do it?" I asked Lyte afterward. "You knew he had you beaten when he drew two cards. Besides, you never looked at your own draw."

'"I didn't have to look," was Lyte's answer. "I knew they were two clubs all the time. They just had to be two clubs. Do you think I was going to let that big Dutchman beat me? It was impossible that he should beat me. It is not my way to be beaten. I just have to win. Why, I'd have been the most surprised man in this world if they hadn't been all clubs."

'That was Lyte's way, and maybe it will help you to appreciate his colossal optimism. As he put it, he just had to succeed, to fare well, to prosper. And in that same incident, as in ten thousand others, he found his sanction. The thing was that he did succeed, did prosper. That was why he was afraid of nothing. Nothing could ever happen to him. He knew it, because nothing had ever happened to him. That time the *Luga* was lost and he swam thirty miles, he was in the water two whole nights and a day. And during all that terrible stretch of time he never lost hope once, never once doubted the outcome. He just knew he was going to make the land. He told me so himself, and I know it was the truth.

'Well, that is the kind of a man Lyte Gregory was. He was of a different race from ordinary, ailing mortals. He was a lordly being, untouched by common ills and misfortunes. Whatever he wanted he got. He won his wife – one of the Caruthers, a little beauty – from a dozen rivals. And she settled down and made him the finest wife in the world. He wanted a boy. He got it. He wanted a girl and another boy. He got them. And they were just right, without spot or blemish, with chests like little barrels, and with all the inheritance of his own health and strength.

'And then it happened. The mark of the beast was laid upon him. I watched it for a year. It broke my heart. But he did not know it, nor did anybody else guess it except that cursed *hapahaole*, Stephen Kaluna. He knew it, but I did not know that he did. And – yes – Doc Strowbridge knew it. He was the federal physician, and he had developed the leper eye. You see, part of his business was to examine suspects and order them to the receiving station at Honolulu. And Stephen Kaluna had developed the leper eye. The disease ran strong in his family, and four or five of his relatives were already on Molokai.

'The trouble arose over Stephen Kaluna's sister. When she became suspect, and before Doc Strowbridge could get hold of her, her brother spirited her away to some hiding place. Lyte was Sheriff of Kona, and it was his business to find her.

'We were all over at Hilo that night, in Ned Austin's. Stephen Kaluna was there when we came in, by himself, in his cups, and quarrelsome. Lyte was laughing over some joke – that huge, happy laugh of a giant boy. Kaluna spat contemptuously on the floor. Lyte noticed, so did everybody; but he ignored the fellow.

Kaluna was looking for trouble. He took it as a personal grudge that Lyte was trying to apprehend his sister. In half a dozen ways he advertised his displeasure at Lyte's presence, but Lyte ignored him. I imagined Lyte was a bit sorry for him, for the hardest duty of his office was the apprehension of lepers. It is not a nice thing to go into a man's house and tear away a father, mother or child, who has done no wrong, and to send such a one to perpetual banishment on Molokai. Of course, it is necessary as a protection to society, and Lyte, I do believe, would have been the first to apprehend his own father did he become suspect.

'Finally, Kaluna blurted out: "Look here, Gregory, you think you're going to find Kalaniweo, but you're not."

'Kalaniweo was his sister. Lyte glanced at him when his name was called, but he made no answer. Kaluna was furious. He was working himself up all the time.

'"I'll tell you one thing," he shouted. "You'll be on Molokai yourself before ever you get Kalaniweo there. I'll tell you what you are. You've no right to be in the company of honest men. You've made a terrible fuss talking about your duty, haven't you? You've sent many lepers to Molokai, and knowing all the time you belonged there yourself."

'I'd seen Lyte angry more than once, but never quite so angry as at that moment. Leprosy with us, you know, is not a thing to jest about. He made one leap across the floor, dragging Kaluna out of his chair with a clutch on his neck. He shook him back and forth savagely, till you could hear the half-caste's teeth rattling.

'"What do you mean?" Lyte was demanding. "Spit it out, man, or I'll choke it out of you!"

'You know, in the West there is a certain phrase that a man must smile while uttering. So with us of the islands, only our phrase is related to leprosy. No matter what Kaluna was, he was no coward. As soon as Lyte eased the grip on his throat he answered:

'"I'll tell you what I mean. You are a leper yourself."

'Lyte suddenly flung the half-caste sidewise into a chair, letting him down easily enough. Then Lyte broke out into honest, hearty laughter. But he laughed alone, and when he discovered it he looked around at our faces. I had reached his side and was trying to get him to come away, but he took no notice of me. He was gazing, fascinated, at Kaluna, who was brushing at his own throat in a flurried, nervous way, as if to brush off the contamination of the fingers that had clutched him. The action was unreasoned, genuine.

'Lyte looked around at us, slowly passing from face to face.

'"My God, fellows! My God!" he said.

'He did not speak it. It was more a hoarse whisper of fright and horror. It was fear that fluttered in his throat, and I don't think that ever in his life before he had known fear.

'Then his colossal optimism asserted itself, and he laughed again.

'"A good joke – whoever put it up," he said. "The drinks are on me. I had a scare for a moment. But, fellows, don't do it again, to anybody. It's too serious. I tell you I died a thousand deaths in that moment. I thought of my wife and the kids, and . . ."

'His voice broke, and the half-caste, still throat-brushing, drew his eyes. He was puzzled and worried.

'"John," he said, turning toward me.

'His jovial, rotund voice rang in my ears. But I could not answer. I was swallowing hard at that moment, and besides, I knew my face didn't look just right.

'"John," he called again, taking a step nearer.

'He called timidly, and of all nightmares of horrors the most frightful was to hear timidity in Lyte Gregory's voice.

'"John, John, what does it mean?" he went on, still more timidly. "It's a joke, isn't it? John, here's my hand. If I were a leper would I offer you my hand? Am I a leper, John?"

'He held out his hand, and what in high heaven or hell did I care? He was my friend. I took his hand, though it cut me to the heart to see the way his face brightened.

'"It was only a joke, Lyte,' I said. "We fixed it up on you. But you're right. It's too serious. We won't do it again."

'He did not laugh this time. He smiled, as a man awakened

from a bad dream and still oppressed by the substance of the dream.

'"All right, then," he said. "Don't do it again, and I'll stand for the drinks. But I may as well confess that you fellows had me going south for a moment. Look at the way I've been sweating."

'He sighed and wiped the sweat from his forehead as he started to step toward the bar.

'"It is no joke," Kaluna said abruptly.

'I looked murder at him, and I felt murder, too. But I dared not speak or strike. That would have precipitated the catastrophe which I somehow had a mad hope of still averting.

'"It is no joke,' Kaluna repeated. "You are a leper, Lyte Gregory, and you've no right putting your hands on honest men's flesh – on the clean flesh of honest men."

'Then Gregory flared up.

'"The joke has gone far enough! Quit it! Quit it, I say, Kaluna, or I'll give you a beating!"

'"You undergo a bacteriological examination," Kaluna answered, "and then you can beat me – to death, if you want to. Why, man, look at yourself there in the glass. You can see it. Anybody can see it. You're developing the lion face. See where the skin is darkened there over your eyes."

'Lyte peered and peered, and I saw his hands trembling.

'"I can see nothing," he said finally, then turned on the *hapa-haole*. "You have a black heart, Kaluna. And I am not ashamed to say that you have given me a scare that no man has the right to give another. I take you at your word. I am going to settle this thing now. I am going straight to Doc Strowbridge. And when I come back, watch out."

'He never looked at us, but started for the door.

'"You wait here, John," he said, waving me back from accompanying him.

'We stood around like a group of ghosts.

'"It is the truth," Kaluna said. "You could see it for yourselves."

'They looked at me, and I nodded. Harry Burnley lifted his glass to his lips, but lowered it untasted. He spilled half of it over the bar. His lips were trembling like a child that is about to cry. Ned Austin made a clatter in the ice-chest. He wasn't looking for anything. I don't think he knew what he was doing. Nobody spoke. Harry Burnley's lips were trembling harder than ever. Suddenly, with a most horrible, malignant expression he drove his fist into Kaluna's face. He followed it up. We made no attempt to separate them. We didn't care if he killed the half-caste. It was a terrible beating. We weren't interested. I don't even remember when Burnley ceased and let the poor devil crawl away. We were all too dazed.

'Doc Strowbridge told me about it afterward. He was working late over a report when Lyte came into his office. Lyte had already recovered his optimism, and came swinging in, a trifle angry with Kaluna to be sure, but very certain of himself. "What could I do?" Doc asked me. "I knew he had it. I had seen it coming on for months. I couldn't answer him. I couldn't say yes. I don't mind telling you I broke down and cried. He pleaded for the bacteriological test. "Snip out a piece of skin and make the test."

'The way Doc Strowbridge cried must have convinced Lyte. The *Claudine* was leaving next morning for Honolulu. We caught him when he was going aboard. You see, he was headed for Honolulu to give himself up to the Board of Health. We could do nothing with him. He had sent too many to Molokai to hang back himself. We argued for Japan. But he wouldn't hear of it. "I've got to take my medicine, fellows," was all he would say, and he said it over and over. He was obsessed with the idea.

'He wound up all his affairs from the Receiving Station at Honolulu, and went down to Molokai. He didn't get on well there. The resident physician wrote us that he was a shadow of his old self. You see he was grieving about his wife and the kids. He knew we were taking care of them, but it hurt him just the same. After six months or so I went down to Molokai. I sat on one side a plate-glass window, and he on the other. We looked at each other through the glass, and talked through what might be called a speaking tube. But it was hopeless. He had made up his mind to remain. Four mortal hours I argued. I was exhausted at the end. My steamer was whistling for me, too.

'But we couldn't stand it. Three months later we chartered the schooner *Halcyon*. She was an opium smuggler, and she sailed like a witch. Her master was a squarehead who would do anything for money, and we made a charter to China worth his while. He sailed from San Francisco, and a few days later we took out Landhouse's sloop for a cruise. She was only a five-ton yacht, but we slammed her fifty miles to windward into the northeast trade. Seasick? I never suffered so in my life. Out of sight of land we picked up the *Halcyon*, and Burnley and I went aboard.

'We ran down to Molokai, arriving about eleven at night. The schooner hove to and we landed through the surf in a whale-boat at Kalawao – the place, you know, where Father Damien died. That squarehead was game. With a couple of revolvers strapped on him he came right along. The three of us crossed the peninsula to Kalaupapa, something like two miles. Just imagine hunting in the dead of night for a man in a settlement of over a thousand lepers. You see, if the alarm was given, it was all off with us. It was strange ground, and pitch dark. The lepers' dogs came out and bayed at us, and we stumbled around till we got lost.

'The squarehead solved it. He led the way into the first detached house. We shut the door after us and struck a light. There were six lepers. We routed them up, and I talked in native. What I wanted was a *kokua*. A *kokua* is, literally, a helper, a native who is clean that lives in the settlement and is paid by the Board of Health to nurse the lepers, dress their sores and such things. We stayed in the house to keep track of the inmates, while the squarehead led one of them off to find a *kokua*. He got him, and he brought him along at the point of his revolver. But the *kokua* was all right. While the squarehead guarded the house, Burnley and I were guided by the *kokua* to Lyte's house. He was all alone.

'"I thought you fellows would come," Lyte said. "Don't touch me, John. How's Ned, and Charley, and all the crowd? Never mind, tell me afterward. I am ready to go now. I've had nine months of it. Where's the boat?"

'We started back for the other house to pick up the squarehead. But the alarm had got out. Lights were showing in the houses, and doors were slamming. We had agreed that there was to be no shooting unless absolutely necessary, and when we were halted we went at it with our fists and the butts of our revolvers. I found myself tangled up with a big man. I couldn't keep him off of me, though twice I smashed him fairly in the face with my fist. He grappled with me, and we went down, rolling and scrambling and struggling for grips. He was getting away with me, when someone came running up with a lantern. Then I saw his face. How shall I describe the horror of it! It was not a face – only wasted or wasting features – a living ravage, noseless, lipless, with one ear swollen and distorted, hanging down to the shoulder. I was frantic. In a clinch he hugged me close to him until that ear flapped in my face. Then I guess I went insane. It was too terrible. I began striking him with my revolver. How it happened I don't know, but just as I was getting clear he fastened upon me with his teeth. The whole side of my hand was in that lipless mouth. Then I struck him with the revolver butt squarely between the eyes, and his teeth relaxed.'

Cudworth held his hand to me in the moonlight, and I could see the scars. It looked as if it had been mangled by a dog.

'Weren't you afraid?' I asked.

'I was. Seven years I waited. You know, it takes that long for the disease to incubate. Here in Kona I waited, and it did not come. But there was never a day of those seven years, and never a night, that I did not look out on . . . on all this . . .' His voice broke as he swept his eyes from the moon-bathed sea beneath to the snowy summits above. 'I could not bear to think of losing it, of never again beholding Kona. Seven years! I stayed clean. But that is why I am single. I was engaged. I could not dare to marry while I was in doubt. She did not understand. She went away to the States, and married. I have never seen her since.

'Just at the moment I got free of the leper policeman there was rush and clatter of hoofs like a cavalry charge. It was the squarehead. He had been afraid of a rumpus and he had improved his time by making those blessed lepers he was guarding saddle up four horses. We were ready for him. Lyte had accounted for three *kokuas*, and between us we untangled Burnley from a couple more. The whole settlement was in an uproar by that time, and as we dashed away somebody opened up on us with a Winchester. It must have been Jack McVeigh, the superintendent of Molokai.

'That was a ride! Leper horses, leper saddles, leper bridles, pitch-black darkness, whistling bullets, and a road none of the best. And the squarehead's horse was a mule, and he didn't know how to ride, either. But we made the whale-boat, and as we shoved off through the surf we could hear the horses coming down the hill from Kalaupapa.

'You're going to Shanghai. You look Lyte Gregory up. He is employed in a German firm there. Take him out to dinner. Open up wine. Give him everything of the best, but don't let him pay for anything. Send the bill to me. His wife and the kids are in Honolulu, and he needs the money for them. I know. He sends most of his salary, and lives like an anchorite. And tell him about Kona. There's where his heart is. Tell him all you can about Kona.'

KOOLAU THE LEPER

'Because we are sick they take away our liberty. We have obeyed the law. We have done no wrong. And yet they would put us in prison. Molokai is a prison. That you know. Niuli, there, his sister was sent to Molokai seven years ago. He has not seen her since. Nor will he ever see her. She must stay there until she dies. This is not her will. It is not Niuli's will. It is the will of the white men who rule the land. And who are these white men?

'We know. We have it from our fathers and our fathers' fathers. They came like lambs, speaking softly. Well might they speak softly, for we were many and strong, and all the islands were ours. As I say, they spoke softly. They were of two kinds. The one kind asked our permission, our gracious permission, to preach to us the word of God. The other kind asked our permission, our gracious permission, to trade with us. That was the beginning. To-day all the islands are theirs, all the land, all the cattle – everything is theirs. They that preached the word of God and they that preached the word of Rum have foregathered and become great chiefs. They live like kings in houses of many rooms, with multitudes of servants to care for them. They who had nothing have everything, and if you, or I, or any Kanaka be hungry, they sneer and say, "Well, why don't you work? There are the plantations."'

Koolau paused. He raised one hand, and with gnarled and twisted fingers lifted up the blazing wreath of hibiscus that crowned his black hair. The moonlight bathed the scene in silver. It was a night of peace, though those who sat about him and listened had all the seeming of battle-wrecks. Their faces were leonine. Here a space yawned in a face where should have been a nose, and there an arm-stump showed where a hand had rotted off. They were men and women beyond the pale, the thirty of them, for upon them had been placed the mark of the beast.

They sat, flower-garlanded, in the perfumed, luminous night, and their lips made uncouth noises and their throats rasped approval of Koolau's speech. They were creatures who once had been men and women. But they were men and women no longer. They were monsters – in face and form grotesque caricatures of everything human. They were hideously maimed and distorted, and had the seeming of creatures that had been racked in millenniums of hell. Their hands, when they possessed them, were like harpy-claws. Their faces were the misfits and slips, crushed and bruised by some mad god at play in the machinery of life. Here and there were features which the mad god had smeared half away, and one woman wept scalding tears from twin pits of horror, where her eyes had once been. Some were in pain and groaned from their chests. Others coughed, making sounds like the tearing of tissue. Two were idiots, more like huge apes marred in the making, until even an ape were an angel. They mowed and gibbered in the moonlight, under crowns of drooping, golden blossoms. One, whose bloated ear-lobe flapped like a fan upon his shoulder, caught up a gorgeous flower of orange and scarlet and with it decorated the monstrous ear that flip-flapped with his every movement.

And over these things Koolau was king. And this was his kingdom – a flower-throttled gorge, with beetling cliffs and crags, from which floated the blattings of wild goats. On three sides the grim walls rose, festooned in fantastic draperies of tropic vegetation and pierced by cave-entrances – the rocky lairs of Koolau's subjects. On the fourth side the earth fell away into a tremendous abyss, and, far below, could be seen the summits of lesser peaks and crags, at whose bases foamed and rumbled the Pacific surge. In fine weather a boat could land on the rocky beach that marked the entrance of Kalalau Valley, but the weather must be very fine. And a cool-headed mountaineer might climb from the beach to the head of Kalalau Valley, to this pocket among the peaks where Koolau ruled; but such a mountaineer must be very cool of head, and he must know the wild-goat trails as well. The marvel was that the mass of human wreckage that constituted

Koolau's people should have been able to drag its helpless misery over the giddy goat-trails to this inaccessible spot.

'Brothers,' Koolau began.

But one of the mowing, apelike travesties emitted a wild shriek of madness, and Koolau waited while the shrill cachinnation was tossed back and forth among the rocky walls and echoed distantly through the pulseless night.

'Brothers, is it not strange? Ours was the land, and behold, the land is not ours. What did these preachers of the word of God and the word of Rum give us for the land? Have you received one dollar, as much as one dollar, any one of you, for the land? Yet it is theirs, and in return they tell us we can go to work on the land, their land, and that what we produce by our toil shall be theirs. Yet in the old days we did not have to work. Also, when we are sick, they take away our freedom.'

'Who brought the sickness, Koolau?' demanded Kiloliana, a lean and wiry man with a face so like a laughing faun's that one might expect to see the cloven hoofs under him. They were cloven, it was true, but the cleavages were great ulcers and livid putrefactions. Yet this was Kiloliana, the most daring climber of them all, the man who knew every goat-trail and who had led Koolau and his wretched followers into the recesses of Kalalau.

'Ay, well questioned,' Koolau answered. 'Because we would not work the miles of sugar-cane where once our horses pastured, they brought the Chinese slaves from over seas. And with them came the Chinese sickness – that which we suffer from and because of which they would imprison us on Molokai. We were born on Kauai. We have been to the other islands, some here and some there, to Oahu, to Maui, to Hawaii, to Honolulu. Yet always did we come back to Kauai. Why did we come back? There must be a reason. Because we love Kauai. We were born here. Here we have lived. And here shall we die – unless – unless – there be weak hearts amongst us. Such we do not want. They are fit for Molokai. And if there be such, let them not remain. To-morrow the soldiers land on the shore. Let the weak hearts go down to them. They will be sent swiftly to Molokai. As for us, we shall stay and fight. But know that we will not die. We have rifles. You know the narrow trails where men must creep, one by one. I, alone, Koolau, who was once a cowboy on Niihau, can hold the trail against a thousand men. Here is Kapahei, who was once a judge over men and a man with honor, but who is now a hunted rat, like you and me. Hear him. He is wise.'

Kapahei arose. Once he had been a judge. He had gone to college at Punahou. He had sat at meat with lords and chiefs and the high representatives of alien powers who protected the interests of traders and missionaries. Such had been Kapahei. But now, as Koolau had said, he was a hunted rat, a creature outside the law, sunk so deep in the mire of human horror that he was above the law as well as beneath it. His face was featureless, save for gaping orifices and for the lidless eyes that burned under hairless brows.

'Let us not make trouble,' he began. 'We ask to be left alone. But if they do not leave us alone, then is the trouble theirs, and the penalty. My fingers are gone, as you see.' He held up his stumps of hands that all might see. 'Yet have I the joint of one thumb left, and it can pull a trigger as firmly as did its lost neighbor in the old days. We love Kauai. Let us live here, or die here, but do not let us go to the prison of Molokai. The sickness is not ours. We have not sinned. The men who preached the word of God and the word of Rum brought the sickness with the coolie slaves who work the stolen land. I have been a judge. I know the law and the justice, and I say to you it is unjust to steal a man's land, to make that man sick with the Chinese sickness, and then to put that man in prison for life.'

'Life is short, and the days are filled with pain,' said Koolau. 'Let us drink and dance and be happy as we can.'

From one of the rocky lairs calabashes were produced and passed around. The calabashes were filled with the fierce distillation of the root of the *ti*-plant; and as the liquid fire coursed through them and mounted to their brains, they forgot that they had once been men and women, for they were men and women once more. The woman who wept scalding tears from open eye-pits was indeed a woman apulse with life as she plucked the strings of an *ukulele* and lifted her voice in a barbaric love-call such as might have come from the dark forest-depths of the primeval world. The air tingled with her cry, softly imperious and seductive. Upon a mat, timing his rhythm to the woman's song, Kiloliana danced. It was unmistakable. Love danced in all his movements, and, next, dancing with him on the mat, was a woman whose heavy hips and generous breast gave the lie to her disease-corroded face. It was a dance of the living dead, for in their disintegrating bodies life still loved and longed. Ever the woman whose sightless eyes ran scalding tears chanted her love-cry, ever the dancers danced of love in the warm night, and ever the calabashes went around till in all their brains were maggots crawling of memory and desire. And with the woman on the mat danced a slender maid whose face was beautiful and unmarred, but whose twisted arms that rose and fell marked the disease's ravage. And the two idiots, gibbering and mouthing strange noises, danced apart, grotesque, fantastic, travestying love as they themselves had been travestied by life.

But the woman's love-cry broke midway, the calabashes were lowered, and the dancers ceased, as all gazed into the abyss above the sea, where a rocket flared like a wan phantom through the moonlit air.

'It is the soldiers,' said Koolau. 'To-morrow there will be fighting. It is well to sleep and be prepared.'

The lepers obeyed, crawling away to their lairs in the cliff, until only Koolau remained, sitting motionless in the moonlight, his rifle across his knees, as he gazed far down to the boats landing on the beach.

The far head of Kalalau Valley had been well chosen as a refuge. Except Kiloliana, who knew back-trails up the precipitous walls, no man could win to the gorge save by advancing across a knife-edged ridge. This passage was a hundred yards in length. At best, it was a scant twelve inches wide. On either side yawned the abyss. A slip, and to right or left the man would fall to his death. But once across he would find himself in an earthly paradise. A sea of vegetation laved the landscape, pouring its green billows from wall to wall, dripping from the cliff-lips in great vine-masses, and flinging a spray of ferns and air-plants into the multitudinous crevices. During the many months of Koolau's rule, he and his followers had fought with this vegetable sea. The choking jungle, with its riot of blossoms, had been driven back from the bananas, oranges and mangoes that grew wild. In little clearings grew the wild arrowroot; on stone terraces, filled with soil scrapings, were the *taro* patches and the melons; and in every open space where the sunshine penetrated, were *papaia* trees burdened with their golden fruit.

Koolau had been driven to this refuge from the lower valley by the beach. And if he were driven from it in turn, he knew of gorges among the jumbled peaks of the inner fastnesses where he could lead his subjects and live. And now he lay with his rifle beside him, peering down through a tangled screen of foliage at the soldiers on the beach. He noted that they had large guns with them, from which the sunshine flashed as from mirrors. The knife-edged passage lay directly before him. Crawling upward along the trail that led to it he could see tiny specks of men. He knew they were not the soldiers, but the police. When they failed, then the soldiers would enter the game.

He affectionately rubbed a twisted hand along his rifle barrel and made sure that the sights were clean. He had learned to shoot as a wild-cattle hunter on Niihau, and on that island his skill as a marksman was unforgotten. As the toiling specks of men grew nearer and larger, he estimated the range, judged the deflection of the wind that swept at right angles across the line of fire, and calculated the chances of overshooting marks that were so far below his level. But he did not shoot. Not until they reached the beginning of the passage did he make his presence known. He did not disclose himself, but spoke from the thicket.

'What do you want?' he demanded.

'We want Koolau, the leper,' answered the man who led the native police, himself a blue-eyed American.

'You must go back,' Koolau said.

He knew the man, a deputy sheriff, for it was by him that he had been harried out of Niihau, across Kauai, to Kalalau Valley and out of the valley to the gorge.

'Who are you?' the sheriff asked.

'I am Koolau, the leper,' was the reply.

'Then come out. We want you. Dead or alive, there is a thousand dollars on your head. You cannot escape.'

Koolau laughed aloud in the thicket.

'Come out!' the sheriff commanded, and was answered by silence.

He conferred with the police, and Koolau saw that they were preparing to rush him.

'Koolau,' the sheriff called. 'Koolau, I am coming across to get you.'

'Then look first and well about you at the sun and sea and sky, for it will be the last time you behold them.'

'That's all right, Koolau,' the sheriff said soothingly. 'I know you're a dead shot. But you won't shoot me. I have never done you any wrong.'

Koolau grunted in the thicket.

'I say, you know, I've never done you any wrong, have I?' the sheriff persisted.

'You do me wrong when you try to put me in prison,' was the reply. 'And you do me wrong when you try for the thousand dollars on my head. If you will live, stay where you are.'

'I've got to come across and get you. I'm sorry. But it is my duty.'

'You will die before you get across.'

The sheriff was no coward. Yet was he undecided. He gazed into the gulf on either side, and ran his eyes along the knife-edge he must travel. Then he made up his mind.

'Koolau,' he called.

But the thicket remained silent.

'Koolau, don't shoot. I am coming.'

The sheriff turned, gave some orders to the police, then started on his perilous way. He advanced slowly. It was like walking a tight rope. He had nothing to lean upon but the air. The lava rock crumbled under his feet, and on either side the dislodged fragments pitched downward through the depths. The sun blazed upon him, and his face was wet with sweat. Still he advanced, until the halfway point was reached.

'Stop!' Koolau commanded from the thicket. 'One more step and I shoot.'

The sheriff halted, swaying for balance as he stood poised above the void. His face was pale, but his eyes were determined. He licked his dry lips before he spoke.

'Koolau, you won't shoot me. I know you won't.'

He started once more. The bullet whirled him half about. On his face was an expression of querulous surprise as he reeled to the fall. He tried to save himself by throwing his body across the knife-edge; but at that moment he knew death. The next moment the knife-edge was vacant. Then came the rush, five policemen, in single file, with superb steadiness, running along the knife-edge. At the same instant the rest of the posse opened fire on the thicket. It was madness. Five times Koolau pulled the trigger, so rapidly that his shots constituted a rattle. Changing his position and crouching low under the bullets that were biting and singing through the bushes, he peered out. Four of the police had followed the sheriff. The fifth lay across the knife-edge, still alive. On the farther side, no longer firing, were the surviving police. On the naked rock there was no hope for them. Before they could clamber down Koolau could have picked off the last man. But he did not fire, and, after a conference, one of them took off a white undershirt and waved it as a flag. Followed by another, he advanced along the knife-edge to their wounded comrade. Koolau gave no sign, but watched them slowly withdraw and become specks as they descended into the lower valley.

Two hours later, from another thicket, Koolau watched a body of police trying to make the ascent from the opposite side of the valley. He saw the wild goats flee before them as they climbed higher and higher, until he doubted his judgment and sent for Kiloliana who crawled in beside him.

'No, there is no way,' said Kiloliana.

'The goats?' Koolau questioned.

'They come over from the next valley, but they cannot pass to this. There is no way. Those men are not wiser than goats. They may fall to their deaths. Let us watch.'

'They are brave men,' said Koolau. 'Let us watch.'

Side by side they lay among the morning-glories, with the yellow blossoms of the *hau* dropping upon them from overhead, watching the motes of men toil upward, till the thing happened, and three of them, slipping, rolling, sliding, dashed over a cliff-lip and fell sheer half a thousand feet.

Kiloliana chuckled.

'We will be bothered no more,' he said.

'They have war guns,' Koolau made answer. 'The soldiers have not yet spoken.'

In the drowsy afternoon, most of the lepers lay in their rock dens asleep. Koolau, his rifle on his knees, fresh-cleaned and ready, dozed in the entrance to his own den. The maid with the twisted arm lay below in the thicket and kept watch on the knife-edge passage. Suddenly Koolau was startled wide awake by the sound of an explosion on the beach. The next instant the atmosphere was incredibly rent asunder. The terrible sound frightened him. It was as if all the gods had caught the envelope of the sky in their hands and were ripping it apart as a woman rips apart a sheet of cotton cloth. But it was such an immense ripping, growing swiftly nearer. Koolau glanced up apprehensively, as if expecting to see the thing. Then high up on the cliff overhead the shell burst in a fountain of black smoke. The rock was shattered, the fragments falling to the foot of the cliff.

Koolau passed his hand across his sweaty brow. He was terribly shaken. He had had no experience with shell-fire, and this was more dreadful than anything he had imagined.

'One,' said Kapahei, suddenly bethinking himself to keep count.

A second and a third shell flew screaming over the top of the wall, bursting beyond view. Kapahei methodically kept the count. The lepers crowded into the open space before the caves. At first they were frightened, but as the shells continued their flight overhead the leper folk became reassured and began to admire the spectacle. The two idiots shrieked with delight, prancing wild antics as each air-tormenting shell went by. Koolau began to recover his confidence. No damage was being done. Evidently they could not aim such large missiles at such long range with the precision of a rifle.

But a change came over the situation. The shells began to fall short. One burst below in the thicket by the knife-edge. Koolau remembered the maid who lay there on watch, and ran down to see. The smoke was still rising from the bushes when he crawled in. He was astounded. The branches were splintered and broken. Where the girl had lain was a hole in the ground. The girl herself was in shattered fragments. The shell had burst right on her.

First peering out to make sure no soldiers were attempting the passage, Koolau started back on the run for the caves. All the time the shells were moaning, whining, screaming by, and the valley was rumbling and reverberating with the explosions. As he came in sight of the caves, he saw the two idiots cavorting about, clutching each other's hands with their stumps of fingers. Even as he ran, Koolau saw a spout of black smoke rise from the ground, near to the idiots. They were flung apart bodily by the explosion. One lay motionless, but the other was dragging himself by his hands toward the cave. His legs trailed out helplessly behind him, while the blood was pouring from his body. He seemed bathed in blood, and as he crawled he cried like a little dog. The rest of the lepers, with the exception of Kapahei, had fled into the caves.

'Seventeen,' said Kapehei. 'Eighteen,' he added.

This last shell had fairly entered into one of the caves. The explosion caused all the caves to empty. But from the particular cave no one emerged. Koolau crept in through the pungent, acrid smoke. Four bodies, frightfully mangled, lay about. One of them was the sightless woman whose tears till now had never ceased.

Outside, Koolau found his people in a panic and already beginning to climb the goat trail that led out of the gorge and on among the jumbled heights and chasms. The wounded idiot, whining feebly and dragging himself along on the ground by his hands, was trying to follow. But at the first pitch of the wall his helplessness overcame him and he fell back.

'It would be better to kill him,' said Koolau to Kapahei, who still sat in the same place.

'Twenty-two,' Kapahei answered. 'Yes, it would be a wise thing to kill him. Twenty-three – twenty-four.'

The idiot whined sharply when he saw the rifle leveled at him. Koolau hesitated, then lowered the gun.

'It is a hard thing to do,' he said.

'You are a fool, twenty-six, twenty-seven,' said Kapahei. 'Let me show you.'

He arose and, with a heavy fragment of rock in his hand, approached the wounded thing. As he lifted his arm to strike, a shell burst full upon him, relieving him of the necessity of the act and at the same time putting an end to his count.

Koolau was alone in the gorge. He watched the last of his people drag their crippled bodies over the brow of the height and disappear. Then he turned and went down to the thicket where the maid had been killed. The shell-fire still continued, but he remained; for far below he could see the soldiers climbing up. A shell burst twenty feet away. Flattening himself into the earth, he heard the rush of the fragments above his body. A shower of *hau* blossoms rained upon him. He lifted his head to peer down the trail, and sighed. He was very much afraid. Bullets from rifles would not have worried him, but this shell-fire was abominable. Each time a shell shrieked by he shivered and crouched; but each time he lifted his head again to watch the trail.

At last the shells ceased. This, he reasoned, was because the soldiers were drawing near. They crept along the trail in single file, and he tried to count them until he lost track. At any rate, there were a hundred or so of them – all come after Koolau the leper. He felt a fleeting prod of pride. With war guns and rifles, police and soldiers, they came for him, and he was only one man, a crippled wreck of a man at that. They offered a thousand dollars for him, dead or alive. In all his life he had never possessed that much money. The thought was a bitter one. Kapahei had been right. He, Koolau, had done no wrong. Because the *haoles* wanted labor with which to work the stolen land, they had brought in the Chinese coolies, and with them had come the sickness. And now, because he had caught the sickness, he was worth a thousand dollars – but not to himself. It was his worthless carcass, rotten with disease or dead from a bursting shell, that was worth all that money.

When the soldiers reached the knife-edged passage, he was prompted to warn them. But his gaze fell upon the body of the murdered maid, and he kept silent. When six had ventured on the knife-edge, he opened fire. Nor did he cease when the knife-edge was bare. He emptied his magazine, reloaded, and emptied it again. He kept on shooting. All his wrongs were blazing in his brain, and he was in a fury of vengeance. All down the goat trail the soldiers were firing, and though they lay flat and sought to shelter themselves in the shallow inequalities of the surface, they were exposed marks to him. Bullets whistled and thudded about him, and an occasional ricochet sang sharply through the air. One bullet ploughed a crease through his scalp, and a second burned across his shoulder-blade without breaking the skin.

It was a massacre, in which one man did the killing. The soldiers began to retreat, helping along their wounded. As Koolau picked them off he became aware of the smell of burnt meat. He glanced about him at first, and then discovered that it was his own hands. The heat of the rifle was doing it. The leprosy had destroyed most of the nerves in his hands. Though his flesh burned and he smelled it, there was no sensation.

He lay in the thicket, smiling, until he remembered the war guns. Without doubt they would open up on him again, and this time upon the very thicket from which he had inflicted the damage. Scarcely had he changed his position to a nook behind a small shoulder of the wall where he had noted that no shells fell, than the bombardment recommenced. He counted the shells. Sixty more were thrown into the gorge before the war-guns ceased. The tiny area was pitted with their explosions, until it seemed impossible that any creature could have survived. So the soldiers thought, for, under the burning afternoon sun, they climbed the goat trail again. And again the knife-edged passage was disputed, and again they fell back to the beach.

For two days longer Koolau held the passage, though the soldiers contented themselves with flinging shells into his retreat. Then Pahau, a leper boy, came to the top of the wall at the back of the gorge and shouted down to him that Kiloliana, hunting goats that they might eat, had been killed by a fall, and that the women were frightened and knew not what to do. Koolau called the boy down and left him with a spare gun with which to guard the passage. Koolau found his people disheartened. The majority of them were too helpless to forage food for themselves under such forbidding circumstances, and all were starving. He selected two women and a man who were not too far gone with the disease, and sent them back to the gorge to bring up food and mats. The rest he cheered and consoled until even the weakest took a hand in building rough shelters for themselves.

But those he had dispatched for food did not return, and he started back for the gorge. As he came out on the brow of the wall, half a dozen rifles cracked. A bullet tore through the fleshy part of his shoulder, and his cheek was cut by a sliver of rock where a second bullet smashed against the cliff. In the moment that this happened, and he leaped back, he saw that the gorge was alive with soldiers. His own people had betrayed him. The shell-fire had been too terrible, and they had preferred the prison of Molokai.

Koolau dropped back and unslung one of his heavy cartridge-belts. Lying among the rocks, he allowed the head and shoulders of the first soldier to rise clearly into view before pulling trigger. Twice this happened, and then, after some delay, in place of a head and shoulders a white flag was thrust above the edge of the wall.

'What do you want?' he demanded.

'I want you, if you are Koolau the leper,' came the answer.

Koolau forgot where he was, forgot everything, as he lay and marvelled at the strange persistence of these *haoles* who would have their will though the sky fell in. Ay, they would have their will over all men and all things, even though they died in getting it. He could not but admire them, too, what of that will in them that was stronger than life and that bent all things to their bidding. He was convinced of the hopelessness of his struggle. There was no gainsaying that terrible will of the *haoles*. Though he killed a thousand, yet would they rise like the sands of the sea

and come upon him, ever more and more. They never knew
when they were beaten. That was their fault and their virtue. It
was where his own kind lacked. He could see, now, how the
handful of the preachers of God and the preachers of Rum had
conquered the land. It was because –

'Well, what have you got to say? Will you come with me?'

It was the voice of the invisible man under the white flag.
There he was, like any *haole*, driving straight toward the end
determined.

'Let us talk,' said Koolau.

The man's head and shoulders arose, then his whole body. He
was a smooth-faced, blue-eyed youngster of twenty-five, slender
and natty in his captain's uniform. He advanced until halted,
then seated himself a dozen feet away:

'You are a brave man,' said Koolau wonderingly. 'I could kill
you like a fly.'

'No, you couldn't,' was the answer.

'Why not?'

'Because you are a man, Koolau, though a bad one. I know
your story. You kill fairly.'

Koolau grunted, but was secretly pleased.

'What have you done with my people?' he demanded. 'The
boy, the two women and the man?'

'They gave themselves up, as I have now come for you to do.'

Koolau laughed incredulously.

'I am a free man,' he announced. 'I have done no wrong. All I
ask is to be left alone. I have lived free, and I shall die free. I will
never give myself up.'

'Then your people are wiser than you,' answered the young
captain. 'Look – they are coming now.'

Koolau turned and watched the remnant of his band approach.
Groaning and sighing, a ghastly procession, it dragged its
wretchedness past. It was given to Koolau to taste a deeper
bitterness, for they hurled imprecations and insults at him as
they went by; and the panting hag who brought up the rear
halted, and with skinny, harpy-claws extended, shaking her
snarling death's head from side to side, she laid a curse upon

him. One by one they dropped over the lip-edge and surrendered to the hiding soldiers.

'You can go now,' said Koolau to the captain. 'I will never give myself up. That is my last word. Good-by.'

The captain slipped over the cliff to his soldiers. The next moment, and without a flag of truce, he hoisted his hat on his scabbard, and Koolau's bullet tore through it. That afternoon they shelled him out from the beach, and as he retreated into the inaccessible pockets beyond, the soldiers followed him.

For six weeks they hunted him from pocket to pocket, over the volcanic peaks and along the goat trails. When he hid in the lantana jungle, they formed lines of beaters, and through lantana jungle and guava scrub they drove him like a rabbit. But ever he turned and doubled and eluded. There was no cornering him. When pressed too closely, his sure rifle held them back and they carried their wounded down the goat trails to the beach. There were times when they did the shooting as his brown body showed for a moment through the underbrush. Once, five of them caught him on an exposed goat trail between pockets. They emptied their rifles at him as he limped and climbed along his dizzy way. Afterward they found blood-stains and knew that he was wounded. At the end of six weeks they gave up. The soldiers and police returned to Honolulu, and Kalalau Valley was left to him for his own, though head-hunters ventured after him from time to time and to their own undoing.

Two years later, and for the last time, Koolau crawled into a thicket and lay down among the *ti*-leaves and wild ginger blossoms. Free he had lived, and free he was dying. A slight drizzle of rain began to fall, and he drew a ragged blanket about the distorted wreck of his limbs. His body was covered with an oilskin coat. Across his chest he laid his Mauser rifle, lingering affectionately for a moment to wipe the dampness from the barrel. The hand with which he wiped had no fingers left upon it with which to pull the trigger.

He closed his eyes, for, from the weakness in his body and the fuzzy turmoil in his brain, he knew that his end was near. Like a wild animal he had crept into hiding to die. Half-conscious, aimless and wandering, he lived back in his life to his early manhood on Niihau. As life faded and the drip of the rain grew dim in his ears, it seemed to him that he was once more in the thick of the horse-breaking, with raw colts rearing and bucking under him, his stirrups tied together beneath, or charging madly about the breaking corral and driving the helping cowboys over the rails. The next instant, and with seeming naturalness, he found himself pursuing the wild bulls of the upland pastures, roping them and leading them down to the valleys. Again the sweat and dust of the branding pen stung his eyes and bit his nostrils.

All his lusty, whole-bodied youth was his, until the sharp pangs of impending dissolution brought him back. He lifted his monstrous hands and gazed at them in wonder. But how? Why? Why should the wholeness of that wild youth of his change to this? Then he remembered, and once again, and for a moment, he was Koolau, the leper. His eyelids fluttered wearily down and the drip of the rain ceased in his ears. A prolonged trembling set up in his body. This, too, ceased. He half-lifted his head, but it fell back. Then his eyes opened, and did not close. His last thought was of his Mauser, and he pressed it against his chest with his folded, fingerless hands.

THE BONES OF KAHEKILI

From over the lofty Koolau Mountains, vagrant wisps of the trade wind drifted, faintly swaying the great, unwhipped banana leaves, rustling the palms, and fluttering and setting up a whispering among the lace-leaved algaroba trees. Only intermittently did the atmosphere so breathe – for breathing it was, the suspiring of the languid, Hawaiian afternoon. In the intervals between the soft breathings, the air grew heavy and balmy with the perfume of flowers and the exhalations of fat, living soil.

Of humans about the low bungalow-like house, there were many; but one only of them slept. The rest were on the tense tiptoes of silence. At the rear of the house a tiny babe piped up a thin blatting wail that the quickly thrust breast could not appease. The mother, a slender *hapa-haole* (half-white), clad in a loose-flowing *holoku* of white muslin, hastened away swiftly among the banana and papaia trees to remove the babe's noise by distance. Other women, *hapa-haole* and full native, watched her anxiously as she fled.

At the front of the house, on the grass, squatted a score of Hawaiians. Well-muscled, broad-shouldered, they were all strapping men. Brown-skinned, with luminous brown eyes and black, their features large and regular, they showed all the signs of being as good-natured, merry-hearted and soft-tempered as the climate. To all of which a seeming contradiction was given by the ferociousness of their accoutrement. Into the tops of their rough leather leggings were thrust long knives, the handles projecting. On their heels were huge-rowelled Spanish spurs. They had the appearance of banditti, save for the incongruous wreaths of flowers and fragrant *maile* that encircled the crowns of their flopping cowboy hats. One of them, deliciously and roguishly handsome as a faun, with the eyes of a faun, wore a flaming double-hibiscus bloom coquettishly tucked over his ear.

Above them, casting a shelter of shade from the sun, grew a wide-spreading canopy of *Ponciana regia*, itself a flame of blossoms, out of each of which sprang pom-poms of feathery stamens. From far off, muffled by distance, came the faint stamping of their tethered horses. The eyes of all were intently fixed upon the solitary sleeper who lay on his back on a *lauhala* mat a hundred feet away under the monkey-pod trees.

Large as were the Hawaiian cowboys, the sleeper was larger. Also, as his snow-white hair and beard attested, he was much older. The thickness of his wrist and the greatness of his fingers made authentic the mighty frame of him hidden under loose dungaree pants and cotton shirt, buttonless, open from midriff to Adam's apple, exposing a chest matted with a thatch of hair as white as that of his head and face. The depth and breadth of that chest, its resilience, and its relaxed and plastic muscles, tokened the knotty strength that still resided in him. Further, no bronze and beat of sun and wind availed to hide the testimony of his skin that he was all *haole* – a white man.

On his back, his great white beard, thrust skyward, untrimmed of barbers, stiffened and subsided with every breath, while with the outblow of every exhalation the white mustache erected perpendicularly like the quills of a porcupine and subsided with each intake. A young girl of fourteen, clad only in a single shift, or *muumuu*, herself a granddaughter of the sleeper, crouched beside him and with a feathered fly-flapper brushed away the flies. In her face were depicted solicitude, and nervousness, and awe, as if she attended on a god.

And truly, Hardman Pool, the sleeping whiskery one, was to her, and to many and sundry, a god – a source of life, a source of food, a fount of wisdom, a giver of law, a smiling beneficence, a blackness of thunder and punishment – in short, a man-master whose record was fourteen living and adult sons and daughters, six great-grandchildren, and more grandchildren than could he in his most lucid moments enumerate.

Fifty-one years before, he had landed from an open boat at Laupahoehoe on the windward coast of Hawaii. The boat was the one surviving one of the whaler *Black Prince* of New Bedford.

Himself New Bedford born, twenty years of age, by virtue of his driving strength and ability he had served as second mate on the lost whaleship. Coming to Honolulu and casting about for himself, he had first married Kalama Mamaiopili, next acted as pilot of Honolulu Harbour, after that started a saloon and boarding house, and, finally, on the death of Kalama's father, engaged in cattle ranching on the broad pasture lands she had inherited.

For over half a century he had lived with the Hawaiians, and it was conceded that he knew their language better than did most of them. By marrying Kalama, he had married not merely her land, but her own chief rank, and the fealty owed by the commoners to her by virtue of her genealogy was also accorded him. In addition, he possessed of himself all the natural attributes of chiefship: the gigantic stature, the fearlessness, the pride; and the high hot temper that could brook no impudence nor insult, that could be neither bullied nor awed by any utmost magnificence of power that walked on two legs, and that could compel service of lesser humans, not by any ignoble purchase by bargaining, but by an unspoken but expected condescending of largesse. He knew his Hawaiians from the outside and the in, knew them better than themselves, their Polynesian circumlocutions, faiths, customs and mysteries.

And at seventy-one, after a morning in the saddle over the ranges that began at four o'clock, he lay under the monkey-pods in his customary and sacred siesta that no retainer dared to break, nor would dare permit any equal of the great one to break. Only to the King was such a right accorded, and, as the King had early learned, to break Hardman Pool's siesta was to gain awake a very irritable and grumpy Hardman Pool who would talk straight from the shoulder and say unpleasant but true things that no king would care to hear.

The sun blazed down. The horses stamped remotely. The fading trade-wind wisps sighed and rustled between longer intervals of quiescence. The perfume grew heavier. The woman brought back the babe, quiet again, to the rear of the house. The monkey-pods folded their leaves and swooned to a siesta of their own in the soft air above the sleeper. The girl, breathless as ever from the enormous solemnity of her task, still brushed the flies away; and the score of cowboys still intently and silently watched.

Hardman Pool awoke. The next out-breath, expected of the long rhythm, did not take place. Neither did the white, long mustache rise up. Instead, the cheeks, under the whiskers, puffed; the eyelids lifted, exposing blue eyes, choleric and fully and immediately conscious; the right hand went out to the half-smoked pipe beside him, while the left hand reached the matches.

'Get me my gin and milk,' he ordered, in Hawaiian, of the little maid, who had been startled into a tremble by his awakening.

He lighted the pipe, but gave no sign of awareness of the presence of his waiting retainers until the tumbler of gin and milk had been brought and drunk.

'Well?' he demanded abruptly, and in the pause, while twenty faces wreathed in smiles and twenty pairs of dark eyes glowed luminously with well-wishing pleasure, he wiped the lingering drops of gin and milk from his hairy lips. 'What are you hanging around for? What do you want? Come over here.'

Twenty giants, most of them young, uprose and with a great clanking and jangling of spurs and spur-chains strode over to him. They grouped before him in a semicircle, trying bashfully to wedge their shoulders, one behind another's, their faces a-grin and apologetic, and at the same time expressing a casual and unconscious democraticness. In truth, to them Hardman Pool was more than mere chief. He was elder brother, or father, or patriarch; and to all of them he was related, in one way or another, according to Hawaiian custom, through his wife and through the many marriages of his children and grandchildren. His slightest frown might perturb them, his anger terrify them, his command compel them to certain death; yet, on the other hand, not one of them would have dreamed of addressing him otherwise than intimately by his first name, which name, 'Hardman,' was transmuted by their tongues into Kanaka Oolea.

At a nod from him, the semicircle seated itself on the *manienie* grass, and with further deprecatory smiles waited his pleasure.

'What do you want?' he demanded, in Hawaiian, with a brusqueness and sternness they knew were put on.

They smiled more broadly, and deliciously squirmed their broad shoulders and great torsos with the appeasingness of so many wriggling puppies. Hardman Pool singled out one of them.

'Well, Iliiopoi, what do *you* want?'

'Ten dollars, Kanaka Oolea.'

'Ten dollars!' Pool cried, in apparent shock at mention of so vast a sum. 'Does it mean you are going to take a second wife? Remember the missionary teaching. One wife at a time, Iliiopoi; one wife at a time. For he who entertains a plurality of wives will surely go to hell.'

Giggles and flashings of laughing eyes from all greeted the joke.

'No, Kanaka Oolea,' came the reply. 'The devil knows I am hard put to get *kow-kow* for one wife and her several relations.'

'*Kow-kow?*' Pool repeated the Chinese-introduced word for food which the Hawaiians had come to substitute for their own *paina*. 'Didn't you boys get *kow-kow* here this noon?'

'Yes, Kanaka Oolea,' volunteered an old, withered native who had just joined the group from the direction of the house. 'All of them had *kow-kow* in the kitchen, and plenty of it. They ate like lost horses brought down from the lava.'

'And what do you want, Kumuhana?' Pool diverted to the old one, at the same time motioning to the little maid to flap flies from the other side of him.

'Twelve dollars,' said Kumuhana. 'I want to buy a jackass and a second-hand saddle and bridle. I am growing too old for my legs to carry me in walking.'

'You wait,' his *haole* lord commanded. 'I will talk with you about the matter, and about other things of importance, when I am finished with the rest and they are gone.'

The withered old one nodded and proceeded to light his pipe.

'The *kow-kow* in the kitchen was good,' Iliiopoi resumed, licking his lips. 'The *poi* was one-finger, the pig fat, the salmon-belly unstinking, the fish of great freshness and plenty, though the *opihis*' (tiny, rock-climbing shell-fish) 'had been salted and thereby made tough. Never should the *opihis* be salted. Often have I told you, Kanaka Oolea, the *opihis* should never be salted. I am full of good *kow-kow*. My belly is heavy with it. Yet is my heart not light of it because there is no *kow-kow* in my own house, where is my wife, who is the aunt of your fourth son's second wife, and where is my baby daughter, and my wife's old mother, and my wife's old mother's feeding child that is a cripple, and my wife's sister who lives likewise with us along with her three children, the father being dead of a wicked dropsy – '

'Will five dollars save all of you from funerals for a day or several?' Pool testily cut the tale short.

'Yes, Kanaka Oolea, and as well it will buy my wife a new comb and some tobacco for myself.'

From a gold-sack drawn from the hip-pocket of his dungarees, Hardman Pool drew the gold piece and tossed it accurately into the waiting hand.

To a bachelor who wanted six dollars for new leggings, tobacco and spurs, three dollars were given; the same to another who needed a hat; and to a third, who modestly asked for two dollars, four were given with a flowery-worded compliment anent his prowess in roping a recent wild bull from the mountains. They knew, as a rule, that he cut their requisitions in half, therefore they doubled the size of their requisitions. And Hardman Pool knew they doubled, and smiled to himself. It was his way, and, further, it was a very good way with his multitudinous relatives, and did not reduce his stature in their esteem.

'And you, Ahuhu?' he demanded of one whose name meant 'poison-wood'.

'And the price of a pair of dungarees,' Ahuhu concluded his list of needs. 'I have ridden much and hard after your cattle, Kanaka Oolea, and where my dungarees have pressed against the seat of the saddle there is no seat to my dungarees. It is not well that it be said that a Kanaka Oolea cowboy, who is also a cousin of Kanaka Oolea's wife's half-sister, should be shamed to be seen out of the saddle save that he walks backward from all that behold him.'

'The price of a dozen pairs of dungarees be thine, Ahuhu,'

Hardman Pool beamed, tossing to him the necessary sum. 'I am proud that my family shares my pride. Afterward, Ahuhu, out of the dozen dungarees you will give me one, else shall I be compelled to walk backward, my own and only dungarees being in like manner well worn and shameful.'

And in laughter of love at their *haole* chief's final sally, all the sweet-child-minded and physically gorgeous company of them departed to their waiting horses, save the old withered one, Kumuhana, who had been bidden to wait.

For a full five minutes they sat in silence. Then Hardman Pool ordered the little maid to fetch a tumbler of gin and milk, which, when she brought it, he nodded her to hand to Kumuhana. The glass did not leave his lips until it was empty, whereupon he gave a great audible out-breath of 'A-a-ah,' and smacked his lips.

'Much *awa* have I drunk in my time,' he said reflectively. 'Yet is the *awa* but a common man's drink, while the *haole* liquor is a drink for chiefs. The *awa* has not the liquor's hot willingness, its spur in the ribs of feeling, its biting alive of oneself that is very pleasant since it is pleasant to be alive.'

Hardman Pool smiled, nodded agreement, and old Kumuhana continued.

'There is a warmingness to it. It warms the belly and the soul. It warms the heart. Even the soul and the heart grow cold when one is old.'

'You *are* old,' Pool conceded. 'Almost as old as I.'

Kumuhana shook his head and murmured, 'Were I no older than you I would be as young as you.'

'I am seventy-one,' said Pool.

'I do not know ages that way,' was the reply. 'What happened when you were born?'

'Let me see,' Pool calculated. 'This is 1880. Subtract seventy-one, and it leaves nine. I was born in 1809, which is the year Keliimakai died, which is the year the Scotchman, Archibald Campbell, lived in Honolulu.'

'Then I am truly older than you, Kanaka Oolea. I remember the Scotchman well, for I was playing among the grass houses of Honolulu at the time, and already riding a surfboard in the *wahine*' (woman) 'surf at Waikiki. I can take you now to the spot where was the Scotchman's grass house. The Seaman's Mission stands now on the very ground. Yet do I know when I was born. Often my grandmother and my mother told me of it. I was born when Madame Pele' (the Fire Goddess or Volcano Goddess) 'became angry with the people of Paiea because they sacrificed no fish to her from their fish-pool, and she sent down a flow of lava from Huulalai and filled up their pond. For ever was the fish-pond of Paiea filled up. That was when I was born.'

'That was in 1801, when James Boyd was building ships for Kamehameha at Hilo,' Pool cast back through the calendar; 'which makes you seventy-nine, or eight years older than I. You are very old.'

'Yes, Kanaka Oolea,' muttered Kumuhana, pathetically attempting to swell his shrunken chest with pride.

'And you are very wise.'

'Yes, Kanaka Oolea.'

'And you know many of the secret things that are known only to old men.'

'Yes, Kanaka Oolea.'

'And then you know – ' Hardman Pool broke off, the more effectively to impress and hypnotize the other ancient with the set stare of his pale-washed blue eyes. 'They say the bones of Kahekili were taken from their hiding-place and lie to-day in the Royal Mausoleum. I have heard it whispered that you alone of all living men truly know.'

'I know,' was the proud answer. 'I alone know.'

'Well, do they lie there? Yes or no?'

'Kahekili was an *alii*' (high chief). 'It is from this straight line that your wife Kalama came. She is an *alii*.' The old retainer paused and pursed his lean lips in meditation. 'I belong to her, as all my people before me belonged to her people before her. She only can command the great secrets of me. She is wise, too wise ever to command me to speak this secret. To you, O Kanaka Oolea, I do not answer yes, I do not answer no. This is a secret of the *aliis* that even the *aliis* do not know.'

'Very good, Kumuhana,' Hardman Pool commended. 'Yet do

you forget that I am an *alii*, and that what my good Kalama does not dare ask, I command to ask. I can send for her, now, and tell her to command your answer. But such would be a foolishness unless you prove yourself doubly foolish. Tell me the secret, and she will never know. A woman's lips must pour out whatever flows in through her ears, being so made. I am a man, and man is differently made. As you well know, my lips suck tight on secrets as a squid sucks to the salty rock. If you will not tell me alone, then will you tell Kalama and me together, and her lips will talk, her lips will talk, so that the latest *malahini* will shortly know what, otherwise, you and I alone will know.'

Long time Kumuhana sat on in silence, debating the argument and finding no way to evade the fact-logic of it.

'Great is your *haole* wisdom,' he conceded at last.

'Yes? or no?' Hardman Pool drove home the point of his steel.

Kumuhana looked about him first, then slowly let his eyes come to rest on the fly-flapping maid.

'Go,' Pool commanded her. 'And come not back without you hear a clapping of my hands.'

Hardman Pool spoke no further, even after the flapper had disappeared into the house; yet his face adamantly looked: 'Yes? – or no?'

Again Kumuhana looked carefully about him, and up into the monkey-pod boughs as if to apprehend a lurking listener. His lips were very dry. With his tongue he moistened them repeatedly. Twice he essayed to speak, but was inarticulately husky. And finally, with bowed head, he whispered, so low and solemnly that Hardman Pool bent his own head to hear: 'No.'

Pool clapped his hands, and the little maid ran out of the house to him in tremulous, fluttery haste.

'Bring a milk and gin for old Kumuhana, here,' Pool commanded; and, to Kumuhana: 'Now tell me the whole story.'

'Wait,' was the answer. 'Wait till the little *wahine* has come and gone.'

And when the maid was gone, and the gin and milk had traveled the way predestined of gin and milk when mixed together, Hardman Pool waited without further urge for the story. Kumuhana pressed his hand to his chest and coughed hollowly at intervals, bidding for encouragement; but in the end, of himself, spoke out.

'It was a terrible thing in the old days when a great *alii* died. Kahekili was a great *alii*. He might have been king had he lived. Who can tell? I was a young man, not yet married. You know, Kanaka Oolea, when Kahekili died, and you can tell me how old I was. He died when Governor Boki ran the Blonde Hotel here in Honolulu. You have heard?'

'I was still on windward Hawaii,' Pool answered. 'But I have heard. Boki made a distillery, and leased Manoa lands to grow sugar for it, and Kaahumanu, who was regent, canceled the lease, rooted out the cane, and planted potatoes. And Boki was angry, and prepared to make war, and gathered his fighting men, with a dozen whaleship deserters and five brass six-pounders, out at Waikiki – '

'That was the very time Kahekili died,' Kumuhana broke in eagerly. 'You are very wise. You know many things of the old days better than we old *kanakas*.'

'It was 1829,' Pool continued complacently. 'You were twenty-eight years old, and I was twenty, just coming ashore in the open boat after the burning of the *Black Prince*.'

'I was twenty-eight,' Kumuhana resumed. 'It sounds right. I remember well Boki's brass guns at Waikiki. Kahekili died, too, at the time, at Waikiki. The people to this day believe his bones were taken to the *Hale o Keawe*' (mausoleum) 'at Honaunau, in Kona – '

'And long afterward were brought to the Royal Mausoleum here in Honolulu,' Pool supplemented.

'Also, Kanaka Oolea, there are some who believe to this day that Queen Alice has them stored with the rest of her ancestral bones in the big jars in her taboo room. All are wrong. I know. The sacred bones of Kahekili are gone and for ever gone. They rest nowhere. They have ceased to be. And many *kona* winds have whitened the surf at Waikiki since the last man looked upon the last of Kahekili. I alone remain alive of those men. I am the last man, and I was not glad to be at the finish.

'For see! I was a young man, and my heart was white-hot lava for Malia, who was in Kahekili's household. So was Anapuni's heart white-hot for her, though the color of his heart was black, as you shall see. We were drinking that night – Anapuni and I – the night that Kahekili died. Anapuni and I were only common-ers, as were all of us *kanakas* and *wahines* who were at the drinking with the common sailors and whaleship men from before the mast. We were drinking on the mats by the beach at Waikiki, close to the old *heiau*' (temple) 'that is not far from what is now the Wilders' beach place. I learned then and for ever what quantities of drink *haole* sailormen can stand. As for us *kanakas*, our heads were hot and light and rattly as dry gourds with the whiskey and the rum.

'It was past midnight, I remember well, when I saw Malia, whom never had I seen at a drinking, come across the wet-hard sand of the beach. My brain burned like red cinders of hell as I looked upon Anapuni look upon her, he being nearest to her by being across from me in the drinking circle. Oh, I know it was whiskey and rum and youth that made the heat of me; but there, in that moment, the mad mind of me resolved, if she spoke to him and yielded to dance with him first, that I would put both my hands around his throat and throw him down and under the *wahine* surf there beside us, and drown and choke out his life and the obstacle of him that stood between me and her. For know that she had never decided between us, and it was because of him that she was not already and long since mine.

'She was a grand young woman with a body generous as that of a chiefess and more wonderful, as she came upon us, across the wet sand, in the shimmer of the moonlight. Even the *haole* sailormen made pause of silence, and with open mouths stared upon her. Her walk! I have heard you talk, O Kanaka Oolea, of the woman Helen who caused the war of Troy. I say of Malia that more men would have stormed the walls of hell for her than went against that old-time city of which it is your custom to talk over much and long when you have drunk too little milk and too much gin.

'Her walk! In the moonlight there, the soft glow-fire of the jelly-fishes in the surf like the kerosene-lamp footlights I have seen in the new *haole* theatre! It was not the walk of a girl, but a woman. She did not flutter forward like rippling wavelets on a reef-sheltered, placid beach. There was that in her manner of walk that was big and queenlike, like the motion of the forces of nature, like the rhythmic flow of lava down the slopes of Kau to the sea, like the movement of the huge orderly trade-wind seas, like the rise and fall of the four great tides of the year that may be like music in the eternal ear of God, being too slow of occurrence in time to make a tune for ordinary quick-pulsing, brief-living, swift-dying man.

'Anapuni was nearest. But she looked at me. Have you ever heard a call, Kanaka Oolea, that is without sound yet is louder than the conches of God? So called she to me across that circle of the drinking. I half arose, for I was not yet full drunken; but Anapuni's arm caught her and drew her, and I sank back on my elbow and watched and raged. He was for making her sit beside him, and I waited. Did she sit, and, next, dance with him, I knew that ere morning Anapuni would be a dead man, choked and drowned by me in the shallow surf.

'Strange, is it not, Kanaka Oolea, all this heat called "love"? Yet it is not strange. It must be so in the time of one's youth, else would mankind not go on.'

'That is why the desire of woman must be greater than the desire of life,' Pool concurred. 'Else would there be neither men nor women.'

'Yes,' said Kumuhana. 'But it is many a year now since the last of such heat has gone out of me. I remember it as one remembers an old sunrise – a thing that was. And so one grows old, and cold, and drinks gin, not for madness, but for warmth. And the milk is very nourishing.

'But Malia did not sit beside him. I remember her eyes were wild, her hair down and flying, as she bent over him and whispered in his ear. And her hair covered him about and hid him as she whispered, and the sight of it pounded my heart against my ribs and dizzied my head till scarcely could I half-see. And I willed myself with all the will of me that if, in short minutes, she did not come over to me, I would go across the circle and get her.

'It was one of the things never to be. You remember Chief Konukalani? Himself he strode up to the circle. His face was black with anger. He gripped Malia, not by the arm, but by the hair, and dragged her away behind him and was gone. Of that, even now, can I understand not the hâlf. I, who was for slaying Anapuni because of her, raised neither hand nor voice of protest when Konukalani dragged her away by the hair – nor did Anapuni. Of course, we were common men, and he was a chief. That I know. But why should two common men, mad with desire of woman, with desire of woman stronger in them than desire of life, let any one chief, even the highest in the land, drag the woman away by the hair? Desiring her more than life, why should the two men fear to slay then and immediately the one chief? Here is something stronger than life, stronger than woman, but what is it? and why?'

'I will answer you,' said Hardman Pool. 'It is so because most men are fools, and therefore must be taken care of by the few men who are wise. Such is the secret of chiefship. In all the world are chiefs over men. In all the world that has been have there ever been chiefs, who must say to the many fool men: "Do this; do not do that. Work, and work as we tell you, or your bellies will remain empty and you will perish. Obey the laws we set you or you will be beasts and without a place in the world. You would not have been, save for the chiefs before you who ordered and regulated for your fathers. No seed of you will come after you, except that we order and regulate for you now. You must be peace-abiding, and decent, and blow your noses. You must be early to bed of nights, and up early in the morning to work if you would have beds to sleep in and not roost in trees like the silly fowls. This is the season for the yam-planting and you must plant now. We say now, to-day, and not picnicking and hulaing to-day and yam-planting to-morrow or some other day of the many careless days. You must not kill one another, and you must leave your neighbors' wives alone. All this is life for you, because you think but one day at a time, while we, your chiefs, think for you all days and for days ahead."'

'Like a cloud on the mountain-top that comes down and wraps about you and that you dimly see is a cloud, so is your wisdom to me, Kanaka Oolea,' Kumuhana murmured. 'Yet is it sad that I should be born a common man and live all my days a common man.'

'That is because you were of yourself common,' Hardman Pool assured him. 'When a man is born common, and is by nature uncommon, he rises up and overthrows the chiefs and makes himself chief over the chiefs. Why do you not run my ranch, with its many thousands of cattle, and shift the pastures by the rain-fall, and pick the bulls, and arrange the bargaining and the selling of the meat to the sailing ships and war vessels and the people who live in the Honolulu houses, and fight with lawyers, and help make laws, and even tell the King what is wise for him to do and what is dangerous? Why does not any man do this that I do? Any man of all the men who work for me, feed out of my hand, and let me do their thinking for them – me, who works harder than any of them, who eats no more than any of them, and who can sleep on no more than one *lauhala* mat at a time like any of them?'

'I am out of the cloud, Kanaka Oolea,' said Kumuhana, with a visible brightening of countenance. 'More clearly do I see. All my long years have the *aliis* I was born under thought for me. Ever, when I was hungry, I came to them for food, as I come to your kitchen now. Many people eat in your kitchen, and the days of feasts when you slay fat steers for all of us are understandable. It is why I come to you this day, an old man whose labor of strength is not worth a shilling a week, and ask of you twelve dollars to buy a jackass and a second-hand saddle and bridle. It is why twice ten fool men of us, under these monkey-pods half an hour ago, asked of you a dollar or two, or four or five, or ten or twelve. We are the careless ones of the careless days who will not plant the yam in season if our *alii* does not compel us, who will not think one day for ourselves, and who, when we age to worthlessness, know that our *alii* will think *kow-kow* into our bellies and a grass thatch over our heads.'

Hardman Pool bowed his appreciation, and urged:

'But the bones of Kahekili. The Chief Konukalani had just dragged away Malia by the hair of the head, and you and Anapuni sat on without protest in the circle of drinking. What was it Malia whispered in Anapuni's ear, bending over him, her hair hiding the face of him?'

'That Kahekili was dead. That was what she whispered to Anapuni. That Kahekili was dead, just dead, and that the chiefs, ordering all within the house to remain within, were debating the disposal of the bones and meat of him before word of his death should get abroad. That the high priest Eoppo was deciding them, and that she had overheard no less than Anapuni and me chosen as the sacrifices to go the way of Kahekili and his bones and to care for him afterward and for ever in the shadowy other world.'

'The *meopuu*, the human sacrifice,' Pool commented. 'Yet it was nine years since the coming of the missionaries.'

'And it was the year before their coming that the idols were cast down and the taboos broken,' Kumuhana added. 'But the chiefs still practised the old ways, the custom of *hunakele*, and hid the bones of the *aliis* where no men should find them and make fish-hooks of their jaws or arrow heads of their long bones for the slaying of little mice in sport. Behold, O Kanaka Oolea!'

The old man thrust out his tongue, and, to Pool's amazement, he saw the surface of that sensitive organ, from root to tip, tattooed in intricate designs.

'That was done after the missionaries came, several years afterward, when Keopuolani died. Also, did I knock out four of my front teeth, and half-circles did I burn over my body with blazing bark. And whoever ventured out-of-doors that night was slain by the chiefs. Nor could a light be shown in a house or a whisper of noise be made. Even dogs and hogs that made a noise were slain, nor all that night were the ships' bells of the *haoles* in the harbor allowed to strike. It was a terrible thing in those days when an *alii* died.

'But the night that Kahekili died. We sat on in the drinking circle after Konukalani dragged Malia away by the hair. Some of the *haole* sailors grumbled; but they were few in the land in those days and the *kanakas* many. And never was Malia seen of men again. Konukalani alone knew the manner of her slaying, and he never told. And in after years what common men like Anapuni and me should dare to question him?

'Now she had told Anapuni before she was dragged away. But Anapuni's heart was black. Me he did not tell. Worthy he was of the killing I had intended for him. There was a giant harpooner in the circle, whose singing was like the bellowing of bulls; and, gazing on him in amazement while he roared some song of the sea, when next I looked across the circle to Anapuni, Anapuni was gone. He had fled to the high mountains where he could hide with the bird-catchers a week of moons. This I learned afterward.

'I? I sat on, ashamed of my desire of woman that had not been so strong as my slave-obedience to a chief. And I drowned my shame in large drinks of rum and whiskey, till the world went round and round, inside my head and out, and the Southern Cross danced a *hula* in the sky, and the Koolau Mountains bowed their lofty summits to Waikiki and the surf of Waikiki kissed them on their brows. And the giant harpooner was still roaring, his the last sounds in my ear, as I fell back on the *lauhala* mat, and was to all things for the time as one dead.

'When I awoke was at the faint first beginning of dawn. I was being kicked by a hard naked heel in the ribs. What of the enormousness of the drink I had consumed, the feelings aroused in me by the heel were not pleasant. The *kanakas* and *wahines* of the drinking were gone. I alone remained among the sleeping sailormen, the giant harpooner snoring like a whale, his head upon my feet.

'More heel-kicks, and I sat up and was sick. But the one who kicked was impatient, and demanded to know where was Anapuni. And I did not know, and was kicked, this time from both sides by two impatient men, because I did not know. Nor did I know that Kahekili was dead. Yet did I guess something serious was afoot, for the two men who kicked me were chiefs, and no common men crouched behind them to do their bidding. One was Aimoku, of Kaneche; the other Humuhumu, of Manoa.

'They commanded me to go with them, and they were not kind in their commanding; and as I uprose, the head of the giant harpooner was rolled off my feet, past the edge of the mat, into the sand. He grunted like a pig, his lips opened, and all of his tongue rolled out of his mouth into the sand. Nor did he draw it back. For the first time I knew how long was a man's tongue. The sight of the sand on it made me sick for the second time. It is a terrible thing, the next day after a night of drinking. I was afire, dry afire, all the inside of me like a burnt cinder, like *aa* lava, like the harpooner's tongue dry and gritty with sand. I bent for a half-drunk drinking coconut, but Aimoku kicked it out of my shaking fingers, and Humuhumu smote me with the heel of his hand on my neck.

'They walked before me, side by side, their faces solemn and black, and I walked at their heels. My mouth stank of the drink, and my head was sick with the stale fumes of it, and I would have cut off my right hand for a drink of water, one drink, a mouthful even. And, had I had it, I know it would have sizzled in my belly like water spilled on heated stones for the roasting. It is terrible, the next day after the drinking. All the life-time of many men who died young has passed by me since the last I was able to do such mad drinking of youth when youth knows not capacity and is undeterred.

'But as we went on, I began to know that some *alii* was dead. No *kanakas* lay asleep in the sand, nor stole home from their love-making; and no canoes were abroad after the early fish most catchable then inside the reef at the change of the tide. When we came past the *hoiau*' (temple) 'to where the Great Kamehameha used to haul out his brigs and schooners, I saw, under the canoe-sheds, that the mat-thatches of Kahekili's great double-canoe had been taken off, and that even then, at low tide, many men were launching it down across the sand into the water. But all these men were chiefs. And though my eyes swam, and the inside of my head went around and around and the inside of my body was a cinder athirst, I guessed that the *alii* who was dead was Kahekili. For he was old, and most likely of the *aliis* to be dead.'

'It was his death, as I have heard it, more than the intercession of Kekuanaoa, that spoiled Governor Boki's rebellion,' Hardman Pool observed.

'It was Kahekili's death that spoiled it,' Kumuhana confirmed. 'All commoners, when the word slipped out that night of his death, fled into the shelter of the grass houses, nor lighted fire nor pipes, nor breathed loudly, being therein and thereby taboo from use for sacrifice. And all Governor Boki's commoners of fighting men, as well as the *haole* deserters from ships, so fled, so that the brass guns lay unserved and his handful of chiefs of themselves could do nothing.

'Aimoku and Humuhumu made me sit on the sand to the side from the launching of the great double-canoe. And when it was afloat all the chiefs were athirst, not being used to such toil; and I was told to climb the palms beside the canoe-sheds and throw down drinking coconuts. They drank and were refreshed, but me they refused to let drink.

'Then they bore Kahekili from his house to the canoe in a *haole* coffin, oiled and varnished and new. It had been made by a ship's carpenter, who thought he was making a boat that must not leak. It was very tight, and over where the face of Kahekili lay was nothing but thin glass. The chiefs had not screwed on the outside plank to cover the glass. Maybe they did not know the manner of *haole* coffins; but at any rate I was to be glad they did not know, as you shall see.

'"There is but one *moepuu*," said the priest Eoppo, looking at me where I sat on the coffin in the bottom of the canoe. Already the chiefs were paddling out through the reef.

'"The other has run into hiding," Aimoku answered. "This one was all we could get."

'And then I knew. I knew everything. I was to be sacrificed. Anapuni had been planned for the other sacrifice. That was what Malia had whispered to Anapuni at the drinking. And she had been dragged away before she could tell me. And in his blackness of heart he had not told me.

'"There should be two," said Eoppo. "It is the law."

'Aimoku stopped paddling and looked back shoreward as if to return and get a second sacrifice. But several of the chiefs contended no, saying that all commoners were fled to the mountains or were lying taboo in their houses, and that it might take days before they could catch one. In the end Eoppo gave in, though he grumbled from time to time that the law required two *moepuus*.

'We paddled on, past Diamond Head and abreast of Koko Head, till we were in the midway of the Molokai Channel. There was quite a sea running, though the trade wind was blowing light. The chiefs rested from their paddles, save for the steersmen who kept the canoes bow-on to the wind and swell. And, ere they proceeded further in the matter, they opened more coconuts and drank.

'"I do not mind so much being the *moepuu*," I said to Humuhumu; "but I should like to have a drink before I am slain." I got no drink. But I spoke true. I was too sick of the much whiskey and rum to be afraid to die. At least my mouth would stink no more, nor my head ache, nor the inside of me be as dry-hot sand. Almost worst of all, I suffered at the thought of the harpooner's tongue, as last I had seen it lying on the sand and covered with sand. O Kanaka Oolea, what animals young men are with the drink! Not until they have grown old, like you and me, do they control their wantonness of thirst and drink sparingly, like you and me.'

'Because we have to,' Hardman Pool rejoined. 'Old stomachs are worn thin and tender, and we drink sparingly because we dare not drink more. We are wise, but the wisdom is bitter.'

'The priest Eoppo sang a long *mele* about Kahekili's mother and his mother's mother, and all their mothers all the way back to the beginning of time,' Kumuhana resumed. 'And it seemed I must die of my sand-hot dryness ere he was done. And he called upon all the gods of the under world, the middle world and the over world, to care for and cherish the dead *alii* about to be consigned to them, and to carry out the curses – they were terrible curses – he laid upon all living men and men to live after who might tamper with the bones of Kahekili to use them in sport of vermin-slaying.

'Do you know, Kanaka Oolea, the priest talked a language largely different, and I know it was the priest language, the old language. Maui he did not name Maui, but Maui-Tiki-Tiki and Maui-Po-Tiki. And Hina, the goddess-mother of Maui, he named Ina. And Maui's god-father he named sometimes Akalana and sometimes Kanaloa. Strange how one about to die and very thirsty should remember such things! And I remember the priest named Hawaii as Vaii, and Lanai as Ngangai.'

'Those were the Maori names,' Hardman Pool explained, 'and the Samoan and Tongan names, that the priests brought with them in their first voyages from the south in the long ago when they found Hawaii and settled to dwell upon it.'

'Great is your wisdom, O Kanaka Oolea,' the old man accorded solemnly. 'Ku, our Supporter of the Heavens, the priest named Tu, and also Ru; and La, our God of the Sun, he named Ra – '

'And Ra was a sun-god in Egypt in the long ago,' Pool interrupted with a sparkle of interest. 'Truly, you Polynesians have traveled far in time and space since first you began. A far cry it is from Old Egypt, when Atlantis was still afloat, to Young Hawaii in the North Pacific. But proceed, Kumuhana. Do you remember anything also of what the priest Eoppo sang?'

'At the very end,' came the confirming nod, 'though I was near dead myself, and nearer to die under the priest's knife, he sang what I have remembered every word of. Listen! It was thus.'

And in quavering falsetto, with the customary broken-notes, the old man sang.

'A Maori death-chant unmistakable,' Pool exclaimed, 'sung by an Hawaiian with a tattooed tongue! Repeat it once again, and I shall say it to you in English.'

And when it had been repeated, he spoke it slowly in English:

> 'But death is nothing new.
> Death is and has been ever since old Maui died.

Then Pata-tai laughed loud
And woke the goblin-god,
Who severed him in two, and shut him in,
So dusk of eve came on.'

'And at the last,' Kumuhana resumed, 'I was not slain. Eoppo, the killing knife in hand and ready to lift for the blow, did not lift. And I? How did I feel and think? Often, Kanaka Oolea, have I since laughed at the memory of it. I felt very thirsty. I did not want to die. I wanted a drink of water. I knew I was going to die, and I kept remembering the thousand waterfalls falling to waste down the *palis*' (precipices) 'of the windward Koolau Mountains. I did not think of Anapuni. I was too thirsty. I did not think of Malia. I was too thirsty. But continually, inside my head, I saw the tongue of the harpooner, covered dry with sand, as I had last seen it, lying in the sand. My tongue was like that, too. And in the bottom of the canoe rolled about many drinking nuts. Yet I did not attempt to drink, for these were chiefs and I was a common man.

' "No," said Eoppo, commanding the chiefs to throw overboard the coffin. "There are not two *moepuus*, therefore there shall be none."

' "Slay the one," the chiefs cried.

'But Eoppo shook his head, and said: "We cannot send Kahekili on his way with only the tops of the taro."

' "Half a fish is better than none," Aimoku said the old saying.

' "Not at the burying of an *alii*," was the priest's quick reply. "It is the law. We cannot be niggard with Kahekili and cut his allotment of sacrifice in half."

'So, for the moment, while the coffin went overside, I was not slain. And it was strange that I was glad immediately that I was to live. And I began to remember Malia, and to begin to plot a vengeance on Anapuni. And with the blood of life thus freshening in me, my thirst multiplied on itself tenfold, and my tongue and mouth and throat seemed as sanded as the tongue of the harpooner. The coffin being overboard, I was sitting in the bottom of the canoe. A coconut rolled between my legs and I closed them on it. But as I picked it up in my hand, Aimoku smote my hand with the paddle-edge. Behold!'

He held up the hand, showing two fingers crooked from never having been set.

'I had no time to vex over my pain, for worse things were upon me. All the chiefs were crying out in horror. The coffin, head-end up, had not sunk. It bobbed up and down in the sea astern of us. And the canoe, without way on it, bow-on to sea and wind, was drifted down by sea and wind upon the coffin. And the glass of it was to us, so that we could see the face and head of Kahekili through the glass; and he grinned at us through the glass and seemed alive already in the other world and angry with us, and, with other-world power, about to wreak his anger upon us. Up and down he bobbed, and the canoe drifted closer upon him.

'"Kill him!" "Bleed him!" "Thrust to the heart of him!" These things the chiefs were crying out to Eoppo in their fear. "Over with the taro tops!" "Let the *alii* have the half of a fish!"

'Eoppo, priest though he was, was likewise afraid, and his reason weakened before the sight of Kahekili in his *haole* coffin that would not sink. He seized me by the hair, drew me to my feet, and lifted the knife to plunge to my heart. And there was no resistance in me. I knew again only that I was very thirsty, and before my swimming eyes, in mid-air and close up, dangled the sanded tongue of the harpooner.

'But before the knife could fall and drive in, the thing happened that saved me. Akai, half-brother to Governor Boki, as you will remember, was steersman of the canoe, and, therefore, in the stern, was nearest to the coffin and its dead that would not sink. He was wild with fear, and he thrust out with the point of his paddle to fend off the coffined *alii* that seemed bent to come on board. The point of the paddle struck the glass. The glass broke – '

'And the coffin immediately sank,' Hardman Pool broke in; 'the air that floated it escaping through the broken glass.'

'The coffin immediately sank, being builded by the ship's carpenter like a boat,' Kumuhana confirmed. 'And I, who was a *moepuu*, became a man once more. And I lived, though I died a thousand deaths from thirst before we gained back to the beach of Waikiki.

'And so, O Kanaka Oolea, the bones of Kahekili do not lie in the Royal Mausoleum. They are at the bottom of Molokai Channel, if not, long since, they have become floating dust of slime, or, builded into the bodies of the coral creatures dead and gone, are builded into the coral reef itself. Of men I am the one living who saw the bones of Kahekili sink into the Molokai Channel.'

In the pause that followed, wherein Hardman Pool was deep sunk in meditation, Kumuhana licked his dry lips many times. At the last he broke silence:

'The twelve dollars, Kanaka Oolea, for the jackass and the second-hand saddle and bridle?'

'The twelve dollars would be thine,' Pool responded, passing to the ancient one six dollars and a half, 'save that I have in my stable junk the very bridle and saddle for you which I shall give you. These six dollars and a half will buy you the perfectly suitable jackass of the *pake*' (Chinese) 'at Kokako who told me only yesterday that such was the price.'

They sat on, Pool meditating, conning over and over to himself the Maori death-chant he had heard, and especially the line, 'So dusk of eve came on,' finding in it an intense satisfaction of beauty; Kumuhana licking his lips and tokening that he waited for something more. At last he broke the silence.

'I have talked long, O Kanaka Oolea. There is not the enduring moistness in my mouth that was when I was young. It seems that afresh upon me is the thirst that was mine when tormented by the visioned tongue of the harpooner. The gin and milk is very good, O Kanaka Oolea, for a tongue that is like the harpooner's.'

A shadow of a smile flickered across Pool's face. He clapped his hands, and the little maid came running.

'Bring one glass of gin and milk for old Kumuhana,' commanded Hardman Pool.

WHEN ALICE TOLD HER SOUL

This, of Alice Akana, is an affair of Hawaii, not of this day, but of days recent enough, when Abel Ah Yo preached his famous revival in Honolulu and persuaded Alice Akana to tell her soul. But what Alice told concerned itself with the earlier history of the then surviving generation.

For Alice Akana was fifty years old, had begun life early, and, early and late, lived it spaciously. What she knew went back into the roots and foundations of families, businesses and plantations. She was the one living repository of accurate information that lawyers sought out, whether the information they required related to land-boundaries and land gifts, or to marriages, births, bequests or scandals. Rarely, because of the tight tongue she kept behind her teeth, did she give them what they asked; and when she did was when only equity was served and no one was hurt.

For Alice had lived, from early in her girlhood, a life of flowers, and song, and wine, and dance; and, in her later years, had herself been mistress of these revels by office of mistress of the *hula* house. In such atmosphere, where mandates of God and man and caution are inhibited, and where woozled tongues will wag, she acquired her historical knowledge of things never otherwise whispered and rarely guessed. And her tight tongue had served her well, so that, while the old-timers knew she must know, none ever heard her gossip of the times of Kalakaua's boathouse, nor of the high times of officers of visiting warships, nor of the diplomats and ministers and councils of the countries of the world.

So, at fifty, loaded with historical dynamite sufficient, if it were ever exploded, to shake the social and commercial life of the Islands, still tight of tongue, Alice Akana was mistress of the *hula* house, manageress of the dancing girls who *hula*'d for royalty, for *luaus* (feasts), house-parties, *poi* suppers and curious tourists. And, at fifty, she was not merely buxom, but short and fat in the Polynesian peasant way, with a constitution and lack of organic weakness that promised incalculable years. But it was at fifty that she strayed, quite by chance of time and curiosity, into Abel Ah Yo's revival meeting.

Now Abel Ah Yo, in his theology and word wizardry, was as much mixed a personage as Billy Sunday. In his genealogy he was much more mixed, for he was compounded of one-fourth Portuguese, one-fourth Scotch, one-fourth Hawaiian and one-fourth Chinese. The Pentecostal fire he flamed forth was hotter and more variegated than could any one of the four races of him alone have flamed forth. For in him were gathered together the cannyness and the cunning, the wit and the wisdom, the subtlety and the rawness, the passion and the philosophy, the agonizing spirit-groping and the legs up to the knees in the dung of reality, of the four radically different breeds that contributed to the sum of him. His, also, was the clever self-deceivement of the entire clever compound.

When it came to word wizardry, he had Billy Sunday, master of slang and argot of one language, skinned by miles. For in Abel Ah Yo were the live verbs, and nouns, and adjectives, and metaphors of four living languages. Intermixed and living promiscuously and vitally together, he possessed in these languages a reservoir of expression in which a myriad Billy Sundays could drown. Of no race, a mongrel *par excellence*, a heterogeneous scrabble, the genius of the admixture was superlatively Abel Ah Yo's. Like a chameleon, he titubated and scintillated grandly between the diverse parts of him, stunning by frontal attack and surprising and confounding by flanking sweeps the mental homogeneity of the more simply constituted souls who came in to his revival to sit under him and flame to his flaming.

Abel Ah Yo believed in himself and his mixedness, as he believed in the mixedness of his weird concept that God looked as much like him as like any man, being no mere tribal god, but a world god that must look equally like all races of all the world, even if it led to piebaldness. And the concept worked. Chinese,

Korean, Japanese, Hawaiian, Porto Rican, Russian, English, French – members of all races – knelt without friction, side by side, to his revision of deity.

Himself in his tender youth an apostate to the Church of England, Abel Ah Yo had for years suffered the lively sense of being a Judas sinner. Essentially religious, he had foresworn the Lord. Like Judas therefore he was. Judas was damned. Wherefore he, Abel Ah Yo, was damned; and he did not want to be damned. So, quite after the manner of humans, he squirmed and twisted to escape damnation. The day came when he solved his escape. The doctrine that Judas was damned, he concluded, was a misinterpretation of God, who, above all things, stood for justice. Judas had been God's servant, specially selected to perform a particularly nasty job. Therefore Judas, ever faithful, a betrayer only by divine command, was a saint. Ergo, he, Abel Ah Yo, was a saint by very virtue of his apostasy to a particular sect, and he could have access with clear grace any time to God.

This theory became one of the major tenets of his preaching, and was especially efficacious in cleansing the consciences of the back-sliders from all other faiths who else, in the secrecy of their subconscious selves, were being crushed by the weight of the Judas sin. To Abel Ah Yo, God's plan was as clear as if he, Abel Ah Yo, had planned it himself. All would be saved in the end, although some took longer than others, and would win only to back-seats. Man's place in the ever-fluxing chaos of the world was definite and pre-ordained – if by no other token, then by denial that there was any ever-fluxing chaos. This was a mere bugbear of mankind's addled fancy; and, by stinging audacities of thought and speech, by vivid slang that bit home by sheerest intimacy into his listeners' mental processes, he drove the bugbear from their brains, showed them the loving clarity of God's design, and, thereby, induced in them spiritual serenity and calm.

What chance had Alice Akana, herself pure and homogeneous Hawaiian, against his subtle democratic-tinged, four-race-engendered, slang-munitioned attack? He knew, by contact, almost as much as she about the waywardness of living and sinning – having been singing boy on the passenger-ships between Hawaii and California, and, after that, bar boy, afloat and ashore, from the Barbary Coast to Heinie's Tavern. In point of fact, he had left his job of Number One Bar Boy at the University Club to embark on his great preachment revival.

So, when Alice Akana strayed in to scoff, she remained to pray to Abel Ah Yo's god, who struck her hard-headed mind as the most sensible god of which she had ever heard. She gave money into Abel Ah Yo's collection plate, closed up the *hula* house and dismissed the *hula* dancers to more devious ways of earning a livelihood, shed her bright colors and raiments and flower garlands, and bought a Bible.

It was a time of religious excitement in the purlieus of Honolulu. The thing was a democratic movement of the people toward God. Place and caste were invited, but never came. The stupid lowly, and the humble lowly, only, went down on its knees at the penitent form, admitted its pathological weight and hurt of sin, eliminated and purged all its bafflements, and walked forth again upright under the sun, child-like and pure, upborne by Abel Ah Yo's god's arm around it. In short, Abel Ah Yo's revival was a clearing house for sin and sickness of spirit, wherein sinners were relieved of their burdens and made light and bright and spritually healthy again.

But Alice was not happy. She had not been cleared. She bought and dispersed Bibles, contributed more money to the plate, contralto'd gloriously in all the hymns, but would not tell her soul. In vain Abel Ah Yo wrestled with her. She would not go down on her knees at the penitent form and voice the things of tarnish within her – the ill things of good friends of the old days. 'You cannot serve two masters,' Abel Ah Yo told her. 'Hell is full of those who have tried. Single of heart and pure of heart must you make your peace with God. Not until you tell your soul to God right out in meeting will you be ready for redemption. In the meantime you will suffer the canker of the sin you carry about within you.'

Scientifically, though he did not know it and though he continually jeered at science, Abel Ah Yo was right. Not could she be again as a child and become radiantly clad in God's grace, until she had eliminated from her soul, by telling, all the sophistications that had been hers, including those she shared with others. In the Protestant way, she must bare her soul in public, as in the Catholic way it was done in the privacy of the confessional. The result of such baring would be unity, tranquillity, happiness, cleansing, redemption and immortal life.

'Choose!' Abel Ah Yo thundered. 'Loyalty to God, or loyalty to man.' And Alice could not choose. Too long had she kept her tongue locked with the honor of man. 'I will tell all my soul about myself,' she contended. 'God knows I am tired of my soul and should like to have it clean and shining once again as when I was a little girl at Kaneohe – '

'But all the corruption of your soul has been with other souls,' was Abel Ah Yo's invariable reply. 'When you have a burden, lay it down. You cannot bear a burden and be quit of it at the same time.'

'I will pray to God each day, and many times each day,' she urged. 'I will approach God with humility, with sighs and with tears. I will contribute often to the plate, and I will buy Bibles, Bibles, Bibles without end.'

'And God will not smile upon you,' God's mouthpiece retorted. 'And you will remain weary and heavy-laden. For you will not have told all your sin, and not until you have told all will you be rid of any.'

'This rebirth is difficult,' Alice sighed.

'Rebirth is even more difficult than birth.' Abel Ah Yo did anything but comfort her. '"Not until you become as a little child . . ."'

'If ever I tell my soul, it will be a big telling,' she confided.

'The bigger the reason to tell it then.'

And so the situation remained at deadlock, Abel Ah Yo demanding absolute allegiance to God, and Alice Akana flirting on the fringes of paradise.

'You bet it will be a big telling, if Alice ever begins,' the beach-combing and disreputable *kamaainas* (old-timers) gleefully told one another over their Palm Tree gin.

In the clubs the possibility of her telling was of more moment.

The younger generation of men announced that they had applied for front seats at the telling, while many of the older generation of men joked hollowly about the conversion of Alice. Further, Alice found herself abruptly popular with friends who had forgotten her existence for twenty years.

One afternoon, as Alice, Bible in hand, was taking the electric street car at Hotel and Fort, Cyrus Hodge, sugar factor and magnate, ordered his chauffeur to stop beside her. Willy nilly, in excess of friendliness, he had her into his limousine beside him and went three-quarters of an hour out of his way and time personally to conduct her to her destination.

'Good for sore eyes to see you,' he burbled. 'How the years fly! You're looking fine. The secret of youth is yours.'

Alice smiled and complimented in return in the royal Polynesian way of friendliness.

'My, my,' Cyrus Hodge reminisced. 'I was such a boy in those days!'

'*Some* boy,' she laughed acquiescence.

'But knowing no more than the foolishness of a boy in those long-ago days.'

'Remember the night your hack-driver got drunk and left you – '

'S-s-sh!' he cautioned. 'That Jap driver is a high-school graduate and knows more English than either of us. Also, I think he is a spy for his Government. So why should we tell him anything? Besides, I was so very young. You remember . . .'

'Your cheeks were like the peaches we used to grow before the Mediterranean fruit-fly got into them,' Alice agreed. 'I don't think you shaved more than once a week then. You were a pretty boy. Don't you remember the *hula* we composed in your honor, the – '

'S-s-sh!' he hushed her. 'All that's buried and forgotten. May it remain forgotten.'

And she was aware that in his eyes was no longer any of the ingenuousness of youth she remembered. Instead, his eyes were keen and speculative, searching into her for some assurance that she would not resurrect his particular portion of that buried past.

'Religion is a good thing for us as we get along into middle age,' another old friend told her. He was building a magnificent house on Pacific Heights, but had recently married a second time, and was even then on his way to the steamer to welcome home his two daughters just graduated from Vassar.

'We need religion in our old age, Alice. It softens, makes us more tolerant and forgiving of the weakness of others – especially the weakness of youth of – of others, when they played high and low and didn't know what they were doing.'

He waited anxiously.

'Yes,' she said. 'We are all born to sin and it is hard to grow out of sin. But I grow, I grow.'

'Don't forget, Alice, in those other days I always played square. You and I never had a falling out.'

'Not even the night you gave that *luau* when you were twenty-one and insisted on breaking the glassware after every toast. But of course you paid for it.'

'Handsomely,' he asserted almost pleadingly.

'Handsomely,' she agreed. 'I replaced more than double the quantity with what you paid me, so that at the next *luau* I catered one hundred and twenty plates without having to rent or borrow a dish or glass. Lord Mainweather gave that *luau* – you remember him.'

'I was pig-sticking with him at Mana,' the other nodded. 'We were at a two weeks' house-party there. But say, Alice, as you know, I think this religion stuff is all right and better than all right. But don't let it carry you off your feet. And don't get to telling your soul on me. What would my daughters think of that broken glassware!'

'I always did have an *aloha*' (warm regard) 'for you, Alice,' a member of the Senate, fat and bald-headed, assured her.

And another, a lawyer and a grandfather: 'We were always friends, Alice. And remember, any legal advice or handling of business you may require, I'll do for you gladly, and without fees, for the sake of our old-time friendship.'

Came a banker to her late Christmas Eve, with formidable, legal-looking envelopes in his hand which he presented to her.

'Quite by chance,' he explained, 'when my people were looking up land-records in Iapio Valley, I found a mortgage of two thousand on your holdings there – that rice land leased to Ah Chin. And my mind drifted back to the past when we were all young together, and wild – a bit wild, to be sure. And my heart warmed with the memory of you, and, so, just as an *aloha*, here's the whole thing cleared off for you.'

Nor was Alice forgotten by her own people. Her house became a Mecca for native men and women, usually performing pilgrimage privily after darkness fell, with presents always in their hands – squid fresh from the reef, *opihis* and *limu*, baskets of alligator pears, roasting corn of the earliest from windward Cahu, mangoes and star-apples, taro pink and royal of the finest selection, sucking pigs, banana *poi*, breadfruit and crabs caught the very day from Pearl Harbor. Mary Mendana, wife of the Portuguese Consul, remembered her with a five-dollar box of candy and a mandarin coat that would have fetched three-quarters of a hundred dollars at a fire sale. And Elvira Miyahara Makaena Yin Wap, the wife of Yin Wap the wealthy Chinese importer, brought personally to Alice two entire bolts of *piña* cloth from the Philippines and a dozen pairs of silk stockings.

The time passed, and Abel Ah Yo struggled with Alice for a properly penitent heart, and Alice struggled with herself for her soul, while half of Honolulu wickedly or apprehensively hung on the outcome. Carnival week was over, polo and the races had come and gone, and the celebration of Fourth of July was ripening, ere Abel Ah Yo beat down by brutal psychology the citadel of her reluctance. It was then that he gave his famous exhortation which might be summed up as Abel Ah Yo's definition of eternity. Of course, like Billy Sunday on certain occasions, Abel Ah Yo had cribbed the definition. But no one in the Islands knew it, and his rating as a revivalist uprose a hundred per cent.

So successful was his preaching that night, that he reconverted many of his converts, who fell and moaned about the penitent form and crowded for room amongst scores of new converts burnt by the pentecostal fire, including half a company of negro soldiers from the garrisoned Twenty-Fifth Infantry, a dozen troopers from the Fourth Cavalry on its way to the Philippines, as many drunken man-of-war's men, divers' ladies from Iwilei and half the riff-raff of the beach.

Abel Ah Yo, subtly sympathetic himself by virtue of his racial admixture, knowing human nature like a book and Alice Akana even more so, knew just what he was doing when he arose that memorable night and exposited God, hell and eternity in terms of Alice Akana's comprehension. For, quite by chance, he had discovered her cardinal weakness. First of all, like all Polynesians, an ardent lover of nature, he found that earthquake and volcanic eruption were the things of which Alice lived in terror. She had been, in the past, on the Big Island, through cataclysms that had shaken grass houses down upon her while she slept, and she had beheld Madame Pele (the Fire or Volcano Goddess) fling red-fluxing lava down the long slopes of Mauna Loa, destroying fish-ponds on the sea-brim and licking up droves of beef cattle, villages and humans on her fiery way.

The night before, a slight earthquake had shaken Honolulu and given Alice Akana insomnia. And the morning papers had stated that Mauna Kea had broken into eruption, while the lava was rising rapidly in the great pit of Kilauea. So, at the meeting, her mind vexed between the terrors of this world and the delights of the eternal world to come, Alice sat down in a front seat in a very definite state of the 'jumps'.

And Abel Ah Yo arose and put his finger on the sorest part of her soul. Sketching the nature of God in the stereotyped way, but making the stereotyped alive again with his gift of tongues in Pidgin-English and Pidgin-Hawaiian, Abel Ah Yo described the day when the Lord, even His infinite patience at an end, would tell Peter to close his day book and ledgers, command Gabriel to summon all souls to Judgment, and cry out with a voice of thunder: 'Welakahao!'

This anthropomorphic deity of Abel Ah Yo thundering the modern Hawaiian-English slang of welakahao at the end of the world, is a fair sample of the revivalist's speech-tools of discourse.

Welakahao means literally 'hot iron'. It was coined in the Honolulu Ironworks by the hundreds of Hawaiian men there employed, who meant by it 'to hustle', 'to get a move on', the iron being hot meaning that the time had come to strike.

'And the Lord cried "*Welakahao*," and the Day of Judgment began and was over *wiki-wiki*' (quickly) 'just like that; for Peter was a better bookkeeper than any on the Waterhouse Trust Company Limited, and, further, Peter's books were true.'

Swiftly Abel Ah Yo divided the sheep from the goats, and hastened the latter down into hell.

'And now,' he demanded, perforce his language on these pages being properly Englished, 'what is hell like? Oh, my friends, let me describe to you, in a little way, what I have beheld with my own eyes on earth of the possibilities of hell. I was a young man, a boy, and I was at Hilo. Morning began with earthquakes. Throughout the day the mighty land continued to shake and tremble, till strong men became seasick, and women clung to the trees to escape falling, and cattle were thrown down off their feet. I beheld myself a young calf so thrown. A night of terror indescribable followed. The land was in motion like a canoe in a Kona gale. There was an infant crushed to death by its fond mother stepping upon it whilst fleeing her falling house.

'The heavens were on fire above us. We read our Bibles by the light of the heavens, and the print was fine, even for young eyes. Those missionary Bibles were always too small of print. Forty miles away from us, the heart of hell burst from the lofty mountains and gushed red-blood of fire-melted rock toward the sea. With the heavens in vast conflagration and the earth *hulaing* beneath our feet, was a scene too awful and too majestic to be enjoyed. We could think only of the thin bubble-skin of earth between us and the everlasting lake of fire and brimstone, and of God to whom we prayed to save us. There were earnest and devout souls who there and then promised their pastors to give not their shaved tithes, but five-tenths of their all to the church, if only the Lord would let them live to contribute.

'Oh, my friends, God saved us. But first He showed us a foretaste of that hell that will yawn for us on the last day, when

he cries "*Welakahao!*" in a voice of thunder. When the iron is hot!
Think of it! When the iron is hot for sinners!

'By the third day, things being much quieter, my friend the
preacher and I, being calm in the hand of God, journeyed up
Mauna Loa and gazed into the awful pit of Kilauea. We gazed
down into the fathomless abyss to the lake of fire far below,
roaring and dashing its fiery spray into billows and fountaining
hundreds of feet into the air like Fourth of July fireworks you
have all seen, and all the while we were suffocating and made
dizzy by the immense volumes of smoke and brimstone
ascending.

'And I say unto you, no pious person could gaze down upon
that scene without recognizing fully the Bible picture of the Pit
of Hell. Believe me, the writers of the New Testament had
nothing on us. As for me, my eyes were fixed upon the exhibition
before me, and I stood mute and trembling under a sense never
before so fully realized of the power, the majesty, and terror of
Almighty God – the resources of His wrath, and the untold
horrors of the finally impenitent who do not tell their souls and
make their peace with the Creator.*

'But oh, my friends, think you our guides, our native attend-
ants, deep-sunk in heathenism, were affected by such a scene?
No. The devil's hand was upon them. Utterly regardless and
unimpressed, they were only careful about their supper, chatted
about their raw fish, and stretched themselves upon their mats
to sleep. Children of the devil they were, insensible to the
beauties, the sublimities, and the awful terror of God's works.
But you are not heathen I now address. What is a heathen? He
is one who betrays a stupid insensibility to every elevated idea
and to every elevated emotion. If you wish to awaken his
attention, do not bid him to look down into the Pit of Hell. But
present him with a calabash of *poi*, a raw fish, or invite him to
some low, groveling and sensuous sport. Oh, my friends, how
lost are they to all that elevates the immortal soul! But the
preacher and I, sad and sick at heart for them, gazed down into

* See Dibble's *A History of the Sandwich Islands*.

hell. Oh, my friends, it *was* hell, the hell of the Scriptures, the hell of eternal torment for the undeserving . . .'

Alice Akana was in an ecstasy or hysteria of terror. She was mumbling incoherently: 'O Lord, I will give nine-tenths of my all. I will give all. I will give even the two bolts of *piña* cloth, the mandarin coat and the entire dozen silk stockings . . .'

By the time she could lend ear again, Abel Ah Yo was launching out on his famous definition of eternity.

'Eternity is a long time, my friends. God lives, and, therefore, God lives inside eternity. And God is very old. The fires of hell are as old and as everlasting as God. How else could there be everlasting torment for those sinners cast down by God into the Pit on the Last Day to burn for ever and for ever through all eternity? Oh, my friends, your minds are small – too small to grasp eternity. Yet is it given to me, by God's grace, to convey to you an understanding of a tiny bit of eternity.

'The grains of sand on the beach of Waikiki are as many as the stars, and more. No man may count them. Did he have a million lives in which to count them, he would have to ask for more time. Now let us consider a little, dinky, old *minah* bird with one broken wing that cannot fly. At Waikiki the *minah* bird that cannot fly takes one grain of sand in its beak and hops, hops, all day long and for many days, all the day to Pearl Harbor and drops that one grain of sand into the harbor. Then it hops, hops, all day and for many days, all the way back to Waikiki for another grain of sand. And again it hops, hops all the way back to Pearl Harbor. And it continues to do this through the years and centuries, and the thousands and thousands of centuries, until, at last, there remains not one grain of sand at Waikiki and Pearl Harbor is filled up with land and growing coconuts and pine-apples. And then, oh my friends, even then, IT WOULD NOT YET BE SUNRISE IN HELL!'

Here, at the smashing impact of so abrupt a climax, unable to withstand the sheer simplicity and objectivity of such artful measurement of a trifle of eternity, Alice Akana's mind broke down and blew up. She uprose, reeled blindly, and stumbled to her knees at the penitent form. Abel Ah Yo had not finished his preaching, but it was his gift to know crowd psychology, and to feel the heat of the pentecostal conflagration that scorched his audience. He called for a rousing revival hymn from his singers, and stepped down to wade among the hallelujah-shouting negro soldiers to Alice Akana. And, ere the excitement began to ebb, nine-tenths of his congregation and all his converts were down on knees praying and shouting aloud an immensity of contrite-ness and sin.

Word came, via telephone, almost simultaneously to the Pacific and University Clubs, that at last Alice was telling her soul in meeting; and, by private machine and taxi-cab, for the first time Abel Ah Yo's revival was invaded by those of caste and place. The first comers beheld the curious sight of Hawaiian, Chinese and all variegated racial-mixtures of the smelting-pot of Hawaii, men and women, fading out and slinking away through the exits of Abel Ah Yo's tabernacle. But those who were sneaking out were mostly men, while those who remained were avid-faced as they hung on Alice's utterance.

Never was a more fearful and damning community narrative enunciated in the entire Pacific, north and south, than that enunciated by Alice Akana; the penitent Phryne of Honolulu.

'Huh!' the first comers heard her saying, having already disposed of most of the venial sins of the lesser ones of her memory. 'You think this man, Stephen Makekau, is the son of Moses Makekau and Minnie Ah Ling, and has a legal right to the two hundred and eight dollars he draws down each month from Parke Richards Limited, for the lease of the fish-pond to Bill Kong at Amana. Not so. Stephen Makekau is not the son of Moses. He is the son of Aaron Kama and Tillie Naone. He was given as a present, as a feeding child, to Moses and Minnie by Aaron and Tillie. I know. Moses and Minnie and Aaron and Tillie are dead. Yet I know and can prove it. Old Mrs Poepoe is still alive. I was present when Stephen was born, and in the night-time when he was two months old, I myself carried him as a present to Moses and Minnie, and old Mrs Poepoe carried the lantern. This secret has been one of my sins. It has kept me from God. Now I am free of it. Young Archie Makekau, who collects bills for the Gas Company and plays baseball in the afternoon, and drinks too much gin, should get that two hundred and eight dollars the first of each month from Parke Richards Limited. He will blow it on gin and a Ford automobile. Stephen is a good man. Archie is no good. Also he is a liar, and he has served two sentences on the reef, and was in reform school before that. Yet God demands the truth, and Archie will get the money and make a bad use of it.'

And in such fashion Alice rambled on through the experiences of her long and full-packed life. And women forgot they were in the tabernacle, and men too, and faces darkened with passion as they learned for the first time the long-buried secrets of their other halves.

'The lawyers' offices will be crowded tomorrow morning,' MacIlwaine, chief of detectives, paused long enough from storing away useful information to lean and mutter in Colonel Stilton's ear.

Colonel Stilton grinned affirmation, although the chief of detectives could not fail to note the ghastliness of the grin.

'There is a banker in Honolulu. You all know his name. He is 'way up, swell society because of his wife. He owns much stock in General Plantations and Inter-Island.'

MacIlwaine recognized the growing portrait and forbore to chuckle.

'His name is Colonel Stilton. Last Christmas Eve he came to my house with big *aloha*' (love) 'and gave me mortgages on my land in Iapio Valley, all canceled, for two thousand dollars' worth. Now why did he have such big cash *aloha* for me? I will tell you . . .'

And tell she did, throwing the searchlight on ancient business transactions and political deals which from their inception had lurked in the dark.

'This,' Alice concluded the episode, 'has long been a sin upon my conscience, and kept my heart from God.

'And Harold Miles was that time President of the Senate, and next week he bought three town lots at Pearl Harbor, and painted his Honolulu house, and paid up his back dues in his clubs. Also the Ramsay home at Honokiki was left by will to the people if the Government would keep it up. But if the Government, after two years, did not begin to keep it up, then would it go to the Ramsay heirs, whom old Ramsay hated like poison. Well, it went to the heirs all right. Their lawyer was Charley Middleton, and he had me help fix it with the Government men. And their names were . . .' Six names, from both branches of the Legislature, Alice recited, and added: 'Maybe they all painted their houses after that. For the first time have I spoken. My heart is much lighter and softer. It has been coated with an armor of house-paint against the Lord. And there is Harry Werther. He was in the Senate that time. Everybody said bad things about him, and he was never re-elected. Yet his house was not painted. He was honest. To this day his house is not painted, as everybody knows.

'There is Jim Lokendamper. He has a bad heart. I heard him, only last week, right here before you all, tell his soul. He did not tell all his soul, and he lied to God. I am not lying to God. It is a big telling, but I am telling everything. Now Azalea Akau, sitting right over there, is his wife. But Lizzie Lokendamper is his married wife. A long time ago he had the great *aloha* for Azalea. You think her uncle, who went to California and died, left her by will that two thousand five hundred dollars she got. Her uncle did not. I know. Her uncle died broke in California, and Jim Lokendamper sent eighty dollars to California to bury him. Jim Lokendamper had a piece of land in Kohala he got from his mother's aunt. Lizzie, his married wife, did not know this. So he sold it to the Kohala Ditch Company and gave the twenty-five hundred to Azalea Akau – '

Here, Lizzie, the married wife, upstood like a fury long-thwarted, and, in lieu of her husband, already fled, flung herself tooth and nail on Azalea.

'Wait, Lizzie Lokendamper!' Alice cried out. 'I have much weight of you on my heart and some house-paint too . . .'

And when she had finished her disclosure of how Lizzie had painted her house, Azalea was up and raging.

'Wait, Azalea Akau. I shall now lighten my heart about you. And it is not house-paint. Jim always paid that. It is your new bath-tub and modern plumbing that is heavy on me . . .'

Worse, much worse, about many and sundry, did Alice Akana have to say, cutting high in business, financial and social life, as well as low. None was too high nor too low to escape; and not until two in the morning, before an entranced audience that packed the tabernacle to the doors, did she complete her recital of the personal and detailed iniquities she knew of the community in which she had lived intimately all her days. Just as she was finishing, she remembered more.

'Huh!' she sniffed. 'I gave last week one lot worth eight hundred dollars cash market price to Abel Ah Yo to pay running expenses and add up in Peter's books in heaven. Where did I get that lot? You all think Mr Fleming Jason is a good man. He is more crooked than the entrance was to Pearl Lochs before the United States Government straightened the channel. He has liver disease now; but his sickness is a judgment of God, and he will die crooked. Mr Fleming Jason gave me that lot twenty-two years ago, when its cash market price was thirty-five dollars. Because his *aloha* for me was big? No. He never had *aloha* inside of him except for dollars.

'You listen. Mr Fleming Jason put a great sin upon me. When Frank Lomiloli was at my house, full of gin, for which gin Mr Fleming Jason paid me in advance five times over, I got Frank Lomiloli to sign his name to the sale paper of his town land for one hundred dollars. It was worth six hundred then. It is worth twenty thousand now. Maybe you want to know where that town land is. I will tell you and remove it off my heart. It is on King Street, where is now the Come Again Saloon, the Japanese Taxicab Company garage, and Smith & Wilson plumbing shop and the Ambrosia Ice Cream Parlors, with the two more stories big Addison Lodging House overhead. And it is all wood, and always has been well painted. Yesterday they started painting it again. But that paint will not stand between me and God. There are no more paint pots between me and my path to heaven.'

The morning and evening papers of the day following held an unholy hush on the greatest news story of years; but Honolulu was half a-giggle and half aghast at the whispered reports, not always basely exaggerated, that circulated wherever two Honoluluans chanced to meet.

'Our mistake,' said Colonel Stilton, at the club, 'was that we did not, at the very first, appoint a committee of safety to keep track of Alice's soul.'

Bob Cristy, one of the younger islanders, burst into laughter, so pointed and so loud that the meaning of it was demanded.

'Oh, nothing much,' was his reply. 'But I heard, on my way here, that old John Ward had just been run in for drunken and disorderly conduct and for resisting an officer. Now Abel Ah Yo fine-toothcombs the police court. He loves nothing better than soul-snatching a chronic drunkard.'

Colonel Stilton looked at Lask Finneston, and both looked at Gary Wilkinson. He returned to them a similar look.

'The old beach-comber!' Lask Finneston cried. 'The drunken old reprobate! I'd forgotten he was alive. Wonderful constitution. Never drew a sober breath except when he was shipwrecked, and, when I remember him, into every deviltry afloat. He must be going on eighty.'

'He isn't far away from it,' Bob Cristy nodded. 'Still beach-combs, drinks when he gets the price, and keeps all his senses, though he's not spry and has to use glasses when he reads. And his memory is perfect. Now if Abel Ah Yo catches him . . .'

Gary Wilkinson cleared his throat preliminary to speech.

'Now there's a grand old man,' he said. 'A left-over from a forgotten age. Few of his type remain. A pioneer. A true *kamaaina*' (old-timer). 'Helpless and in the hands of the police in his old age! We should do something for him in recognition of his yeoman work in Hawaii. His old home, I happen to know, is Sag Harbor. He hasn't seen it for over half a century. Now why shouldn't he be surprised to-morrow morning by having his fine paid, and by being presented with return tickets to Sag Harbor, and, say, expenses for a year's trip? I move a committee. I appoint Colonel Chilton, Lask Finneston and . . . and myself. As for chairman, who more appropriate than Lask Finneston, who knew the old gentleman so well in the early days? Since there is no objection, I hereby appoint Lask Finneston chairman of the committee for the purpose of raising and donating money to pay the police-court fine and the expenses of a year's travel for the noble pioneer, John Ward, in recognition of a lifetime of devotion of energy to the upbuilding of Hawaii.'

There was no dissent.

'The committee will now go into secret session,' said Lask Finneston, arising and indicating the way to the library.

SHIN-BONES

They have gone down to the pit with their weapons of war, and they have laid their swords under their heads.

'It was a sad thing to see the old lady revert.'

Prince Akuli shot an apprehensive glance sideward to where, under the shade of a *kukui* tree, an old *wahine* (Hawaiian woman) was just settling herself to begin on some work in hand.

'Yes,' he nodded half-sadly to me, 'in her last years Hiwilani went back to the old ways, and to the old beliefs – in secret, of course. And *believe* me, she was some collector herself. You should have seen her bones. She had them all about her bedroom, in big jars, and they constituted most all her relatives, except a half-dozen or so that Kanau beat her out of by getting to them first. The way the pair of them used to quarrel about those bones was awe-inspiring. And it gave me the creeps, when I was a boy, to go into that big, for-ever-twilight room of hers, and know that in this jar was all that remained of my maternal grand-aunt, and that in that jar was my great-grandfather, and that in all the jars were the preserved bone-remnants of the shadowy dust of the ancestors whose seed had come down and been incorporated in the living, breathing me. Hiwilani had gone quite native at the last, sleeping on mats on the hard floor – she'd fired out of the room the great, royal, canopied four-poster that had been presented to her grandmother by Lord Byron, who was the cousin of the Don Juan Byron and came here in the frigate *Blonde* in 1825.

'She went back to all native, at the last, and I can see her yet, biting a bite out of the raw fish ere she tossed them to her women to eat. And she made them finish her *poi*, or whatever else she did not finish of herself. She – '

But he broke off abruptly, and by the sensitive dilation of his nostrils and by the expression of his mobile features I saw that he had read in the air and identified the odor that offended him.

'Deuce take it!' he cried to me. 'It stinks to heaven. And I shall be doomed to wear it until we're rescued.'

There was no mistaking the object of his abhorrence. The ancient crone was making a dearest-loved *lei* (wreath) of the fruit of the *hala* which is the screw-pine or pandanus of the South Pacific. She was cutting the many sections or nut-envelopes of the fruit into fluted bell-shapes preparatory to stringing them on the twisted and tough inner bark of the *hau* tree. It certainly smelled to heaven, but, to me, a *malahini* (new-comer), the smell was wine-woody and fruit-juicy and not unpleasant.

Prince Akuli's limousine had broken an axle a quarter of a mile away, and he and I had sought shelter from the sun in this veritable bowery of a mountain home. Humble and grass-thatched was the house, but it stood in a treasure-garden of begonias that sprayed their delicate blooms a score of feet above our heads, that were like trees, with willowy trunks of trees as thick as a man's arm. Here we refreshed ourselves with drinking-coconuts, while a cowboy rode a dozen miles to the nearest telephone and summoned a machine from town. The town itself we could see, the Lakanaii metropolis of Olokona, a smudge of smoke on the shore-line, as we looked down across the miles of cane-fields, the billow-wreathed reef-lines, and the blue haze of ocean to where the island of Oahu shimmered like a dim opal on the horizon.

Maui is the Valley Isle of Hawaii and Kauai the Garden Isle; but Lakanaii, lying abreast of Oahu, is recognized in the present, and was known of old and always, as the Jewel Isle of the group. Not the largest, nor merely the smallest, Lakanaii is conceded by all to be the wildest, the most wildly beautiful, and, in its size, the richest of all the islands. Its sugar tonnage per acre is the highest, its mountain beef-cattle the fattest, its rainfall the most generous without ever being disastrous. It resembles Kauai in that it is the first-formed and therefore the oldest island, so that it had had time sufficient to break down its lava rock into the richest soil, and to erode the canyons between the ancient craters until they are like Grand Canyons of the Colorado, with number-less waterfalls plunging thousands of feet in the sheer or dissipat-ing into veils of vapor, and evanescing in mid-air to descend softly and invisibly through a mirage of rainbows, like so much dew or gentle shower, upon the abyss-floors.

Yet Lakanaii is easy to describe. But how can one describe Prince Akuli? To know him is to know all Lakanaii most thoroughly. In addition, one must know thoroughly a great deal of the rest of the world. In the first place, Prince Akuli has no recognized nor legal right to be called 'Prince.' Furthermore, 'Akuli' means the 'squid'. So that Prince Squid could scarcely be the dignified title of the straight descendant of the oldest and highest *aliis* (high chiefs) of Hawaii – an old and exclusive stock, wherein, in the ancient way of the Egyptian Pharaohs, brothers and sisters had even wed on the throne for the reason that they could not marry beneath rank, that in all their known world there was none of higher rank, and that, at every hazard, the dynasty must be perpetuated.

I have heard Prince Akuli's singing historians (inherited from his father) chanting their interminable genealogies, by which they demonstrated that he was the highest *alii* in all Hawaii. Beginning with Wakea, who is their Adam, and with Papa, their Eve, through as many generations as there are letters in our alphabet they trace down to Nanakaoko, the first ancestor born in Hawaii and whose wife was Kahihiokalani. Later, but always highest, their generations split from the generations of Ua, who was the founder of the two distinct lines of the Kauai and Oahu kings.

In the eleventh century AD, by the Lakanaii historians, at the time brothers and sisters mated because none existed to excel them, their rank received a boost of new blood of rank that was next to heaven's door. One Hoikemaha, steering by the stars and the ancient traditions, arrived in a great double-canoe from Samoa. He married a lesser *alii* of Lakanaii, and when his three sons were grown, returned with them to Samoa to bring back his own youngest brother. But with him he brought back Kumi, the son of Tui Manua, which latter's rank was highest in all

Polynesia, and barely second to that of the demigods and gods. So the estimable seed of Kumi, eight centuries before, had entered into the *aliis* of Lakanaii, and been passed down by them in the undeviating line to reposit in Prince Akuli.

Him I first met, talking with an Oxford accent, in the officers' mess of the Black Watch in South Africa. This was just before that famous regiment was cut to pieces at Magersfontein. He had as much right to be in that mess as he had to his accent, for he was Oxford-educated and held the Queen's Commission. With him, as his guest, taking a look at the war, was Prince Cupid, so nicknamed, but the true prince of all Hawaii, including Lakanaii, whose real and legal title was Prince Jonah Kuhio Kalanianaole, and who might have been the living King of Hawaii Nei had it not been for the *haole* (white man) Revolution and Annexation – this, despite the fact that Prince Cupid's *alii* genealogy was lesser to the heaven-boosted genealogy of Prince Akuli. For Prince Akuli might have been King of Lakanaii, and of all Hawaii, perhaps, had not his grandfather been soundly thrashed by the first and greatest of the Kamehamehas.

This had occurred in the year 1810, in the booming days of the sandalwood trade, and in the same year that the King of Kauai came in, and was good, and ate out of Kamehameha's hand. Prince Akuli's grandfather, in that year, had received his trouncing and subjugating because he was 'old school'. He had not imaged island empire in terms of gunpowder and *haole* gunners. Kamehameha, farther-visioned, had annexed the service of *haoles*, including such men as Isaac Davis, mate and sole survivor of the massacred crew of the schooner *Fair American*, and John Young, captured boatswain of the snow *Eleanor*. And Isaac Davis, and John Young, and others of their waywardly adventurous ilk, with six-pounder brass carronades from the captured *Iphigenia* and *Fair American*, had destroyed the war canoes and shattered the morale of the King of Lakanaii's land-fighters, receiving duly in return from Kamehameha, according to agreement: Isaac Davis, six hundred mature and fat hogs; John Young, five hundred of the same described pork on the hoof that was split.

And so, out of all incests and lusts of the primitive cultures and beast-man's gropings toward the stature of manhood, out of all red murders, and brute battlings, and matings with the younger brothers of the demigods, world-polished, Oxford-accented, twentieth century to the tick of the second, comes Prince Akuli, Prince Squid, pure-veined Polynesian, a living bridge across the thousand centuries, comrade, friend and fellow-traveler out of his wrecked seven-thousand-dollar limousine, marooned with me in a begonia paradise fourteen hundred feet above the sea, and his island metropolis of Olokona, to tell me of his mother, who reverted in her old age to ancientness of religious concept and ancestor worship, and collected and surrounded herself with the charnel bones of those who had been her forerunners back in the darkness of time.

'King Kalakaua started this collecting fad, over on Oahu,' Prince Akuli continued. 'And his queen, Kapiolani, caught the fad from him. They collected everything – old *makaloa* mats, old *tapas*, old calabashes, old double-canoes and idols which the priests had saved from the general destruction in 1819. I haven't seen a pearl-shell fish-hook in years, but I swear that Kalakaua accumulated ten thousand of them, to say nothing of human jaw-bone fish-hooks, and feather cloaks, and capes and helmets, and stone adzes, and *poi*-pounders of phallic design. When he and Kapiolani made their royal progresses around the islands, their hosts had to hide away their personal relics. For to the king, in theory, belongs all property of his people; and with Kalakaua, when it came to the old things, theory and practice were one.

'From him my father, Kanau, got the collecting bee in his bonnet, and Hiwilani was likewise infected. But father was modern to his finger-tips. He believed neither in the gods of the *kahunas*' (priests) 'nor of the missionaries. He didn't believe in anything except sugar stocks, horse-breeding, and that his grand-father had been a fool in not collecting a few Isaac Davises and John Youngs and brass carronades before he went to war with Kamehameha. So he collected curios in the pure collector's spirit; but my mother took it seriously. That was why she went in for bones. I remember, too, she had an ugly old stone-idol she used to yammer to and crawl around on the floor before. It's in the

Deacon Museum now. I sent it there after her death, and her collection of bones to the Royal Mausoleum in Olokona.

'I don't know whether you remember her father was Kaaukuu. Well, he was, and he was a giant. When they built the Mausoleum, his bones, nicely cleaned and preserved, were dug out of their hiding-place, and placed in the Mausoleum. Hiwilani had an old retainer, Ahuna. She stole the key from Kanau one night, and made Ahuna go and steal her father's bones out of the Mausoleum. I know. And he must have been a giant. She kept him in one of her big jars. One day, when I was a tidy size of a lad, and curious to know if Kaaukuu was as big as tradition had him, I fished his intact lower jaw out of the jar, and the wrappings, and tried it on. I stuck my head right through it, and it rested around my neck and on my shoulders like a horse collar. And every tooth was in the jaw, whiter than procelain, without a cavity, the enamel unstained and unchipped. I got the walloping of my life for that offence, although she had to call old Ahuna in to help give it to me. But the incident served me well. It won her confidence in me that I was not afraid of the bones of the dead ones, and it won for me my Oxford education. As you shall see, if that car doesn't arrive first.

'Old Ahuna was one of the real old ones with the hall-mark on him and branded into him of faithful born-slave service. He knew more about my mother's family, and my father's, than did both of them put together. And he knew, what no living other knew, the burial-place of centuries, where were hid the bones of most of her ancestors and of Kanau's. Kanau couldn't worm it out of the old fellow, who looked upon Kanau as an apostate.

'Hiwilani struggled with the old codger for years. How she ever succeeded is beyond me. Of course, on the face of it, she was faithful to the old religion. This might have persuaded Ahuna to loosen up a little. Or she may have jolted fear into him; for she knew a lot of the line of chatter of the old Huni sorcerers, and she could make a noise like being on terms of utmost intimacy with Uli, who is the chiefest god of sorcery of all the sorcerers. She could skin the ordinary *kahuna lapaau*' (medicine man) 'when it came to praying to Lonopuha and Koleamoku; read dreams and visions and signs and omens and indigestions to beat the band; make the practitioners under the medicine god, Maiola, look like thirty cents; pull off a *pule hee* incantation that would make them dizzy; and she claimed to a practice of *kahuna hoenoho*, which is modern spiritism, second to none. I have myself seen her drink the wind, throw a fit, and prophesy. The *aumakuas* were brothers to her when she slipped offerings to them across the altars of the ruined *heiaus*' (temples) 'with a line of prayer that was as unintelligible to me as it was hair-raising. And as for old Ahuna, she could make him get down on the floor and yammer and bite himself when she pulled the real mystery dope on him.

'Nevertheless, my private opinion is that it was the *anaana* stuff that got him. She snipped off a lock of his hair one day with a pair of manicure scissors. This lock of hair was what we call the *maunu*, meaning the bait. And she took jolly good care to let him know she had that bit of his hair. Then she tipped it off to him that she had buried it, and was deeply engaged each night in her offerings and incantations to Uli.'

'That was the regular praying-to-death?' I queried in the pause of Prince Akuli's lighting his cigarette.

'Sure thing,' he nodded. 'And Ahuna fell for it. First he tried to locate the hiding-place of the bait of his hair. Failing that, he hired a *pahiuhiu* sorcerer to find it for him. But Hiwilani queered that game by threatening to the sorcerer to practise *apo leo* on him, which is the art of permanently depriving a person of the power of speech without otherwise injuring him.

'Then it was that Ahuna began to pine away and get more like a corpse every day. In desperation he appealed to Kanau. I happened to be present. You have heard what sort of a man my father was.

'"Pig!" he called Ahuna. "Swine-brains! Stinking fish! Die and be done with it. You are a fool. It is all nonsense. There is nothing in anything. The drunken *haole*, Howard, can prove the missionaries wrong. Square-face gin proves Howard wrong. The doctors say he won't last six months. Even square-face gin lies. Life is a liar, too. And here are hard times upon us, and a slump in sugar. Glanders has got into my brood mares. I wish I could lie down and sleep for a hundred years, and wake up to find sugar up a hundred points."

'Father was something of a philosopher himself, with a bitter wit and a trick of spitting out staccato epigrams. He clapped his hands. "Bring me a high-ball," he commanded; "no, bring me two high-balls." Then he turned on Ahuna. "Go and let yourself die, old heathen, survival of darkness, blight of the Pit that you are. But don't die on these premises. I desire merriment and laughter, and the sweet tickling of music, and the beauty of youthful motion, not the croaking of sick toads and googly-eyed corpses about me still afoot on their shaky legs. I'll be that way soon enough if I live long enough. And it will be my everlasting regret if I don't live long enough. Why in hell did I sink that last twenty thousand into Curtis's plantation? Howard warned me the slump was coming, but I thought it was the square-face making him lie. And Curtis has blown his brains out, and his head *luna* has run away with his daughter, and the sugar chemist has got typhoid, and everything's going to smash."

'He clapped his hands for his servants, and commanded: "Bring me my singing boys. And the *hula* dancers – plenty of them. And send for old Howard. Somebody's got to pay, and I'll shorten his six months of life by a month. But above all, music. Let there be music. It is stronger than drink, and quicker than opium."

'He with his music druggery! It was his father, the old savage, who was entertained on board a French frigate, and for the first time heard an orchestra. When the little concert was over, the captain, to find which piece he liked best, asked which piece he'd like repeated. Well, when grandfather got done describing, what piece do you think it was?'

I gave up, while the Prince lighted a fresh cigarette.

'Why, it was the first one, of course. Not the real first one, but the tuning up that preceded it.'

I nodded, with eyes and face mirthful of appreciation, and Prince Akuli, with another apprehensive glance at the old *wahine* and her half-made *hala lei*, returned to his tale of the bones of his ancestors.

'It was somewhere around this stage of the game that old Ahuna gave in to Hiwilani. He didn't exactly give in. He compromised. That's where I come in. If he would bring her the bones of her mother, and of her grandfather (who was the father of Kaaukuu, and who by tradition was rumored to have been even bigger than his giant son), she would return to Ahuna the bait of his hair she was praying him to death with. He, on the other hand, stipulated that he was not to reveal to her the secret burial-place of all the *alii* of Lakanaii all the way back. Nevertheless, he was too old to dare the adventure alone, must be helped by some one who of necessity would come to know the secret, and I was that one. I was the highest *alii*, beside my father and mother, and they were no higher than I.

'So I came upon the scene, being summoned into the twilight room to confront those two dubious old ones who dealt with the dead. They were a pair – mother fat to despair of helplessness, Ahuna thin as a skeleton and as fragile. Of her one had the impression that if she lay down on her back she could not roll over without the aid of block-and-tackle; of Ahuna one's impression was that the tooth-pickedness of him would shatter to splinters if one bumped into him.

'And when they had broached the matter, there was more *pilikia*' (trouble). 'My father's attitude stiffened my resolution. I refused to go on the bone-snatching expedition. I said I didn't care a whoop for the bones of all the *aliis* of my family and race. You see, I had just discovered Jules Verne, loaned me by old Howard, and was reading my head off. Bones? When there were North Poles, and Centres of Earths, and hairy comets to ride across space among the stars! Of course I didn't want to go on any bone-snatching expedition. I said my father was able-bodied, and he could go, splitting equally with her whatever bones he brought back. But she said he was only a blamed collector – or words to that effect, only stronger.

'"I know him," she assured me. "He'd bet his mother's bones on a horse-race or an ace-full."

'I stood with father when it came to modern scepticism, and I told her the whole thing was rubbish. "Bones?" I said. "What are bones? Even field mice, and many rats, and cockroaches have bones, though the roaches wear their bones outside their meat instead of inside. The difference between man and other animals," I told her, "is not bones, but brain. Why, a bullock has bigger bones than a man, and more than one fish I've eaten has more bones, while a whale beats creation when it comes to bone."

'It was frank talk, which is our Hawaiian way, as you have long since learned. In return, equally frank, she regretted she hadn't given me away as a feeding child when I was born. Next she bewailed that she had ever borne me. From that it was only a step to *anaana* me. She threatened me with it, and I did the bravest thing I have ever done. Old Howard had given me a knife of many blades, and corkscrews, and screw-drivers, and all sorts of contrivances, including a tiny pair of scissors. I proceeded to pare my finger-nails.

'"There," I said, as I put the parings into her hand. "Just to show you what I think of it. There's bait and to spare. Go on and *anaana* me if you can."

'I have said it was brave. It was. I was only fifteen, and I had lived all my days in the thick of the mystery stuff, while my scepticism, very recently acquired, was only skin-deep. I could be a sceptic out in the open in the sunshine. But I was afraid of the dark. And in that twilight room, the bones of the dead all about me in the big jars, why, the old lady had me scared stiff. As we say to-day, she had my goat. Only I was brave and didn't let on. And I put my bluff across, for my mother flung the parings into my face and burst into tears. Tears in an elderly woman weighing three hundred and twenty pounds are scarcely impressive, and I hardened the brassiness of my bluff.

'She shifted her attack, and proceeded to talk with the dead. Nay, more, she summoned them there, and, though I was all ripe to see but couldn't, Ahuna saw the father of Kaaukuu in the corner and lay down on the floor and yammered. Just the same, although I almost saw the old giant, I didn't quite see him.

'"Let him talk for himself," I said. But Hiwilani persisted in doing the talking for him, and in laying upon me his solemn injunction that I must go with Ahuna to the burial-place and bring back the bones desired by my mother. But I argued that if the dead ones could be invoked to kill living men by wasting sicknesses, and that if the dead ones could transport themselves from their burial-crypts into the corner of her room, I couldn't see why they shouldn't leave their bones behind them, there in her room and ready to be jarred, when they said good-by and departed for the middle world, the over world, or the under world, or wherever they abided when they weren't paying social calls.

'Whereupon mother let loose on poor old Ahuna, or let loose upon him the ghost of Kaaukuu's father, supposed to be crouching there in the corner, who commanded Ahuna to divulge to her the burial-place. I tried to stiffen him up, telling him to let the old ghost divulge the secret himself, than whom nobody else knew it better, seeing that he had resided there upwards of a century. But Ahuna was old school. He possessed no iota of scepticism. The more Hiwilani frightened him, the more he rolled on the floor and the louder he yammered.

'But when he began to bite himself, I gave in. I felt sorry for him; but, over and beyond that, I began to admire him. He was sterling stuff, even if he was a survival of darkness. Here, with the fear of mystery cruelly upon him, believing Hiwilani's dope implicitly, he was caught between two fidelities. She was his living *alii*, his *alii kapo*' (sacred chiefess). 'He must be faithful to her, yet more faithful must he be to all the dead and gone *aliis* of her line who depended solely on him that their bones should not be disturbed.

'I gave in. But I, too, imposed stipulations. Steadfastly had my father, new school, refused to let me go to England for my education. That sugar was slumping was reason sufficient for him. Steadfastly had my mother, old school, refused, her heathen mind too dark to place any value on education, while it was shrewd enough to discern that education led to unbelief in all that was old. I wanted to study, to study science, the arts, philosophy, to study everything old Howard knew, which enabled him, on the edge of the grave, undauntedly to sneer at superstition, and to give me Jules Verne to read. He was an Oxford man before he went wild and wrong, and it was he who had set the Oxford bee buzzing in my noddle.

'In the end Ahuna and I, old school and new school leagued together, won out. Mother promised that she'd make father send me to England, even if she had to pester him into a prolonged drinking that would make his digestion go back on him. Also, Howard was to accompany me, so that I could decently bury him in England. He was a queer one, old Howard, an individual if there ever was one. Let me tell you a little story about him. It was when Kalakaua was starting on his trip around the world. You remember, when Armstrong, and Judd, and the drunken valet of a German baron accompanied him. Kalakaua made the proposition to Howard . . .'

But here the long-apprehended calamity fell upon Prince Akuli. The old *wahine* had finished her *lei hala*. Barefooted, with no adornment of femininity, clad in a shapeless shift of much-washed cotton, with age-withered face and labor-gnarled hands, she cringed before him and crooned a *mele* in his honor, and, still cringing, put the *lei* around his neck. It is true the *hala* smelled most freshly strong, yet was the act beautiful to me, and the old woman herself beautiful to me. My mind leapt into the Prince's narrative so that to Ahuna I could not help likening her.

Oh, truly, to be an *alii* in Hawaii, even in this second decade of the twentieth century, is no light thing. The *alii*, utterly of the new, must be kindly and kingly to those old ones absolutely of the old. Nor did the Prince without a kingdom, his loved island long since annexed by the United States and incorporated into a territory along with the rest of the Hawaiian Islands – nor did the Prince betray his repugnance for the odor of the *hala*. He bowed his head graciously; and his royal condescending words of pure Hawaiian I knew would make the old woman's heart warm until she died with remembrance of the wonderful occasion. The wry grimace he stole to me would not have been made had he felt any uncertainty of its escaping her.

'And so,' Prince Akuli resumed, after the *wahine* had tottered away in an ecstasy, 'Ahuna and I departed on our grave-robbing adventure. You know the Iron-bound Coast.'

I nodded, knowing full well the spectacle of those lava leagues of weather coast, truly iron-bound so far as landing-places or anchorages were concerned, great forbidding cliff-walls thousands of feet in height, their summits wreathed in cloud and rain squall, their knees hammered by the trade-wind billows into spouting, spuming white, the air, from sea to rain-cloud, spanned by a myriad leaping waterfalls, provocative, in day or night, of countless sun and lunar rainbows. Valleys, so called, but fissures rather, slit the cyclopean walls here and there, and led away into a lofty and madly vertical back country, most of it inaccessible to the foot of man and trod only by the wild goat.

'Precious little you know of it,' Prince Akuli retorted, in reply to my nod. 'You've seen it only from the decks of steamers. There are valleys there, inhabited valleys, out of which there is no exit by land, and perilously accessible by canoe only on the selected days of two months in the year. When I was twenty-eight I was over there in one of them on a hunting trip. Bad weather, in the auspicious period, marooned us for three weeks. Then five of my party and myself swam for it out through the surf. Three of us made the canoes waiting for us. The other two were flung back on the sand, each with a broken arm. Save for us, the entire party remained there until the next year, ten months afterward. And one of them was Wilson, of Wilson & Wall, the Honolulu sugar factors. And he was engaged to be married.

'I've seen a goat, shot above by a hunter above, land at my feet a thousand yards underneath. *Believe* me, that landscape seemed to rain goats and rocks for ten minutes. One of my canoemen fell off the trail between the two little valleys of Aipio and Luno. He hit first fifteen hundred feet beneath us, and fetched up in a ledge three hundred feet farther down. We didn't bury him. We couldn't get to him, and flying machines had not yet been invented. His bones are there now, and barring earthquake and volcano, will be there when the Trumps of Judgment sound.

'Goodness me! Only the other day, when our Promotion

Committee, trying to compete with Honolulu for the tourist trade, called in the engineers to estimate what it would cost to build a scenic drive around the Iron-bound Coast, the lowest figures were a quarter of a million dollars a mile!

'And Ahuna and I, an old man and a young boy, started for that stern coast in a canoe paddled by old men! The youngest of them, the steersman, was over sixty, while the rest of them averaged seventy at the very least. There were eight of them, and we started in the night-time, so that none should see us go. Even those old ones, trusted all their lives, knew no more than the fringe of the secret. To the fringe, only, could they take us.

'And the fringe was – I don't mind telling that much – the fringe was Ponuloo Valley. We got there the third afternoon following. The old chaps weren't strong on the paddles. It was a funny expedition, into such wild waters, with now one and now another of our ancient-mariner crew collapsing and even fainting. One of them actually died on the second morning out. We buried him overside. It was positively uncanny, the heathen ceremonies those gray ones pulled off in burying their gray brother. And I was only fifteen, *alii kapo* over them by blood of heathenness and right of hereditary heathen rule, with a penchant for Jules Verne and shortly to sail for England for my education! So one learns. Small wonder my father was a philosopher, in his own lifetime spanning the history of man from human sacrifice and idol worship, through the religions of man's upward striving, to the Medusa of rank atheism at the end of it all. Small wonder that, like old Ecclesiastes, he found vanity in all things and surcease in sugar stocks, singing boys and *hula* dancers.'

Prince Akuli debated with his soul for an interval.

'Oh, well,' he sighed, 'I have done some spanning of time myself.' He sniffed disgustedly of the odor of the *hala lei* that stifled him. 'It stinks of the ancient,' he vouchsafed. 'I? I stink of the modern. My father was right. The sweetest of all is sugar up a hundred points, or four aces in a poker game. If the Big War lasts another year, I shall clean up three-quarters of a million over a million. If peace breaks to-morrow, with the consequent slump, I could enumerate a hundred who will lose my direct bounty, and go into the old natives' homes my father and I long since endowed for them.'

He clapped his hands, and the old *wahine* tottered toward him in an excitement of haste to serve. She cringed before him, as he drew pad and pencil from his breast pocket.

'Each month, old woman of our old race,' he addressed her, 'will you receive, by rural free delivery, a piece of written paper that you can exchange with any storekeeper anywhere for ten dollars gold. This shall be so for as long as you live. Behold! I write the record and the remembrance of it, here and now, with this pencil on this paper. And this is because you are of my race and service, and because you have honored me this day with your mats to sit upon and your thrice-blessed and thrice-delicious *lei hala*.'

He turned to me a weary and sceptical eye, saying:

'And if I die to-morrow, not alone will the lawyers contest my disposition of my property, but they will contest my benefactions and my pensions accorded, and the clarity of my mind.

'It was the right weather of the year; but even then, with our old weak ones at the paddles, we did not attempt the landing until we had assembled half the population of Ponuloo Valley down on the steep little beach. Then we counted our waves, selected the best one, and ran in on it. Of course, the canoe was swamped and the outrigger smashed, but the ones on shore dragged us up unharmed beyond the wash.

'Ahuna gave his orders. In the night-time all must remain within their houses, and the dogs be tied up and have their jaws bound so that there should be no barking. And in the night-time Ahuna and I stole out on our journey, no one knowing whether we went to the right or left or up the valley toward its head. We carried jerky, and hard *poi* and dried *aku*, and from the quantity of the food I knew we were to be gone several days. Such a trail! A Jacob's ladder to the sky, truly, for that first *pali*' (precipice), 'almost straight up, was three thousand feet above the sea. And we did it in the dark!

'At the top, beyond the sight of the valley we had left, we slept until daylight on the hard rock in a hollow nook Ahuna knew, and that was so small that we were squeezed. And the old fellow, for fear that I might move in the heavy restlessness of lad's sleep, lay on the outside with one arm resting across me. At daybreak, I saw why. Between us and the lip of the cliff scarcely a yard intervened. I crawled to the lip and looked, watching the abyss take on immensity in the growing light and trembling from the fear of height that was upon me. At last I made out the sea, over half a mile straight beneath. And we had done this thing in the dark!

'Down in the next valley, which was a very tiny one, we found evidence of the ancient population, but there were no people. The only way was the crazy foot-paths up and down the dizzy valley walls from valley to valley. But lean and aged as Ahuna was, he seemed untirable. In the second valley dwelt an old leper in hiding. He did not know me, and when Ahuna told him who I was, he groveled at my feet, almost clasping them, and mumbled a *mele* of all my line out of a lipless mouth.

'The next valley proved to be the valley. It was long and so narrow that its floor had caught not sufficient space of soil to grow *taro* for a single person. Also, it had no beach, the stream that threaded it leaping a *pali* of several hundred feet down to the sea. It was a god-forsaken place of naked, eroded lava, to which only rarely could the scant vegetation find root-hold. For miles we followed up that winding fissure through the towering walls, far into the chaos of back country that lies behind the Iron-bound Coast. How far that valley penetrated I do not know, but, from the quantity of water in the stream, I judged it far. We did not go to the valley's head. I could see Ahuna casting glances to all the peaks, and I knew he was taking bearings, known to him alone, from natural objects. When he halted at the last, it was with abrupt certainty. His bearings had crossed. He threw down the portion of food and outfit he had carried, It was the place. I looked on either hand at the hard, implacable walls, naked of vegetation, and could dream of no burial-place possible in such bare adamant.

'We ate, then stripped for work. Only did Ahuna permit me to retain my shoes. He stood beside me at the edge of a deep pool, likewise appareled and prodigiously skinny.

'"You will dive down into the pool at this spot," he said. "Search the rock with your hands as you descend, and, about a fathom and a half down, you will find a hole. Enter it, head-first, but going slowly, for the lava rock is sharp and may cut your head and body."

'"And then?" I queried. "You will find the hole growing larger," was his answer. "When you have gone all of eight fathoms along the passage, come up slowly, and you will find your head in the air, above water, in the dark. Wait there then for me. The water is very cold."

'It didn't sound good to me. I was thinking, not of the cold water and the dark, but of the bones. "You go first," I said. But he claimed he could not. "You are my *alii*, my prince," he said. "It is impossible that I should go before you into the sacred burial-place of your kingly ancestors."

'But the prospect did not please. "Just cut out this prince stuff," I told him. "It isn't what it's cracked up to be. You go first, and I'll never tell on you." "Not alone the living must we please," he admonished, "but, more so, the dead must we please. Nor can we lie to the dead."

'We argued it out, and for half an hour it was stalemate. I wouldn't, and he simply couldn't. He tried to buck me up by appealing to my pride. He chanted the heroic deeds of my ancestors; and, I remember especially, he sang to me of Moko-moku, my great-grandfather and the gigantic father of the gigantic Kaaukuu, telling how thrice in battle Mokomoku leaped among his foes, seizing by the neck a warrior in either hand and knocking their heads together until they were dead. But this was not what decided me. I really felt sorry for old Ahuna, he was so beside himself for fear the expedition would come to naught. And I was coming to a great admiration for the old fellow, not least among the reasons being the fact of his lying down to sleep between me and the cliff-lip.

'So, with true *alii*-authority of command, saying, "You will immediately follow after me," I dived in. Everything he had said was correct. I found the entrance to the subterranean passage, swam carefully through it, cutting my shoulder once on the lava-sharp roof, and emerged in the darkness and air. But before I could count thirty, he broke water beside me, rested his hand on my arm to make sure of me, and directed me to swim ahead of him for the matter of a hundred feet or so. Then we touched bottom and climbed out on the rocks. And still no light, and I remember I was glad that our altitude was too high for centipedes.

'He had brought with him a coconut calabash, tightly stoppered, of whale-oil that must have been landed on Lahaina beach thirty years before. From his mouth he took a water-tight arrangement of a matchbox composed of two empty rifle-cartridges fitted snugly together. He lighted the wicking that floated on the oil, and I looked about, and knew disappointment. No burial-chamber was it, but merely a lava tube such as occurs on all the islands.

'He put the calabash of light into my hands and started me ahead of him on the way, which he assured me was long, but not too long. It was long, at least a mile in my sober judgment, though at the time it seemed five miles; and it ascended sharply. When Ahuna, at the last, stopped me, I knew we were close to our goal. He knelt on his lean old knees on the sharp lava rock, and clasped my knees with his skinny arms. My hand that was free of the calabash lamp he placed on his head. He chanted to me, with his old cracked, quavering voice, the line of my descent and my essential high *alii*-ness. And then he said:

'"Tell neither Kanau nor Hiwilani aught of what you are about to behold. There is no sacredness in Kanau. His mind is filled with sugar and the breeding of horses. I do know that he sold a feather cloak his grandfather had worn to that English collector for eight thousand dollars, and the money he lost the next day betting on the polo game between Maui and Oahu. Hiwilani, your mother, is filled with sacredness. She is too much filled with sacredness. She grows old, and weak-headed, and she traffics over-much with sorceries."

'"No," I made answer. "I shall tell no one. If I did, then I would have to return to this place again. And I do not want ever to return to this place. I'll try anything once. This I shall never try twice."

'"It is well," he said, and arose, falling behind so that I should enter first. Also, he said: "Your mother is old. I shall bring her, as promised, the bones of her mother and of her grandfather. These should content her until she dies; and then, if I die before her, it is you who must see to it that all the bones in her family collection are placed in the Royal Mausoleum."

'I have given all the Islands' museums the once-over,' Prince Akuli lapsed back into slang, 'and I must say that the totality of the collections cannot touch what I saw in our Lakanaii burial-cave. Remember, and with reason and history, we trace back the highest and oldest genealogy in the Islands. Everything that I had ever dreamed or heard of, and much more that I had not, was there. The place was wonderful. Ahuna, sepulchrally mutter-ing prayers and *meles*, moved about, lighting various whale-oil lamp-calabashes. They were all there, the Hawaiian race from the beginning of Hawaiian time. Bundles of bones and bundles of bones, all wrapped decently in *tapa*, until for all the world it was like the parcels-post department at a post office.

'And everything! *Kahilis*, which you may know developed out of the fly-flapper into symbols of royalty until they became larger than hearse-plumes with handles a fathom and a half and over two fathoms in length. And such handles! Of the wood of the *kauila*, inlaid with shell and ivory and bone with a cleverness that had died out among our artificers a century before. It was a centuries-old family attic. For the first time I saw things I had only heard of, such as the *pahoas*, fashioned of whale-teeth and suspended by braided human hair, and worn on the breast only by the highest of rank.

'There were *tapas* and mats of the rarest and oldest; capes and *leis* and helmets and cloaks, priceless all, except the too-ancient ones, of the feathers of the *mamo*, and of the *iwi* and the *akakane* and the *o-o*. I saw one of the *mamo* cloaks that was superior to that finest one in the Bishop Museum in Honolulu, and that they value at between half a million and a million dollars. Goodness

me, I thought at the time, it was lucky Kanau didn't know about
it.

'Such a mess of things! Carved gourds and calabashes, shell-
scrapers, nets of *olona* fiber, a junk of *iè-iè* baskets and fish-hooks
of every bone and spoon of shell. Musical instruments of the
forgotten days – *ukukes* and nose flutes, and *kiokios* which are
likewise played with one unstoppered nostril. Taboo *poi* bowls
and finger bowls, left-handed adzes of the canoe gods, lava-cup
lamps, stone mortars and pestles and *poi*-pounders. And adzes
again, a myriad of them, beautiful ones, from an ounce in wieght
for the finer carving of idols to fifteen pounds for the felling of
trees, and all with the sweetest handles I have ever beheld.

'There were the *kaekeekes* – you know, our ancient drums,
hollowed sections of the coconut tree, covered one end with
shark-skin. The first *kaekeeke* of all Hawaii Ahuna pointed out to
me and told me the tale. It was manifestly most ancient. He was
afraid to touch it for fear the age-rotted wood of it would crumble
to dust, the ragged tatters of the shark-skin head of it still
attached. "This is the very oldest and father of all our *kaekeekes*,"
Ahuna told me. "Kila, the son of Moikeha, brought it back from
far Raiatea in the South Pacific. And it was Kila's own son,
Kahai, who made that same journey, and was gone ten years,
and brought back with him from Tahiti the first breadfruit trees
that sprouted and grew on Hawaiian soil."

'And the bones and bones! The parcel-delivery array of them!
Besides the small bundles of the long bones, there were full
skeletons, *tapa*-wrapped, lying in one-man, and two- and three-
man canoes of precious *koa* wood, with curved outriggers of
wiliwili wood, and proper paddles to hand with the *io*-projection
at the point simulating the continuance of the handle, as if, like
a skewer, thrust through the flat length of the blade. And their
war weapons were laid away by the sides of the lifeless bones
that had wielded them – rusty old horse-pistols, derringers,
pepper-boxes, five-barrelled fantastiques, Kentucky long rifles,
muskets handled in trade by John Company and Hudson's Bay,
shark-tooth swords, wooden stabbing-knives, arrows and spears

bone-headed of the fish and the pig and of man, and spears and arrows wooden-headed and fire-hardened.

'Ahuna put a spear in my hand, headed and pointed finely with the long shin-bone of a man, and told me the tale of it. But first he unwrapped the long bones, arms and legs, of two parcels, the bones, under the wrappings, neatly tied like so many faggots. "This," said Ahuna, exhibiting the pitiful white contents of one parcel, "is Laulani. She was the wife of Akaiko, whose bones, now placed in your hands, much larger and male-like as you observe, held up the flesh of a large man, a three hundred pounder seven-footer, three centuries agone. And this spear-head is made of the shin-bone of Keola, a mighty wrestler and runner of their own time and place. And he loved Laulani, and she fled with him. But in a forgotten battle on the sands of Kalini, Akaiko rushed the lines of the enemy, leading the charge that was successful, and seized upon Keola, his wife's lover, and threw him to the ground, and sawed through his neck to the death with a shark-tooth knife. Thus, in the old days as always, did man combat for woman with man. And Laulani was beautiful; that Keola should be made into a spearhead for her! She was formed like a queen, and her body was a long bowl of sweetness, and her fingers *lomi'd*" (massaged) "to slimness and smallness at her mother's breast. For ten generations have we remembered her beauty. Your father's singing boys to-day sing of her beauty in the *hula* that is named of her. This is Laulani, whom you hold in your hands."

'And, Ahuna done, I could but gaze, with imagination at the one time sobered and fired. Old drunken Howard had lent me his Tennyson, and I had mooned long and often over the *Idyls of the King*. Here were the three, I thought – Arthur, and Launcelot, and Guinevere. This, then, I pondered, was the end of it all, of life and strife and striving and love, the weary spirits of these long-gone ones to be invoked by fat old women and mangy sorcerers, the bones of them to be esteemed of collectors and betted on horse-races and ace-fulls or to be sold for cash and invested in sugar stocks.

'For me it was illumination. I learned there in the burial-cave the great lesson. And to Ahuna I said: "The spear headed with the long bone of Keola I shall take for my own. Never shall I sell it. I shall keep it always."

'"And for what purpose?" he demanded. And I replied: "That the contemplation of it may keep my hand sober and my feet on earth with the knowledge that few men are fortunate enough to have as much of a remnant of themselves as will compose a spear-head when they are three centuries dead."

'And Ahuna bowed his head, and praised my wisdom of judgment. But at that moment the long-rotted *olona*-cord broke and the pitiful woman's bones of Laulani shed from my clasp and clattered on the rocky floor. One shin-bone, in some way deflected, fell under the dark shadow of a canoe-bow, and I made up my mind that it should be mine. So I hastened to help him in the picking up of the bones and the tying, so that he did not notice its absence.

'"This," said Ahuna, introducing me to another of my ancestors, "is your great-grandfather, Mokomoku, the father of Kaaukuu. Behold the size of his bones. He was a giant. I shall carry him, because of the long spear of Keola that will be difficult for you to carry away. And this is Lelemahoa, your grandmother, the mother of your mother, that you shall carry. And day grows short, and we must still swim up through the waters to the sun ere darkness hides the sun from the world."

'But Ahuna, putting out the various calabashes of light by drowning the wicks in the whale-oil, did not observe me include the shin-bone of Laulani with the bones of my grandmother.'

The honk of the automobile, sent up from Olokona to rescue us, broke off the Prince's narrative. We said good-by to the ancient and fresh-pensioned *wahine*, and departed. A half-mile on our way, Prince Akuli resumed.

'So Ahuna and I returned to Hiwilani, and to her happiness, lasting to her death the year following, two more of her ancestors abided about her in the jars of her twilight room. Also, she kept her compact and worried my father into sending me to England. I took old Howard along, and he perked up and confuted the doctors, so that it was three years before I buried him restored to the bosom of his family. Sometimes I think he was the most brilliant man I have ever known. Not until my return from England did Ahuna die, the last custodian of our *alii* secrets. And at his death-bed he pledged me again never to reveal the location in that nameless valley, and never to go back myself.

'Much else I have forgotten to mention did I see there in the cave that one time. There were the bones of Kumi, the near demigod, son of Tui Manua of Samoa, who, in the long before, married into my line and heaven-boosted my genealogy. And the bones of my great-grandmother who had slept in the four-poster presented her by Lord Byron. And Ahuna hinted tradition that there was reason for that presentation, as well as for the historically known lingering of the *Blonde* in Olokona for so long. And I held her poor bones in my hands – bones once fleshed with sensate beauty, informed with sparkle and spirit, instinct with love and love-warmness of arms around and eyes and lips together, that had begat me in the end of the generations unborn. It was a good experience. I am modern, 'tis true. I believe in no mystery stuff of old time nor of the *kahunas*. And yet, I saw in that cave things which I dare not name to you, and which I, since old Ahuna died, alone of the living know. I have no children. With me my long line ceases. This is the twentieth century, and we stink of gasolene. Nevertheless these other and nameless things shall die with me. I shall never revisit the burial-place. Nor in all time to come will any man gaze upon it through living eyes unless the quakes of earth rend the mountains asunder and spew forth the secrets contained in the hearts of the mountains.'

Prince Akuli ceased from speech. With welcome relief on his face, he removed the *lei hala* from his neck, and, with a sniff and a sigh, tossed it into concealment in the thick *lantana* by the side of the road.

'But the shin-bone of Laulani?' I queried softly.

He remained silent while a mile of pasture land fled by us and yielded to caneland.

'I have it now,' he at last said. 'And beside it is Keola, slain ere his time and made into a spear-head for love of the woman whose shin-bone abides near to him. To them, those poor pathetic bones, I owe more than to aught else. I became possessed of them in the period of my culminating adolescence. I know they changed the entire course of my life and trend of my mind. They gave to me a modesty and a humility in the world, from which my father's fortune has ever failed to seduce me.

'And often, when woman was nigh to winning to the empery of my mind over me, I sought Laulani's shin-bone. And often, when lusty manhood stung me into feeling overproud and lusty, I consulted the spearhead remnant of Keola, one-time swift runner, and mighty wrestler and lover, and thief of the wife of a king. The contemplation of them has ever been of profound aid to me, and you might well say that I have founded my religion or practice of living upon them.'

THE WATER BABY

I lent a weary ear to old Kohokumu's interminable chanting of the deeds and adventures of Maui, the Promethean demi-god of Polynesia who fished up dry land from ocean depths with hooks made fast to heaven, who lifted up the sky whereunder previously men had gone on all fours, not having space to stand erect, and who made the sun with its sixteen snared legs stand still and agree thereafter to traverse the sky more slowly – the sun being evidently a trade-unionist and believing in the six-hour day, while Maui stood for the open shop and the twelve-hour day.

'Now this,' said Kohokumu, 'is from Queen Lilliuokalani's own family mele:

> '"Maui became restless and fought the sun
> With a noose that he laid.
> And winter won the sun,
> And summer was won by Maui . . ."'

Born in the Islands myself, I know the Hawaiian myths better than this old fisherman, although I possessed not his memorization that enabled him to recite them endless hours.

'And you believe all this?' I demanded in the sweet Hawaiian tongue.

'It was a long time ago,' he pondered. 'I never saw Maui with my own eyes. But all our old men from all the way back tell us these things, as I, an old man, tell them to my sons and grandsons, who will tell them to their sons and grandsons all the way ahead to come.'

'You believe,' I persisted, 'that whopper of Maui roping the sun like a wild steer, and that other whopper of heaving up the sky from off the earth?'

'I am of little worth, and am not wise, O Lakana,' my fisherman made answer. 'Yet have I read the Hawaiian Bible the

missionaries translated to us, and there have I read that your Big
Man of the Beginning made the earth and sky and sun and moon
and stars, and all manner of animals from horses to cockroaches
and from centipedes and mosquitoes to sea lice and jellyfish, and
man and woman and everything, and all in six days. Why, Maui
didn't do anything like that much. He didn't *make* anything. He
just put things in order, that was all, and it took him a long, long
time to make the improvements. And anyway, it is much easier
and more reasonable to believe the little whopper than the big
whopper.'

And what could I reply? He had me on the matter of
reasonableness. Besides, my head ached. And the funny thing, as
I admitted to myself, was that evolution teaches in no uncertain
voice that man did run on all fours ere he came to walk upright,
that astronomy states flatly that the speed of the revolution of
the earth on its axis has diminished steadily, thus increasing the
length of day, and that the seismologists accept that all the
islands of Hawaii were elevated from the ocean floor by volcanic
action.

Fortunately, I saw a bamboo pole, floating on the surface
several hundred feet away, suddenly up-end and start a very
devil's dance. This was a diversion from the profitless discussion,
and Kohokumu and I dipped our paddles and raced the little
outrigger canoe to the dancing pole. Kohokumu caught the line
that was fast to the butt of the pole and underhanded it in until
a two-foot *ukikiki*, battling fiercely to the end, flashed its wet
silver in the sun and began beating a tattoo on the inside bottom
of the canoe. Kohokumu picked up a squirming, slimy squid
with his teeth, bit a chunk of live bait out of it, attached the bait
to the hook, and dropped line and sinker overside. The stick
floated flat on the surface of the water, and the canoe drifted
slowly away. With a survey of the crescent composed of a score
of such sticks all lying flat, Kohokumu wiped his hands on his
naked sides and lifted the wearisome and centuries-old chant of
Kuali:

> '"Oh, the great fishhook of Maui!
> *Manai-i-ka-lani* – 'made fast to the heavens'!

An earth-twisted cord ties the hook,
Engulfed from lofty Kauiki!
Its bait the red-billed Alae,
The bird to Hina sacred!
It sinks far down to Hawaii,
Struggling and in pain dying!
Caught is the land beneath the water,
Floated up, up to the surface,
But Hina hid a wing of the bird
And broke the land beneath the water!
Below was the bait snatched away
And eaten at once by the fishes,
The Ulua of the deep muddy places!"'

His aged voice was hoarse and scratchy from the drinking of too much swipes at a funeral the night before, nothing of which contributed to make me less irritable. My head ached. The sun glare on the water made my eyes ache, while I was suffering more than half a touch of *mal de mer* from the antic conduct of the outrigger on the blobby sea. The air was stagnant. In the lee of Waihee, between the white beach and the reef, no whisper of breeze eased the still sultriness. I really think I was too miserable to summon the resolution to give up the fishing and go in to shore.

Lying back with closed eyes, I lost count of time. I even forgot that Kohokumu was chanting till reminded of it by his ceasing. An exclamation made me bare my eyes to the stab of the sun. He was gazing down through the water glass.

'It's a big one,' he said, passing me the device and slipping overside feet first into the water.

He went under without splash and ripple, turned over, and swam down. I followed his progress through the water glass, which is merely an oblong box a couple of feet long, open at the top, the bottom sealed water-tight with a sheet of ordinary glass.

Now Kohokumu was a bore, and I was squeamishly out of sorts with him for his volubleness, but I could not help admiring him as I watched him go down. Past seventy years of age, lean as a toothpick and shriveled like a mummy, he was doing what few young athletes of my race would do or could do. It was forty feet to bottom. There, partly exposed, but mostly hidden under the bulge of a coral lump, I could discern his objective. His keen eyes had caught the projecting tentacle of a squid. Even as he swam, the tentacle was lazily withdrawn, so that there was no sign of the creature. But the brief exposure of the portion of one tentacle had advertised its owner as a squid of size.

The pressure at a depth of forty feet is no joke for a young man, yet it did not seem to inconvenience this oldster. I am certain it never crossed his mind to be inconvenienced. Unarmed, bare of body save for a brief *malo* or loin cloth, he was undeterred by the formidable creature that constituted his prey. I saw him steady himself with his right hand on the coral lump, and thrust his left arm into the hole to the shoulder. Half a minute elapsed, during which time he seemed to be groping and rooting around with his left hand. Then tentacle after tentacle, myriad-suckered and wildly waving, emerged. Laying hold of his arm, they writhed and coiled about his flesh like so many snakes. With a heave and a jerk appeared the entire squid, a proper devilfish or octopus.

But the old man was in no hurry for his natural element, the air above the water. There, forty feet beneath, wrapped about by an octopus that measured nine feet across from tentacle tip to tentacle tip and that could well drown the stoutest swimmer, he coolly and casually did the one thing that gave to him his empery over the monster. He shoved his lean, hawklike face into the very center of the slimy, squirming mass, and with his several ancient fangs bit into the heart and life of the matter. This accomplished, he came upward slowly, as a swimmer should who is changing atmospheres from the depths. Alongside the canoe, still in the water and peeling off the grisly clinging thing, the incorrigible old sinner burst into the *pule* of triumph which had been chanted by countless squid-catching generations before him:

> '"O Kanaloa of the taboo nights!
> Stand upright on the solid floor!
> Stand upon the floor where lies the squid!

> Stand up to take the squid of the deep sea!
> Rise up, O Kanaloa!
> Stir up! Stir up! Let the squid awake!
> Let the squid that lies flat awake!
> Let the squid that lies spread out . . .'' '

I closed my eyes and ears, not offering to lend him a hand, secure in the knowledge that he could climb back unaided into the unstable craft without the slightest risk of upsetting it.

'A very fine squid,' he crooned. 'It is a wahine squid. I shall now sing to you the song of the cowrie shell, the red cowrie shell that we used as a bait for the squid – '

'You were disgraceful last night at the funeral,' I headed him off. 'I heard all about it. You made much noise. You sang till everybody was deaf. You insulted the son of the widow. You drank swipes like a pig. Swipes are not good for your extreme age. Some day you will wake up dead. You ought to be a wreck to-day – '

'Ha!' he chuckled. 'And you, who drank no swipes, who was a babe unborn when I was already an old man, who went to bed last night with the sun and the chickens – this day you are a wreck. Explain me that. My ears are as thirsty to listen as was my throat thirsty last night. And here to-day, behold, I am, as that Englishman who came here in his yacht used to say, I am in fine form, in devilish fine form.'

'I give you up,' I retorted, shrugging my shoulders. 'Only one thing is clear, and that is that the devil doesn't want you. Report of your singing has gone before you.'

'No,' he pondered the idea carefully. 'It is not that. The devil will be glad for my coming, for I have some very fine songs for him, and scandals and old gossips of the high aliis that will make him scratch his sides. So let me explain to you the secret of my birth. The Sea is my mother. I was born in a double canoe, during a Kona gale, in the channel of Kahoolawe. From her, the Sea, my mother, I received my strength. Whenever I return to her arms, as for a breast clasp, as I have returned this day, I grow strong again and immediately. She, to me, is the milk giver, the life source – '

'Shades of Antæus!' thought I.

'Some day,' old Kohokumu rambled on, 'when I am really old, I shall be reported of men as drowned in the sea. This will be an idle thought of men. In truth, I shall have returned into the arms of my mother, there to rest under the heart of her breast until the second birth of me, when I shall emerge into the sun a flashing youth of splendor like Maui himself when he was golden young.'

'A queer religion,' I commented.

'When I was younger I muddled my poor head over queerer religions,' old Kohokumu retorted. 'But listen, O Young Wise One, to my elderly wisdom. This I know: as I grow old I seek less for the truth from without me, and find more of the truth from within me. Why have I thought this thought of my return to my mother and of my rebirth from my mother into the sun? You do not know. I do not know, save that, without whisper of man's voice or printed word, without prompting from other-where, this thought has arisen from within me, from the deeps of me that are as deep as the sea. I am not a god. I do not make things. Therefore I have not made this thought. I do not know its father or its mother. It is of old time before me, and therefore it is true. Man does not make truth. Man, if he be not blind, only recognizes truth when he sees it. Is this thought that I have thought a dream?'

'Perhaps it is you that are a dream,' I laughed. 'And that I and sky and sea and the iron-hard land are dreams, all dreams.'

'I have often thought that,' he assured me soberly. 'It may well be so. Last night I dreamed I was a lark bird, a beautiful singing lark of the sky like the larks on the upland pastures of Haleakala. And I flew up, up toward the sun, singing, singing, as old Kohokumu never sang. I tell you now that I dreamed I was a lark bird singing in the sky. But may not I, the real I, be the lark bird? And may not the telling of it be the dream that I, the lark bird, am dreaming now? Who are you to tell me ay or no? Dare you tell me I am not a lark bird asleep and dreaming that I am old Kohokumu?'

I shrugged my shoulders, and he continued triumphantly:

'And how do you know but what you are old Maui himself asleep and dreaming that you are John Lakana talking with me in a canoe? And may you not awake, old Maui yourself, and scratch your sides and say that you had a funny dream in which you dreamed you were a haole?'

'I don't know,' I admitted. 'Besides, you wouldn't believe me.'

'There is much more in dreams than we know,' he assured me with great solemnity. 'Dreams go deep, all the way down, maybe to before the beginning. May not old Maui have only dreamed he pulled Hawaii up from the bottom of the sea? Then would this Hawaii land be a dream, and you and I and the squid there only parts of Maui's dream? And the lark bird, too?'

He sighed and let his head sink on his breast.

'And I worry my old head about the secrets undiscoverable,' he resumed, 'until I grow tired and want to forget, and so I drink swipes, and go fishing, and sing old songs, and dream I am a lark bird singing in the sky. I like that best of all, and often I dream it when I have drunk much swipes – '

In great dejection of mood he peered down into the lagoon through the water glass.

'There will be no more bites for a while,' he announced. 'The fish-sharks are prowling around, and we shall have to wait until they are gone. And so that the time shall not be heavy, I will sing you the canoe-hauling song to Lono. You remember:

> '"Give to me the trunk of the tree, O Lono!
> Give me the tree's main root, O Lono!
> Give me the ear of the tree, O Lono! – "'

'For the love of mercy, don't sing!' I cut him short. 'I've got a headache, and your singing hurts. You may be in devilish fine form to-day, but your throat is rotten. I'd rather you talked about dreams, or told me whoppers.'

'It is too bad that you are sick, and you so young,' he conceded cheerily. 'And I shall not sing any more. I shall tell you something you do not know and have never heard; something that is no dream and no whopper, but is what I know to have happened. Not very long ago there lived here, on the beach beside this very lagoon, a young boy whose name was Keikiwai, which, as you know, means Water Baby. He was truly a water baby. His gods were the sea and fish gods, and he was born with knowledge of the language of fishes, which the fishes did not know until the sharks found it out one day when they heard him talk it.

'It happened this way. The word had been brought, and the commands, by swift runners, that the king was making a progress around the island, and that on the next day a luau was to be served him by the dwellers here of Waihee. It was always a hardship, when the king made a progress, for the few dwellers in small places to fill his many stomachs with food. For he came always with his wife and her women, with his priests and sorcerers, his dancers and flute-players and hula singers and fighting men and servants, and his high chiefs with their wives and sorcerers and fighting men and servants.

'Sometimes, in small places like Waihee, the path of his journey was marked afterward by leanness and famine. But a king must be fed, and it is not good to anger a king. So, like warning in advance of disaster, Waihee heard of his coming, and all food-getters of field and pond and mountain and sea were busied with getting food for the feast. And behold, everything was got, from the choicest of royal taro to sugar-cane joints for the roasting, from opihis to limu, from fowl to wild pig and poi-fed puppies – everything save one thing. The fishermen failed to get lobsters.

'Now be it known that the king's favorite food was lobster. He esteemed it above all *kai-kai* (food), and his runners had made special mention of it. And there were no lobsters, and it is not good to anger a king in the belly of him. Too many sharks had come inside the reef. That was the trouble. A young girl and an old man had been eaten by them. And of the young men who dared dive for lobsters, one was eaten, and one lost an arm, and another lost one hand and one foot.

'But here was Keikiwai, the Water Baby, only eleven years old, but half fish himself and talking the language of fishes.

To his father the head men came, begging him to send the Water Baby to get lobsters to fill the king's belly and divert his anger.

'Now this, what happened, was known and observed. For the fishermen and their women, and the taro growers and the bird catchers, and the head men, and all Waihee, came down and stood back from the edge of the rock where the Water Baby stood and looked down at the lobsters far beneath on the bottom.

'And a shark, looking up with its cat's eyes, observed him, and sent out the shark-call of "fresh meat" to assemble all the sharks in the lagoon. For the sharks work thus together, which is why they are strong. And the sharks answered the call till there were forty of them, long ones and short ones and lean ones and round ones, forty of them by count; and they talked to one another, saying: "Look at that titbit of a child, that morsel delicious of human-flesh sweetness without the salt of the sea in it, of which salt we have too much, savory and good to eat, melting to delight under our hearts as our bellies embrace it and extract from it its sweet."

'Much more they said, saying: "He has come for the lobsters. When he dives in he is for one of us. Not like the old man we ate yesterday, tough to dryness with age, nor like the young men whose members were too hard-muscled, but tender, so tender that he will melt in our gullets ere our bellies receive him. When he dives in, we will all rush for him, and the lucky one of us will get him, and, gulp, he will be gone, one bite and one swallow, into the belly of the luckiest one of us."

'And Keikiwai, the Water Baby, heard the conspiracy, knowing the shark language; and he addressed a prayer, in the shark language, to the shark god Moku-Halii, and the sharks heard and waved their tails to one another and winked their cat's eyes in token that they understood his talk. And then he said: "I shall now dive for a lobster for the king. And no hurt shall befall me, because the shark with the shortest tail is my friend and will protect me."

'And, so saying, he picked up a chunk of lava rock and tossed it into the water, with a big splash, twenty feet to one side. The forty sharks rushed for the splash, while he dived, and by the time they discovered they had missed him, he had gone to the bottom and come back and climbed out, within his hand a fat lobster, a wahine lobster, full of eggs, for the king.

'"Ha!" said the sharks, very angry. "There is among us a traitor. The titbit of a child, the morsel of sweetness, has spoken, and has exposed the one among us who has saved him. Let us now measure the length of our tails!"

'Which they did, in a long row, side by side, the shorter-tailed ones cheating and stretching to gain length on themselves, the longer-tailed ones cheating and stretching in order not to be out-cheated and out-stretched. They were very angry with the one with the shortest tail, and him they rushed upon from every side and devoured till nothing was left of him.

'Again they listened while they waited for the Water Baby to dive in. And again the Water Baby made his prayer in the shark language to Moku-Halii, and said: "The shark with the shortest tail is my friend and will protect me." And again the Water Baby tossed in a chunk of lava, this time twenty feet away off to the other side. The sharks rushed for the splash, and in their haste ran into one another, and splashed with their tails till the water was all foam and they could see nothing, each thinking some other was swallowing the titbit. And the Water Baby came up and climbed out with another fat lobster for the king.

'And the thirty-nine sharks measured tails, devouring the one with the shortest tail, so that there were only thirty-eight sharks. And the Water Baby continued to do what I have said, and the sharks to do what I have told you, while for each shark that was eaten by his brothers there was another fat lobster laid on the rock for the king. Of course, there was much quarreling and argument among the sharks when it came to measuring tails; but in the end it worked out in rightness and justice, for, when only two sharks were left, they were the two biggest of the original forty.

'And the Water Baby again claimed the shark with the shortest tail was his friend, fooled the two sharks with another lava chunk, and brought up another lobster. The two sharks each claimed the other had the shorter tail, and each fought to eat the other, and the one with the longer tail won – '

'Hold, O Kohokumu!' I interrupted. 'Remember that that shark had already – '

'I know just what you are going to say,' he snatched his recital back from me. 'And you are right. It took him so long to eat the thirty-ninth shark, for inside the thirty-ninth shark were already the nineteen other sharks he had eaten, and inside the fortieth shark were already the nineteen other sharks he had eaten, and he did not have the appetite he had started with. But do not forget he was a very big shark to begin with.

'It took him so long to eat the other shark, and the nineteen sharks inside the other shark, that he was still eating when darkness fell and the people of Waihee went away home with all the lobsters for the king. And didn't they find the last shark on the beach next morning dead and burst wide open with all he had eaten?'

Kohokumu fetched a full stop and held my eyes with his own shrewd ones.

'Hold, O Lakana!' he checked the speech that rushed to my tongue. 'I know what next you would say. You would say that with my own eyes I did not see this, and therefore that I do not know what I have been telling you. But I do know, and I can prove it. My father's father knew the grandson of the Water Baby's father's uncle. Also, there, on the rocky point to which I point my finger now, is where the Water Baby stood and dived. I have dived for lobsters there myself. It is a great place for lobsters. Also, and often, have I seen sharks there. And there, on the bottom, as I should know, for I have seen and counted them, are the thirty-nine lava rocks thrown in by the Water Baby as I have described.'

'But – ' I began.

'Ha!' he baffled me. 'Look! While we have talked the fish have begun again to bite.'

He pointed to three of the bamboo poles erect and devil-dancing in token that fish were hooked and struggling on the lines beneath. As he bent to his paddle, he muttered, for my benefit:

'Of course I know. The thirty-nine lava rocks are still there. You can count them any day for yourself. Of course I know, and I know for a fact.'

AFTERWORD: JACK LONDON'S
LIFE AND WORKS

Jack London was born on 12 January 1876, in San Francisco,
the only child of a spiritualist and music teacher, Flora Wellman.
His father was probably a wandering astrologer called William
Henry Chaney. His mother was soon married to a widower and
Civil War veteran, John London, who had two young daughters
with him, Eliza and Ida. Flora's son was given his stepfather's
name, John Griffith London.

Jack London's boyhood was spent in Oakland and on small
farms near San Francisco Bay. His parents' schemes for making
money failed and the family returned to live in a succession of
poorhouses in Oakland. To earn a few dollars, Jack worked as a
newsboy and in a skittle alley, and later in a cannery. He had an
early love of books and of sailing in a skiff on the bay. By the age
of fifteen, he was a delinquent and an oyster pirate – a time
which he was to romanticize in a book for boys, *The Cruise of the
Dazzler* (1902). He also briefly joined the side of the law against
his old comrades and later wrote of his adventures in *Tales of the
Fish Patrol* (1905).

In 1893, he set off for a seven-month sealing voyage on the
schooner *Sophie Sutherland*. This hard life among sailors engaged
in a bloody task gave him the experience to write and publish his
first story, about a typhoon off Japan – and the material for his
best novel about the struggle of men against nature and each
other, *The Sea-Wolf* (1904).

The next year, 1894, he joined Kelly's detachment of Coxey's
Army of the unemployed, which tried to march on Washington.
His experiences as a Road Kid and a vagrant are recounted in
The Road (1907), the forerunner of the work of Dos Passos and
Kerouac. The thirty days he spent in jail in the Erie Country
Penitentiary marked him all his life. He became determined to

use his brains to keep out of the degradation forced on the jobless.

He returned to high school in Oakland, became a radical, joined the Socialist Labor Party, and spent one semester at the University of California at Berkeley. He fell deeply under the influence of Spencer's social Darwinism and also Marxism, as preached by the Oakland socialists and the circle gathering round Anna Strunsky, one of his early loves.

In 1897, Jack London went on the Klondike Gold Rush, caught scurvy, and returned to California after a 2,000-mile voyage down the Yukon River. He applied himself to writing as a profession, nearly starving and working incessantly. A partly autobiographical account of these harsh years can be found in his novel *Martin Eden* (1909).

His Klondike stories soon attracted attention. After publishing his first three collections of them, *The Son of the Wolf* (1900), *The God of His Fathers* (1901) and *Children of the Frost* (1902), he found himself famous. If his first novel, *A Daughter of the Snows*, was a failure, *The Call of the Wild* (1903) was his masterpiece as a short novel and gave him international recognition, enhanced by another collection of Alaskan stories, *The Faith of Men* (1904).

In 1900, he had married Elizabeth (Bess) Maddern, mainly for biological reasons, as he declared in his collaboration with Anna Strunsky, *The Kempton-Wace Letters* (1903). His wife bore him two daughters, Joan and Becky. In 1902, he fell in love with Anna Strunsky, but lost her when he left for London, where he wrote his emotional account of the poor in the East End, *The People of the Abyss*. Reconciled with his wife on his return, he soon left her for the older Charmian Kittredge, an emancipated and courageous Californian.

In 1904, he became a correspondent for the Hearst newspapers in the Russo-Japanese war, and recognized the threat of Asia to the world dominance of Europe. The Russian revolution of 1905 inflamed his radicalism, so that he gave a series of socialist lectures, later published in two important collections of essays, *War of the Classes* and *Revolution*. His divorce and his instant remarriage, to Charmian Kittredge, put him even more in the news.

He continued to write intensively, inventing the American boxing novel in *The Game* (1905), recreating primitive existence in *Before Adam* (1907) and continuing to mine his lucrative Klondike vein with *Moon-Face* and *Love of Life and Other Stories*. His greatest success after *The Sea-Wolf* was another short novel, *White Fang* (1906), which told the story of a wild dog tamed by civilization, the reverse of *The Call of the Wild*. Yet his most original contribution was *The Iron Heel* (1908), a chilling prophecy of the Fascist period to come.

At the peak of his influence and powers, Jack London decided to build his own sailing boat, the *Snark*, and to cruise round the world with Charmian as his 'mate'. The San Francisco earthquake of 1906 doubled the costs and delayed the start of the voyage, so that Jack was nearly bankrupt when he sailed to Hawaii, the Marquesas, Tahiti, Samoa and the Solomon Islands. The two-year voyage, interrupted by a short return home to rescue his finances, was a saga of accidents and disease ending in the complete collapse of Jack's health. He abandoned the *Snark* and started some disastrous arsenic treatments in Australia, which damaged his nerves and kidneys. He sailed back to California in 1909. It was the first public defeat of a man who had created the image of a superman and now was trapped within it.

During the last seven years of his life, Jack lived in deteriorating health and devoted his energies to developing his ranch near Glen Ellen in Northern California and to building his stone 'Wolf House'. Always short of money for his increasing expenses, he lived a disciplined life, writing every day. He returned to the profitable theme of Alaska in *Lost Face* and *Burning Daylight* (1910) and *Smoke Bellew* (1912). His long sea voyage produced the autobiographical *The Cruise of the Snark* and, between 1911 and 1913, a succession of Pacific stories and novels: *When God Laughs, Adventure, South Sea Tales, A Son of the Sun* and *The House of Pride*. If the quality of his work deteriorated with his health, yet his style and professionalism kept him popular and respected.

In 1912, he sailed round Cape Horn on the *Dirigo*, the basis of his grisly novel *The Mutiny of the Elsinore*. Charmian miscarried for the second time, removing any chance of his having a male child. He had quarrelled with his first wife and two daughters, and his last misfortune was to lose the completed Wolf House by fire. His story of his own problems with alcohol, *John Barleycorn* (1913), showed his writing and his self-awareness at their best, while his new devotion to the land and life on his ranch was portrayed in two novels, *The Valley of the Moon* (1913) and *The Little Lady of the Big House* (1916). His life at Glen Ellen had truly become the centre of his existence, devotedly run by Charmian and his stepsister Eliza, who acted as his ranch manager.

Some of his best short stories were written in his declining years, particularly those in *The Strength of the Strong* (1914), which contains 'South of the Slot', 'The Dream of Debs', 'The Sea-Farmer' and 'Samuel'. Other collections of stories were *The Night Born* and *The Turtles of Tasman*. He continued his boxing novels with *The Abysmal Brute* and his science fiction with *The Scarlet Plague* (1915) and the haunting *The Red One* (1918). Yet his most extraordinary feat of imagination was his novel of prison life and time travel, *The Star Rover* (1915).

His physical condition was made even worse by a severe attack of dysentery while he was reporting the Mexican Revolution in 1914. Hardly alive and existing on huge quantities of fluid and pain-killing drugs, Jack spent the last two years of his life becoming conscious of the many contradictions of his character. His animal novels *Jerry of the Islands* and *Michael, Brother of Jerry*, were run-of-the-mill, but his psychological stories, after his reading of Freud and Jung, proved to be some of his finer work, published in *On the Makaloa Mat* (1919). His notes for a projected novel on his dead Shire stallion and for 'Farthest Distant: The Last Novel of Them All' promised great works to come.

Unfortunately, long stays in Hawaii could not help his internal maladies and increasing sense of disgust with life. He resigned from the Socialist Party in 1916 and shortly afterward took an overdose of the drugs prescribed for his kidney and bladder problems. He had done this many times before, but this time his weakened body could not take the strain. He lapsed into a coma and died on 22 November 1916.

NOTE ON THE TEXTS

In all Jack London's works, there are differences between the versions printed in periodicals and in books. The first book edition, however, is the version on which London himself put his stamp of authority, and this version has been chosen as the basis of these texts. Only a few changes into modern usage in spelling and punctuation have been included.

'The Chinago' is taken from *The Chinago*, published by the Macmillan Company in New York in 1911. 'The House of Mapuhi', 'The Whale Tooth', 'Mauki' and 'The Seed of McCoy' were published in *South Sea Tales* by the Macmillan Company in 1911. 'Good-By, Jack', 'The Sheriff of Kona' and 'Koolau the Leper' were published in *The House of Pride and Other Tales of Hawaii* by the Macmillan Company in 1912. And 'The Bones of Kahekili', 'When Alice Told Her Soul', 'Shin-Bones' and 'The Water Baby' were published in *On the Makaloa Mat* by the Macmillan Company in 1919 after Jack London's death.